DANGEROUS
BOYS

DANGEROUS BOYS

ABIGAIL HAAS

SIMON AND SCHUSTER

First published in Great Britain in 2014 by Simon and Schuster UK Ltd
A CBS COMPANY

1 3 5 7 9 10 8 6 4 2

Simon & Schuster UK Ltd
1st Floor, 222 Gray's Inn Road
London
WC1X 8HB

www.simonandschuster.co.uk

Simon & Schuster Australia, Sydney
Simon & Schuster India, New Delhi

A CIP catalogue record for this book
is available from the British Library

PB ISBN: 978-1-47111-916-3
EBOOK ISBN: 978-1-47111-917-0

Printed and bound by CPI Group (UK) Ltd, Croydon, CR0 4YY

ACKNOWLEDGEMENTS

I'm so grateful that so many people worked to help make this book possible. Thanks to my rock-star agents, Rebecca Friedman and Amanda Preston. A huge thank you to the team from S&S UK for your enthusiasm and expertise, you've been a dream to work with: Ingrid Selberg, Eleanor Willis, Kat McKenna, Rachel Mann, Elv Moody, Emma Young, and Paul Coomey (for my amazing covers). Thanks to my family for everything, and to Abby Schulman, Brandy Colbert, Nadine Nettman-Semerau, Julia Collard, Elisabeth Donnelly, Laurie Farrugia and Lane Shadgett, for your friendship and support.

Finally, a huge thank you to the readers and bloggers who have tirelessly championed my books: the queen of promo Dahlia Adler, Racquel (Book Barbie), Estelle (Rather Be Reading), Blythe (Finding Bliss in Books), Leah Raeder, Wendy (Book Scents), Stormy (Book.Blog.Bake), Alexa Loves Books, and everyone else who has fought to spread the word. I am so blessed to have you on my team!

THE END

Our lives are made up of choices. Big ones, small ones, strung together by the thin air of good intentions; a line of dominoes, ready to fall. Which shirt to wear on a cold winter's morning, what crappy junk food to eat for lunch. It starts out so innocently, you don't even notice: go to this party or that movie, listen to this song, or read that book, and then, somehow, you've chosen your college and career; your boyfriend or wife.

So many choices, we stop counting after a while. They blur into an endless stream, leading seamlessly to the next question, the next decision – yes, no, no, yes. The line of dominoes falling one by one. Click, click, click, they tumble faster until you can only see the two that really mattered:

The beginning, and this, the end.

Oliver, and Ethan, and I.

"What are you doing, baby brother?" Oliver takes half a step towards us. "You're scaring Chloe." He looks from me to Ethan and back again, and I can see him trying to assess the scene, his brain ticking quickly behind those sharp blue eyes. "Just calm down."

"I am calm!"

"We can talk about this." Oliver tries to soothe him.

"No!" Ethan insists, his voice a hoarse yell. The sound sends shivers of fear through me. I've never seen him like this before, so wild and erratic. Out of control. "I'm not listening to your lies anymore. It's all bullshit, every word of it. You can't talk your way out of this!"

"I'm sorry," I whisper, crumpled in the corner. "I'm so, so sorry. I never meant ... I never meant to hurt you."

"It's too late for that!" Ethan screams.

I flinch back, shaking, looking desperately for some escape. But I'm trapped with Ethan standing between me and the door. Oliver is closer, he could go and get help; I catch his eye, trying to gesture, but instead of leaving, he just inches towards us.

"Shh, Ethan, it's OK." Oliver holds his hands up, a sign of submission. "We won't talk, we don't have to do anything. Just put the knife down."

Ethan looks at the blade in his hand, like he'd forgotten it was there. The steel glints, bright in the candlelight, so pretty I could almost forget what ugly truths it could write.

"Ethan, please," I beg. "Don't hurt us."

DISPATCH: **Nine one one, what's your emergency?**

CALLER: **Please, you have to send someone. An ambulance, please, he's bleeding!**

DISPATCH: **OK, we'll send help. Just calm down, and tell me where you are.**

CALLER: **I ... I don't know what to do. There's so much blood, I can't make it stop.**

DISPATCH: **Where are you, honey? What happened?**

CALLER: **Up by Echo Point, by the lake. I tried to get him out, and now ... (*sobbing*) Please, he's not moving!**

DISPATCH: **I'm sending an ambulance now. Tell me what happened, where is he hurt?**

(*Silence*)

DISPATCH: **Honey? Are you there? Talk to me.**

(*Silence*)

CALLER: **It's burning. Everything's on fire.**

THE BEGINNING

It was three weeks until the end of summer, and I was counting down, the way I always used to as a kid. Then, the countdown was to keep fall at bay; measuring every precious moment of summer, as if somehow charting the days out in neat red marks in my journal would give them weight enough to make them real, anchor them steady in my life instead of letting them drift, aimlessly by, into the front porch popsicle haze that was already gone.

Now, I counted towards the end of summer because I couldn't wait for school to start. Marking out the weeks in an afternoon lull at the diner, day by day, planning my escape.

Three weeks until freshman orientation. Three weeks until I could be done with Haverford, Indiana, for good: the single-stoplight Main Street, the shuttered stores on the out-skirts of town, and the house that stood too quiet – filled with torn photographs and the ticking time-bomb that was my mother. Three weeks until my real life could finally begin.

"Can I grab a drop of that refill, sweetheart?"

I looked up from my paper napkin calendar with a start. Sheriff Weber was in his usual booth by the windows, nurs-ing a cup of coffee as he leafed slowly through the local paper, chewing absently on the end of a ballpoint pen. Most afternoons, he would be there, flipping through paperwork or settled in with his word puzzles. He often would say – yawn-ing, stretching – leave the chasing down criminals to the younger deputies; people knew where they could find him.

"Sure, sorry." I rounded the counter and poured him more, glimpsing the scribbles on his crossword page.

"Thanks. You know a five-letter word for discordant, on edge?"

I paused, seeing the letters take shape in my mind. "Sharp?"

Weber nodded slowly, writing in the answer along the edge of the box.

"Why don't you fill it in?" I asked, curious. Now that I was up close, I saw he had almost the whole page covered with notes, but nothing written in the grid itself.

"I like to wait until I've got it all figured out." Weber gave me a conspiratorial smile, his weathered face drooping above the crisp blue of his uniform; a dark, basset hound face. "Saves going back and making a mess with the crossings out."

I lingered by the cherry-red booth. The diner was quiet, it always was this time of day: a haven of sunshine and pie displays, and swinging Sixties pop on the old-school jukebox. Now that most of the summer crowds had decamped from their lakeshore vacation homes, Haverford seemed in limbo, the streets empty where only days ago, they'd bustled with the busy throngs of day-trippers and summer kids, tracking sand across the floors, dripping melted ice cream across the cracked vinyl seats for me to clean.

"You'll be off soon?" Weber asked. I'd known him for ever. His daughter was my best friend and this year, I'd spent more time than was polite over at their house under the guise of studying and after-school hang-outs.

I nodded. "I leave a few days after Alisha, I think."

"It's too soon. Although, don't let her know her old dad said that." Weber gave me a rueful smile. "She says we're acting like it's the end of the world, not college. I expect your folks are the same."

I tensed at the mention of my parents. "Something like that," I answered vaguely, but Weber must have realized his mistake, because he coughed, awkward.

"Say, what's the pie today?" He changed the subject.

"Blueberry." I smiled quickly. "It's good, you want a slice?"

"Sure, why not? I've got some time before dinner."

"Coming right up."

I headed back behind the counter. One thing I wouldn't be missing about this town was the way everybody knew everyone's business – even if they pretended like they didn't. Nobody had said a word to me about the events of this spring, but I'd caught the curious glances around town, and overheard snatched murmurs of gossip in line at the store. *"No, they never knew . . . Yup, out in San Diego, due in the fall."*

I slammed the coffee pot back under the drip, swallowing down the anger that bubbled, treacherous, every time I let my thoughts wander.

Three weeks. Just three more weeks to go.

"Wow, what did that coffee pot ever do to you?"

I spun around. The boy was back, walking over from the front door and slinging himself down on one of the stools by the counter, the same way he had done every day so far that week.

"Oh, hey." I swallowed, looking away. "What can I get you?"

The boy reached over and slid a menu closer, glancing over the peeling laminate sheet even though I already knew what he'd be ordering.

"Tuna melt, mustard, mayo, pickle on the side." The boy gave me an easy smile, a flash of white against his tanned face and sandy-brown hair. His eyes were blue: kind eyes, guile-less, and today his gaze drifted past me, up to the specials board hung overhead. "Throw in one of those root beer floats."

"You sure?" I raised an eyebrow. We kept all the old-fash-ioned soda shop specials written up on the chalkboard, but nobody ever ordered them. They all knew better.

"What can I say, I'm a dare-devil," the boy grinned. "A risk-taker. I live life on the edge."

"Really?"

"Nope." The boy laughed. "But it sounds good, doesn't it?"

"I'll get you a milkshake," I decided, placing his order on the back bar and hitting the bell to call José back from his not-so-secret cigarette break. "Chocolate OK?"

"Yes ma'am."

I took my time fixing the drink, scooping the ice cream and running the blender on loud as I snuck a glance back to him. He waited at the counter, perfectly at ease. He didn't bring a book or a paper, I noticed, or endlessly scroll through his phone like the other regulars who came in alone. He just sat, calm and still, watching the occasional pedestrian stroll past outside the windows.

"Here you go." I delivered his shake, served in a tall glass with whipped cream spiraling into a snowy peak.

His eyes widened at the sight. "Damn, that's something. You think I should drink it or scale the thing?"

"Up to you," I laughed. I pulled out the bottles of ketchup and began setting them on end, filling old containers with the new. "I'll send a search party if you're not back by dawn."

The boy grinned. "I'm Ethan, by the way. I figure, since I've been in every day . . ." He looked awkward for a moment, waiting for my reply.

"Hey." I reached to shake his outstretched hand. "Chloe."

"Good to meet you, Chloe." Ethan took a slurp of his shake. "You're officially my first friend in Haverford."

"Welcome to town."

He smiled again, easy. "We just moved here. Dad's developing the tract out past Echo Point."

I nodded. Kids from high school would head out there to get high and drink cheap beer, blowing off steam with their fathers' guns. I'd never been invited, I didn't run in those crowds, but I'd see the debris when I went out running around the lake sometimes, the ashes from the campfire and the twists of empty cans.

"It's going to be four luxury properties," Ethan continued. "Rustic cabin style, but all the mod-cons. Fifteen hundred square foot a piece." He stopped, looking bashful. "Sorry, construction talk."

"You're working on the site?" I asked, studying him. His plaid shirt was crisp, and his face was more cleanly shaven than some of the construction guys who stopped by for breaks, all scruffy beards and dirty nails.

He nodded. "Kind of, more the office for now. Learning the ropes. I graduated this summer and went straight into the job. Suddenly, I'm supposed to be an adult, just because I'm earning a paycheck." He gave me a rueful grin and I nodded.

"It's strange, isn't it? They give you a diploma and then you're supposed to magically know what you're doing. I'm leaving for college soon," I added.

"Shame," Ethan said. "Not the college part, but ..." He coughed, looking bashful. "Who'll keep me in tuna melts?"

"I don't make them." I felt myself blush.

"But you do cut the crusts off for me," Ethan grinned, a teasing glint in his eyes.

I turned to straighten up the back counter, shielding my face from him for a moment. I'd been thinking of him as "the boy" all week, but he was more than that, I realized. Eighteen, nineteen – Ethan was a man. It shouldn't have seemed like such a foreign discovery, but it was. This was the year it had changed: my classmates suddenly filling out from gangly boys to broad-shouldered, solid-chested guys with a new certainty to their stride, a sense of physicality, occupying their space in the world with ease.

Ethan was one of them: tall and solid, and watching me with a blatant interest in his eyes I couldn't ignore; an interest that felt thrilling and uneasy all the same. The boys in school never looked at me like that, they knew better; that I wasn't one of the girls who partied by the lake, or hooked up in a basement on a Friday night. I was careful, determined that nothing would distract me from my future plans.

But Ethan didn't know that. He didn't know anything about me at all – and still, he looked at me like I was someone worth watching.

José slid his order through the hatch and I busied myself slicing off the crusts and folding a paper napkin before bracing myself and turning back to the counter. I placed the food in front of Ethan and his eyes flicked down to my chest for the briefest of split-seconds before locking eyes with me again.

"Thanks. So when do you head out?"

I blinked a moment. "Oh, end of the month."

"Whereabouts?"

"Connecticut," I replied. "Mills."

"Wow." Ethan bit off a corner of his sandwich and chewed. "You must be smart."

I paused. I never knew what to say to that. Often, it sounded like an insult coming from guys, as if I was supposed to back-track and stutter, no, no, I wasn't smart at all.

"Chloe?" Weber's voice came. I turned, remembering.

"The pie! I'm sorry."

"Don't worry about it, I've got to get going." He tucked away his phone and rose out of the booth, shrugging on his jacket. "Damn kids spray-painting at the Seven-Eleven again. Broad daylight." He shook his head with a sigh. "What do I owe you?"

"On the house." I waved it away.

Weber shook his head and placed a five-dollar bill down on the table. "You take care," he said. "And come over for dinner sometime this week. We should have a goodbye with you girls before you leave."

"I will." I moved to wipe down his table. He'd left the newspaper, so I checked the crossword: filled in, every box marked with neat black lettering.

"Friendly town." Ethan spoke up when I returned to my spot behind the counter. "We've been moving around so much, I forgot places like this existed."

"I guess . . ." I nodded. "I've never been anywhere else. Not yet."

"You're lucky. Last place we lived, I never saw our neighbors once. Except the time they tossed dead wood over the fence into our backyard, nearly knocked my brains out," Ethan added.

I thought of the world out there waiting for me, filled with cities where I wouldn't know a soul and could lose myself on streets I didn't know by heart. It sounded like bliss to me, but I knew that if I said so, Ethan would only ask why, so I busied myself with wiping down the rest of the tables instead, daydreaming in the warm, bright diner until he finished his sandwich and the afternoon rush (which was more of a trickle these days) started up, and I had to deal with the cluster of junior high kids all ordering bottomless dollar sodas and single portions of fries, cluttering the booths with their vibrant sling of bags and jackets and the breathless buzz of their cellphones.

"Hey, Chloe?" Ethan lingered awkwardly by the door as I delivered a tray of drinks, trying not to spill. "You, umm, maybe want to go out sometime?"

I stopped, taken by surprise. Behind me, I could hear a table of teenage girls burst into excited whispers, but I wavered, unsure, clutching my empty tray to my chest.

"I don't know . . . I'm leaving in a few weeks."

"So you're busy every night until then?" Ethan teased.

I smiled. "No, but . . ." I trailed off, not sure how to explain that I didn't want to put down any more roots in this town, not when I couldn't wait to cut my last ties loose.

"Look, the way I see it, you can't lose." Ethan grinned.

"Really?" I had to laugh at his confidence.

"Sure, it's zero risk," Ethan explained. "If it turns out you can't stand the sight of me, you won't have to. You'll be hundreds of miles away. What do you say, dinner and a movie?"

My mind raced. He looked good, standing there, backlit by the afternoon sun, gold in his hair and a hopeful smile on his face. Solid and easy.

But I was already a hundred miles away.

"I can't," I mumbled, looking down. "But, thanks."

He blinked, his face falling. "Well, here, take my number." He grabbed a napkin and scribbled it down. "In case you change your mind." I took the paper, slowly folding it into my pocket. "See you around."

I watched him go, back out on to the sidewalk and across the street to where a brand-new blue pick-up truck sat waiting. He was unhurried and sure in the sunlight. I wondered if I'd made a mistake.

But the red marks on my calendar were counting down, closer to the life that was waiting for me in Connecticut. Men wearing thick cable-knit sweaters and parka coats, fall leaves, freshman dorms. I had weeks to kill here, sure, but what was the point in starting something new when part of me was already gone?

NOW

You can never really know someone.

Maybe you think that sounds trite, or perhaps you already learned it a long time ago. But me, I didn't really grasp it until now: huddled in the corner of the ambulance, watching the medics try to shock life back into a motionless body.

The sirens are blaring, but everything drifts away from me. The noise and the blood, the hands tugging at my body; the light they shine in my eyes and the shock of pure oxygen from the mask strapped over my face.

We're all strangers, in the end.

I remember something, from a book Oliver gave me months ago. It said that we're all irrevocably trapped inside our own minds: just as it's impossible for anyone to truly know us, we can't begin to hope to know anyone else.

I understand it now.

You can be a part of someone's life for years, your parent or brother or friend, and then one day they turn around and do something so unconscionable, a crime so great, that suddenly, they're a stranger to you. You think that their goodness is innate, embedded in their DNA, so you take it for granted, right up until the terrible moment when everything changes. Only then do you realize, those good deeds were actions. Actions that can stop, change on a dime at any time.

You don't know what's behind that smile. You can't imagine who someone will turn out to be. We assume the sun will rise every morning just because it has done every other day, but what happens when you wake up to darkness? When you open your eyes and find, today is the one different day?

I watch them fix the paddles in place on his chest, yell out, and stand clear. I watch the shock jerk through him, the flatline stretching on and on and on.

You can never know anyone at all.

THEN

I cycled home from the diner, looping slowly through the quiet streets of the neighborhood. Our house was at the end of the block, sitting in the shadow of one of the old maple trees that slanted more precariously every year. My father had always threatened to get it taken down, lest another storm send it crashing through their roof, but me and Mom would protest about history and preservation until he let the subject drop. It was ironic that, in the end, he'd been the one to wreak destruction, more thoroughly than any freak storm could have managed.

The car was still in the drive, not moved an inch from when I left that morning.

I felt it hit me all at once: the heavy resignation, and bitterness too. I took a breath and braced myself as I unlocked the door and stepped into the house.

It was silent.

On the good days – the days I hadn't even realized were good, until they were gone – the house had echoed with sound. The moment I arrived home from school, I would step into bustle and warmth, my mother in the kitchen keeping one eye on the stove, talking on the phone or singing along to country music on the radio. Now I could only hope for the sound of the TV, if any hint of life at all.

"Mom?" I called out, walking slowly down the hall, checking the living room. Nothing. "I'm home."

The house was still, my cereal bowl still in the sink and the trash I'd bagged by the back door, waiting to be taken out.

I climbed the stairs, then paused outside my mother's bedroom door. "Mom?" I tapped lightly.

No reply.

I longed to keep walking, down the hall to my room. I would make dinner and spend the night watching TV, pretending as if I was really alone in the house instead of just alone in every way that really mattered.

But the door had been closed that morning, and all of the day before.

I pushed it open and stepped into the room.

The drapes were drawn, heavy. It took a moment for my eyes to adjust to the dim. There were spaces on the dresser and bookshelves where Dad's things had been, the closet door open, half empty.

And Mom, curled under the covers, staring blankly at the wall.

"Are you hungry?" I strode over to the windows, my voice ringing out, bright and false. I yanked back the drapes, even though it would be dark in an hour. Clothing was scattered on the floor, so I picked it up, dropping it in the laundry hamper. "I can fix you something for dinner. Some soup, we're running low on everything else. Maybe you can run to the store tomorrow?"

Still, silence.

I felt fear bloom in my chest, the metallic edge I'd been keeping at bay all summer long.

"Mom?" My voice wavered, cracking. Mom finally turned her head, as if it took all the effort she could muster.

"I'm not hungry, sweetie."

"You need to eat."

"I'm fine." Mom turned her head again, slowly closing her eyes. "I'm just tired, that's all. You make whatever you want."

She lay there, motionless. The conversation was over.

I slipped out of the room, walking slowly down the hall

to my room. I sat on the very edge of my bed and took a breath. My hands were shaking, and I clenched them into two small fists, looking around the room. I'd started packing already, as if that would make the time pass faster. My books were in boxes, my favorites carefully selected to make the trip out to the East Coast. I'd deliberated for hours, weighing each of my collection like favored children, leaving the remainders stacked, lonely on the shelf.

It looked like my mother's room now. Like the whole fucking house. Abandoned.

What would she do once I was at college?

Fear drove me to pick up my cellphone and make the call I'd been avoiding.

It took eight rings for Dad to answer. I almost hung up, when suddenly, his voice came, flustered on the other end of the line. "Pumpkin, hi – just give me a moment."

There was silence, muffled voices in the background and then he was there again. "Sorry, we're just heading out the door."

I felt the ache in my chest tighten. "I can call back later."

"No, no, I've got time. I'm glad you called. What's up?"

I took a breath. "It's Mom," I said carefully. "I'm . . . worried about her."

It felt wrong, to talk about her like this, behind her back, but I didn't know what else to do. All summer, I'd been telling myself it would pass, this depression, but instead, Mom was sinking lower, disappearing from sight into that bundle of bedcovers and listless grief. "She's not doing so good, Daddy." My voice caught, but I pressed on. "I'm really worried."

"Chloe ..." Dad's voice changed, impatience replacing his earlier enthusiasm. "I'm sorry, but I don't know what you expect me to do. Your mother's her own woman, she has to make her own choices now."

"But ..." My protest died on my lips.

"I know this hasn't been easy for her," Dad sighed. "And with you going off to college now ..."

I froze. "Are you saying this is my fault?"

"No, of course not, sweetie," he replied quickly. "Nobody's to blame. We're all just trying to make the best of the situation."

I let the words sit there, too tired to even be angry. I often wondered, could he hear himself? Or did he believe the lies, even now?

He told me first.

That was the one thing I couldn't forgive him for, even as it all unfolded, one unforgivable crime after the next. He'd sat down to dinner one night, splitting a pizza with me while Mom worked late at the hospital, and he'd told me, his eyes fixed on some point just beyond my head. He was leaving.

There was a woman in California, they'd met on a business trip. They'd fallen in love. He was leaving to be with her.

"I was going to wait until you left for college," he'd said apologetically, as if the timing was the problem, and not the fact of his betrayal. "But it's not fair on Rochelle, to keep going on like this. I can't pretend anymore."

I sat there, sick to my stomach with guilt. Because he'd made a liar of me too. For those next few awful hours, Mom was out there, oblivious. She was processing paperwork and going to get coffee; chatting with her co-workers on a break. And all the while, her life was about to fall apart, and I was the one who knew it. I was complicit in my father's crimes now, and oh, how I hated him for it.

After that, there were tears and yelling and recrimination, back and forth for days on end. Mom, furious then wretched then terrified, and my father, strangely resolute. I closed the door on them, not sure which disgusted me most: the unwavering insistence of Dad that he was leaving, or the naked panic in Mom's voice as she begged him to stay, try counseling, do anything to make it work again.

And then it came out, the real reason for his urgency. This woman was pregnant. He wanted to go and marry her, and raise this other child.

"I didn't mean for any of this to happen," he told me, looking weary but self-righteous. He'd pulled his shirts from the closet to fill the cases on the bed, neatly folding them even in the midst of the chaos. "Now I'm just trying to do the right thing."

It still chilled me, that to Dad, this was the noble choice. To switch one wife for another; trade a daughter for his future son.

"But, about Mom . . ." I tried again now, needing him to understand. "She's not going in to work. She's not doing anything these days. She just lays there, or watches TV."

"I'm sure she'll be fine," Dad insisted, as if he hadn't heard a word. "You just focus on your own plans, you must have a lot to get ready. Did you find out your dorm assignment yet?" he segued smoothly, suddenly upbeat again. "We were looking at the brochure again, just the other night. The campus looks great. And if you can't make it out for Thanksgiving, we'll come visit in the spring, after the baby comes. You'll want to meet your brother. Rochelle can't wait."

I listened to him chatter happily about college courses and their latest pre-natal visit, and wondered how he could be so oblivious. It seemed cruel, callous even, to go from dismissing Mom's agony to sharing news about his own new life without even pausing for breath. But if there was one thing I'd learned in the months since his leaving, it was that my father was gifted with a breathtaking ability for denial. It was as if he'd created a shield around himself, and all the damage and hurt and pain simply slid off, never piercing him the way it sliced through the rest of us.

"I should go." I cut him off, unable to listen anymore. "I don't want to keep you."

"It was great talking to you, sweetie," Dad said, unaware of the crushing emptiness that settled around me, the empty house, and the fear of that closed bedroom door. "Don't worry so much about your mom, I'm sure she'll be fine."

There was a voice in the background, *her* voice, and then the line went dead and he was gone.

I sat, not moving, for another minute. Then I forced myself to change clothes and head back down the stairs to the kitchen. I turned on all the lights in the house, until the rooms were filled with a warm golden glow; twisting the old-fashioned dial on the radio until I found the country station again, playing songs I recognized from years ago. I took out the trash, and ran the dishwasher; fixed soup, and a plate of buttered toast, and a pot of hot tea.

I left a tray by Mom's bed and then ate alone in front of the TV, flipping through stations of endless noise and laughter, quiz shows and reality scandals. None of it distracted me from the silence upstairs, or the life that my father was living in a house a thousand miles away.

Ethan's face rose up in my mind: the eagerness of his smile. The curiosity in his gaze.

I felt a restless itch and bounced up again. I found my work jeans, crumpled in the laundry – the napkin folded up in my pocket.

I smoothed it out. Ethan's handwriting was firm and sure: his phone number dark on the page.

I hesitated another moment, and then I dialed.

THEN

I waited on the front porch, a little nervous, and wishing I wasn't. Ethan arrived on the stroke of seven, just as promised. He pulled up to the curb in his pick-up truck, but when I got up to climb in, he shut off the engine and came down to open my door.

"Thanks," I murmured, surprised by the old-fashioned gesture.

"Always," Ethan grinned. He'd changed his shirt and taken a shower, his hair still pressed damp against his scalp. "You look nice."

I was only wearing a top and jeans, but I still felt a tiny rush at his compliment. I blushed, climbing up into the cab of the truck and letting Ethan close the door behind me. I looked around, taking stock as he crossed back around to the driver's side. The front seats were swept clean, but behind me, there was a crumple of fast-food wrappers, spare sweaters, loose change.

It struck me suddenly just how little I knew about this guy. He'd breezed into town, an outsider, and now I was sitting in his truck, trusting him to take me where he said we would go. Everyone here knew everyone else, but he was a stranger. A blank slate.

And I was one too.

The thought was strangely reassuring, after months of ducking questions and avoiding the sympathy on everyone's faces. Ethan wouldn't know a thing about my family's history, or the sadness lurking behind my front door. I could be anyone I wanted with him tonight.

I might not even have to lie to him at all.

"Hartley OK?" he asked, naming the nearest town with a movie theatre, about thirty minutes away. He started the engine and casually reached to rest his hand on the back of my seat as he turned and reversed out of the drive.

"Sure." I reached for the stereo tuner, but then saw it was hooked up to his iPod with a snaking wire.

"Here, take your pick." Ethan passed me the handset. I scrolled through, glad of the ice-breaker. Now we would chat about music, talk about our favorite bands and confess the weird, uncool songs lurking in our collections. I could do that, easy and inconsequential.

"But you've got to promise not to judge me," he added with a grin.

"You've got some guilty secrets?" I teased.

"Doesn't everyone?"

I glanced across and saw a dark, solemn glint in his eyes. Then Ethan laughed. "No, I'm just messing with you. I'm an open book, nothing much to hide."

"Not even your love for Blakely Ray?" I smirked, landing on a list of songs by the latest teen pop star craze.

"What? She's crazy catchy," Ethan protested. Other guys might have gotten ruffled, but he just laughed when I set one of the songs to play, lip-synching along with faux sincerity. "C'mon girl, get into it!"

"OK, OK, you win!" I laughed and changed the track, and then guitar chords were drifting, light and gentle, out through the open windows into the crisp evening air. I turned my head to watch the world slide past, Haverford quickly receding behind us as the highway snaked past the modern development on the outskirts of town, then into the wide open bleed of woods and fields, ramshackle ranch houses dotted behind overgrown hedgerows.

I breathed in, and felt the sharp knot in my chest ease, just a little.

"Where did you move from?" I turned my head back to Ethan, finding him idly tapping the steering wheel in time with the music. He drove with an ease I envied, his broad shoulders relaxed, one elbow resting out the window.

"Columbus," he replied, shooting me a brief, rueful grin. "Then before that, Chicago, Atlanta, we did a few months in Nashville my junior year ... Dad moves around a lot for the business, and Mom doesn't like us all to be apart for too long."

"How was it, moving around so much?" I studied him carefully, looking for some sign of conflict beneath the casual smile.

Ethan shrugged. "It sucked to begin with, but I got the hang of it after a while. I'd join the basketball team, or go out for whatever sport was in season, and things would settle down pretty quick."

"Guys don't know how lucky they are." I shook my head, thinking of my own high school life: the cliques and strange, shifting hierarchies that I'd barely managed to get a handle on before we were tossing our graduation caps in the air, suddenly free.

"What do you mean?" Ethan looked over.

"Just ... girls are different," I explained. "You guys can shoot some hoops and swing by a kegger, and suddenly you're in. But, I've lived in that town my whole life, and I still don't know if I fit in."

"Sure you do." Ethan corrected me. "I've seen you at the diner, chatting with all the regulars. People love you."

I didn't reply. It was easy to think of Haverford as a picture postcard town, but nowhere was perfect. Sure, I could see the same people, day in, day out; exchange pleasantries, chat about the weather and the high school football game, but I'd often wondered, how quickly that friendly charm could slip. Last year, there'd been an accident: a car full of kids from the next town over, two dead on an icy stretch of highway at night. First came the platitudes, flowers on the side of the road and a tearful memorial service at the chapel out past Thompsett Falls, but then the whispers started, curling around morning coffee as the town mothers sat, chatting in the front booth; snaking louder across the street, in line at the post office, then finally scrawled in red paint across the lockers of the survivors in school.

Drunk. Slut. Killer.

It didn't take much, in a town like this. I'd seen it for myself, the way even my mother's friends took a half-step back after Dad left. As if the scandal were contagious, Mom somehow to blame for her own trust and ignorance.

I shook off the memories. I'd promised myself I wouldn't think about it tonight. "So, I don't know much about you, aside from your thing for tuna melts," I said.

"Fire away," Ethan laughed. "Like I said, open book."

"Parents?" I asked, thinking of my own tangled family.

"Together, all good as far as I can tell."

"Siblings?" I asked, quickly, to stop him repeating the question back at me. I didn't talk about Mom with anyone; not even my best friend, Alisha knew.

"A brother, older," Ethan replied, tapping on the steering wheel. "He's at Yale," he added, with a wry note in his voice.

"What about you, did you not think about college?"

"Nah." Ethan made a face. "School was never my thing. I've been helping Dad out for years, and business is good again, so I figure, why not? I'll learn more on site than I would sitting in a classroom somewhere, taking notes." He paused. "What about you? What's the big plan?"

"No plan." I hugged my knees up to my chest, toying with the chipped blue polish on my toenails. "I like history, maybe psychology. I'll see once I get there. But enough about school and Haverford." I looked over. "You're supposed to be distracting me from all of that."

Ethan laughed. "I didn't realize, is that the deal?"

"Yes." I smiled. "It's why I agreed to go out with you tonight."

"Well then." Ethan gave me a sideways look. "I'd better not let you down."

*

We saw an action movie in the end, filled with enough brutal fight scenes and bright explosions to send all thoughts from my mind for a couple of hours. I relaxed, adjusting to Ethan's presence beside me, solid in the dark, and when he reached over to take my hand, just as the trailers ended, I didn't pull away. Instead, I curled my fingers through his, feeling the warmth and slight dampness of his palm. My heartbeat sped, faster, as if my body were detached from my brain, feeling each shift of motion in his body and the light press of his thigh against mine with an unfamiliar rush.

He was watching me. I could tell out of the corner of my eye, glancing over under the guise of reaching for the soda. The lights from the screen danced across his face, blue and white; his jawline smudged with stubble, hair now drying with a faint curl. His eyes met mine, and I quickly turned back to the movie, tilting my head so my hair fell, a curtain of privacy between us.

In the dark, I felt his breath quicken, half a beat.

I was still. I knew what was coming, felt the intention from his body even before his arm slid over the back of my seat and he slowly leaned in.

I turned my face up to meet him as his lips found mine. He tasted of salted popcorn and sweet bubblegum, was almost tentative as he parted my lips and slid his tongue deeper into my mouth. I listened to the roar of gunfire on-screen, and kissed him back.

Ethan drove me home and put the truck in park. We kissed for half an hour there, Ethan's hands, clutching at my sweater; my body, pressed against him, until finally he detached himself, catching his breath.

"I should go." He pulled away, running one hand through his mussed-up hair. He looked disoriented, breathing fast, and I felt a curl of satisfaction to see his usual easy calm so flustered. I leaned over the gear shift to kiss an experimental line along his jaw.

"So go," I murmured, reaching his ear and biting down gently on his lobe. He flinched under my touch and I felt a flash of power.

"I have an early start tomorrow," Ethan protested weakly.

"You can go anytime you like," I smiled. I hooked a finger over his top button and tugged him down to meet my mouth. "I'm not stopping you."

"You're dangerous." Ethan let out a chuckle, and then he was kissing me again, cradling my face in his hands, slow and deliberate.

They were goodbye kisses, I could feel it, and with them, my panic began to rise. I hung on to his shirt, feeling the house loom behind me, dark and too still. I wanted to stay, exactly where we were: locked in the front cab of his truck with the music playing low and the engine humming behind every kiss. I was safe here, warm in his arms with the cocktail of adrenalin shivering in my veins, but when I got out of the truck, the night would be over. The temporary, carefree bubble I'd been living in would burst and I'd be left standing on my front step again, back in the cold, sharp darkness of my real world.

"I really have to go." Ethan pulled away again, his voice apologetic. He cupped my cheek, a regretful smile. "Believe me, I'd stay here all night if I could, but I've got to be on the site before the rest of the crew. I can't cut any corners just because I'm the boss's son."

"That's OK." I mustered a smile. I pulled my sneakers back on and tugged my sweater down. "I ... I had fun tonight. Thanks."

I reached for the door handle.

"I'll call you," Ethan said, catching my hand and pressing a kiss into my palm. "I have a meeting tomorrow, but we could go out Friday night. And I'll come by the diner, try and catch you on your lunch break."

I paused. I hadn't been thinking about the future, only tonight. "Ethan ..." I started. "Just because we hung out this one time—"

"I know, I know, you're leaving." Ethan cut me off. He

flashed me a grin. "But you said, you had fun, right? So let's have fun again."

I wavered, still feeling the breathless shiver of attraction in my bloodstream. "I don't know. Maybe. We'll see."

"I'll call you." Ethan released my hand. "Tomorrow. It's a date."

"It's a maybe," I warned him, climbing down.

"You can play hard to get all you like," Ethan joked through the open window. "But I know your secret."

"Oh yeah?" I smiled, amused by his confidence. "What's that?"

"You want me." Ethan winked, gunning the engine and driving away, leaving me alone on the dark sidewalk. I watched him go, headlights disappearing into the black night, until there was nothing but the sound of crickets and the glow from the security light at the Mayhews', one house down, and my own heart, beating just a little faster in my chest.

I turned and slowly walked up the path to my front porch, letting the laughter and fun of the evening dissolve into the crisp night air. I paused, listening through the door. Every time I turned the key in the lock now, it was a question. What would I find on the other side?

Tonight, it was silence again. I exhaled the small breath of hope and closed the door behind me, heading straight upstairs to my room. There was a pale strip of light shining from under Mom's door, but I didn't stop. I knew it would just be the lamp I'd left on for her. She hadn't even gotten out of bed to turn it off before she went to sleep.

I went to my room, closing the door tight behind me, but I couldn't stop the chill creeping around my shoulders. What would happen when I wasn't there to switch her lights on and off, fix her dinner, and coax her into the shower?

My phone buzzed. I checked the message. Ethan.

sweet dreams xo

I hugged my phone to my chest. One more date. Where was the harm in that?

NOW

"Honey, I need to take a look at you now, is that OK?"

The brassy, middle-aged nurse looks familiar, but they all do; faces from around town and the hospital, all those days I waited here for a ride after school, and then, later, the appointments with Mom slumped, glassy-eyed beside me.

Now I'm the unresponsive one, wordless, looking down the corridor they took him last. I can still see his body, terrifyingly still in the midst of all the chaos. Splayed, unmoving on the gurney, his eyes shut and his limbs draped like a broken doll; his chest burned red from the electric shocks, gauze wadded bloody against his wound.

They hustled him away, through the swing of the double doors, and suddenly, I was left in the hallway surrounded by the litter of bandages and medical wrappers, and the pools of blood, smeared red on the yellow linoleum floor.

Blood in the hospital, blood at the house. Blood soaked through my T-shirt, sticky on my hands. I don't know how he's still alive when it's all over me, everything inside him draining out.

Gone.

"Can you hear me, Chloe?"

"She's in shock." The other, younger, nurse speaks up, cinching a strap tight around my upper arm and pressing to inflate it. "Poor girl, hasn't said a word since they came in."

"Where is he now?"

"Surgery," she replies, clucking through her teeth. "Stab wound tore clear through his gut, it's a wonder he didn't bleed out."

"Jasmine! Not in front of her!" There's a disapproving hiss and then the older nurse pats my shoulder gently. "There, there, honey, they're doing their best to help him. He's going to be just fine."

They're silent after that, busy checking me over: fussing over the long cut on my arm, the bruises like a dark necklace at my throat. I sit quietly, barely flinching, even when the sting of alcohol hits my open wounds. They patch on bandages and dab the blood from my face. Then, at last, they take their hands from my body and I can breathe deep again.

Air rasps in my throat and I double over, choking.

"You got a lot of smoke back there. Take this a moment." Jasmine straps another oxygen mask over my face. I accept, relief as sharp as the crisp, clean air that circles through my lungs. I focus on my breathing, in and out, the bright lights stinging my swollen eyes as the women move a couple of steps over and scribble on my chart.

"We'll be needing photos of the bruises," the older nurse murmurs, but not too quiet for me to hear. "All her injuries, for the police."

"What do you think happened?" Jasmine's voice is hushed with speculation. "It was that Reznick boy, I saw them wheel him in."

"Which one?"

"That's right, they're brothers. I don't know his name."

"I've seen them over at the bar over in Portsdale."

"Drinking?"

"Mmmhmm."

"Well . . ."

"Poor girl. She's just a tiny thing, too."

"You heard what happened with her mama?"

I strain to listen, but another orderly comes past, asking about the chart for another patient, and my life is quickly forgotten.

"Is there anyone we can call for you?" The older nurse

returns, lifting the oxygen mask away and offering me a paper cup of water.

I take it with shaking hands, but I don't make a sound.

"It's OK, honey, it's over now," she adds warmly. She doesn't know the half of it. She can't imagine the truth. "You're safe now. Everything will be alright."

I ignore her, watching the bustle of chaos around me: firefighters and the sheriff's department, patients and staff. I look for clues in their expression, a hint of what's to come.

What are they thinking? What have they found?

I watch them, and wonder if I'll ever be safe again.

THEN

I woke with a new determined energy. Today would be different; it had to be. I would be gone soon and Mom would be left here alone. I had to know she could function without me, that she could get up and go to work, and live her life the way she used to. She'd been using sick leave and personal days at work, but they wouldn't last much longer. Time was running out, for both of us.

I quickly dressed, and strode down the hall to Mom's room.

"Good morning!" My voice sounded bright and metallically cheerful. I yanked back the curtains and pulled the covers from her sleeping body. "Time to get up!"

Mom squinted against the light, cringing back. "I'm just

going to sleep a little more . . . " she murmured, but I gritted my teeth.

"No, Mom, you have to go to work today."

I turned away from her limp body and focussed on easier tasks: finding clean underwear in the dresser, pulling down a skirt and blouse from the closet. I laid them out on the chair, then went into the bathroom to get the shower started: a bright mist of steam and hot water.

"Come on," I said loudly, returning to the bedroom. "You're going to be late."

Mom slowly swung her legs over the side of the bed and sat there a moment. "I really don't feel . . ." she whispered softly, hunched over like a reluctant child.

I remembered when I was small, the war Mom would wage trying to get me to kindergarten. I didn't like having to leave home, the bright foreign classroom, or the crowds of noisy, bawling kids. I didn't understand why I couldn't stay playing with my train-set on the living-room floor, and helping Mom with lunch, smearing peanut butter and jelly thickly on to slices of bread. 'I'll make you a special breakfast,' Mom would coo, steering me out of bed in the morning. 'And you can wear your favorite red socks.'

Now, I tried to fix that same beseeching smile on my face. "A shower will feel good, won't it?" I took Mom's hand and led her to the bathroom. "Use some of that rose body wash, it smells great. And I'll make eggs for us, with cheese, the way you like."

Mom wavered in the doorway.

"And some coffee," I added, desperate. "By the time you come downstairs, I'll have everything ready."

Mom turned to me and, for a terrible moment, I thought I'd lost. That there was nothing to drag her out of the listless slump, no matter what I promised. Then Mom's face creased with the ghost of a smile. "A shower would be nice," she said slowly, as if every word was an effort. "And maybe some toast."

"Whatever you want," I told her, eager. "Just ask."

When Mom finally came downstairs, I could have wept with relief. She was back. She wore the simple blouse and skirt, her wet hair pulled back in a braid, panty-hose and pumps on her feet. With makeup, she looked normal: color in her cheeks, mascara and lipstick. Her eyes still flickered around the room, uncertain, but, looking at her, I would never have guessed the truth.

Hope rose in my chest, a flutter, winged and ready to take flight. Mom would be OK now. She just needed to snap out of it, to get back to her normal routine.

"Eggs!" I declared, shoveling half the pan on to a plate. I pushed it in front of her with a fork and some buttered toast. "They're not as good as yours, but I did my best."

"Thank you, sweetheart." Mom blinked at me, as if seeing me for the first time. She went to the coffee pot and poured herself a cup. "I don't know if I have time though, I need to be in by nine."

"I'll make it a sandwich," I said quickly, pulling the plate back. "So you can take it with you. Remember, you used to do that for me?"

Mom smiled. "Of course I remember. You would insist on taking every last bite with you, you didn't want to waste a thing. I blame that fourth-grade teacher of yours, what was her name? She made you watch that documentary on famines in Africa, and you came home crying. What was she thinking?"

It was the longest sentence she'd spoken in weeks.

I watched her move around the kitchen, finding her purse and keys, and pouring another dash of coffee into a travel thermos. Her movements were slow, but deliberate, as if her body was remembering what it meant to stretch and move.

But she was moving. That was something, it had to be.

Mom turned back to me. "Are you going to wrap that? I have to run."

I blinked back to life. "Yes, here." I quickly assembled the breakfast sandwich and wrapped it in foil. "Have a good day!"

"You too, sweetheart." Mom darted back and kissed me on the forehead. "Ride safe."

It was a perfect fall day, blue-skied and crisp. I didn't have time for my usual morning run, so I dressed in my favorite striped knitted sweater and rode the long way into work, pumping hard on the pedals, swooping through the outskirts of the neighborhoods, feeling the stretch in my limbs and the burst of chilled air in my lungs.

I felt free again, the dark weight of the past few months lifting as the blocks melted behind me in a fast blur of red and gold and olive green. Relief beat through me with every heartbeat, a mantra I could cling to.

Mom was OK. We were going to be OK.

My flight was already booked. I had an email from my roommate, a science major from New Jersey, and a catalogue full of freshman classes I'd marked down to take. We were closer now, I was closer.

We were going to be OK.

At the diner, I hummed along with the jukebox, helping Loretta to open up. I lifted the chairs down from the tops of the tables and set them right with a clatter, and the two of us fell into our regular rhythm, setting out pastries fresh-delivered, filling pitchers with ice-water and restocking the napkin dispensers.

"You look happy," Loretta noted, giving me a knowing smile. "I'll bet it has something to do with that boy."

"No," I protested, straightening up. "I'm just in a good mood, that's all."

"Mmmhmm," Loretta smirked. Her dark eyes were full of laughter as she pointed her index finger at me and wagged. "Don't think I haven't seen him in here, every day like clockwork. You know he asked me for your shifts."

I stopped. "He did?"

"Wanted to know when you worked, so he'd be sure he didn't miss you." Loretta paused to select a cherry Danish and take a bite. "He's sweet on you, that's for sure."

"It's nothing." I shrugged off her comments, but even as I was wiping down the counter, my phone buzzed with a new text.

had a great time last night. c u at lunch. xo

Ethan.

He'd been tracking my movements. He'd asked about my schedule.

I wondered what to reply, but soon the diner was buzzing with the steady stream of morning regulars and the text was forgotten. I served and wiped and poured all morning, until the crowd thinned and I could take up my usual spot behind the counter, slipping into daydreams of the life waiting for me, just a few more days away.

"My roommate is crazy."

I looked up as Alisha clattered through the diner, collapsing on a stool by the counter. She dropped an armful of bags, spilling three-ring files and pads of college-ruled paper astray. "They sent me a copy of her application profile," she continued, rolling her dark eyes. "She checked 'nocturnal' under sleeping habits. And she's a vegan too."

"Ouch." I poured her a soda. "Maybe she's faking and thought she'd get a single."

"I hope so." Alisha sighed, slumping lower on the counter. "I want so badly for everything to go right, and the wrong roommate could set me back all year."

Alisha had been planning her escape from Haverford too, for as long as we'd been friends. But while my plans took me as far as college – the rest, a hazy world of possibilities – Alisha had mapped her life with exacting strategy. She'd picked her freshman courses at UCLA before she'd even applied, researched the clubs and activities she wanted to try, and already assembled a list of grad schools for four, five years down the line.

"So, how's your stalker?" Alisha changed the subject. I frowned. "You know, that cute guy who's always in here."

"His name is Ethan and he's not a stalker," I corrected her. I looked away, wiping down the counter. "We actually went out last night."

"What?" Alisha jolted upright. "And you're telling me now?"

I shrugged. "It wasn't a big deal. We went to a movie."

"That's it?" Alisha demanded.

"It was fun, I guess," I offered.

Alisha looked at me for a moment, then shook her head. "Honestly, Chloe. Sometimes I don't understand you at all."

I didn't reply. I knew I was supposed to call her with breathless gossip, poring over Ethan's texts, but the truth was, I didn't feel all that breathless, not now the cloud of hormones from last night had ebbed away. Ethan was nice. It had been a welcome distraction, but feigning excitement would only make me feel like I was putting on a show: play-acting at teen girl swooning, when the truth was far more difficult than that.

The diner bell sounded, distracting Alisha. She looked around then spun back, making a face at me as a girl from our class strode in. Crystal Keller, one of the girls who partied out by the lake. She'd barely showed up in school, slouched in the back of every class, and now, she made a beeline for the back, wearing ratty tight cut-offs and clumpy boots, her bleached hair showing dark at the roots.

"Restrooms are for customers only," I called after her. Crystal ignored me, the bathroom door slamming shut.

Alisha gave me a look. "I can't believe she graduated," she murmured. "Not that she'll do anything now. Except work in the Quik-Stop, get knocked up and have three kids by the time she's twenty."

"'Lish," I warned her, glancing towards the bathroom.

"What? We both know it's true." She yawned, "I heard she fucked two guys on the football team at a party last month, and she let them film it."

"That's ridiculous."

"That's what they're saying." Alisha shrugged, as if she couldn't be held responsible for rumors and gossip.

The bathroom door swung open again. Crystal emerged, this time in a different shirt – a black T-shirt with a giant tongue on the front. It was ripped up in front, showing her bra straps, hot pink, peeking from underneath.

"Real classy," Alisha murmured as she passed us by. If Crystal heard us, she didn't let on. She walked out of the diner without a backwards glance.

Alisha watched her go, a mixture of fascination and smugness on her face. "I'm so glad I'm getting out of this town."

My cellphone rang before I could reply. I fished it out, wondering if it was another message from Ethan, but instead the display showed an unknown number.

"What did I say about those things?" Loretta called, from where she was tallying receipts in a corner booth. "You don't know what kind of damage they're doing to your brain. Radiation waves, and all sorts."

"Sorry!" I moved to the side to answer. I couldn't hear the other voice for a moment, and had to cup my hand around my ear to listen. "Sorry, who is this?"

"It's Beverly, from your mom's office." The voice was tense. I froze. "You need to come pick her up."

THEN

I rode as fast as I could, but it still took forty-five minutes to get out to the hospital. I left my bike unlocked by the back entrance and hurried inside through the labyrinth of hallways to the second-floor offices. Mom had always complained they crammed them into such a small department, barely big enough to fit the reams of paperwork all the insurance companies demanded. Now, I practically skidded down the hall to her office, ignoring the looks from the staff as I passed.

"Mom?" I threw open the door. Her colleague, Beverly, was there, and Mom – *God, Mom* – was crying in the corner, huddled on the floor with her legs splayed out under her body. "What happened?" I demanded. "Did she fall? What's wrong?"

"Shh." Beverly quickly moved to close the door behind her, sending an anxious look out into the hall. "I don't know what happened, someone called me in, said they found her like this. She won't stop."

"Mom?" I approached her gently. I crouched, so our eyes were level. "Are you OK? Are you feeling alright?"

Mom didn't pause for breath. She was weeping, full-out, her body shaking with sobs. I stared at her, horrified. Her makeup was smeared in desperate streaks but, more than that, she looked like a stranger, as if her face had been smudged out of alignment, put back together all wrong. She didn't even look at me, she just kept crying in great ugly gasps.

Fear settled around me, ice cold.

"They wanted to have Psych up," Beverly added, sounding concerned. She was a squat woman, all bright lipstick and spider's legs mascara. "Do an evaluation, maybe give her something to sedate her—"

"No!" I choked out the word. "She'll be fine. Thanks for calling me." I forced myself to act calm. "I've got it from here."

Beverly didn't move.

"I said, I've got it," I insisted, digging my nails into my palms to keep from shaking. I pasted on a smile. "You've done so much already. Don't you need to get back to work?"

Beverly took a breath and then beckoned me outside the

room. "About that . . ." She paused, reluctant in the hallway. "I'm sorry, but I'm going to have to let her go. She's missed so much already, and if she's not coming back . . . I need someone I can rely on."

"Fine." The word was a lie, but I needed to get her out of there. "Whatever you want. I get it." I took a long breath and managed to meet Beverly's eyes. "Now, can you leave us please?" I was shocked at how reasonable I sounded. "I should really get her home."

"Of course." Beverly's head bobbed. "Call me, OK? Let me know how she's doing."

She walked away and I stepped back into the room: left alone with the weeping stranger who used to be my mother.

I swallowed. Panic threatened, welling up like a dark tide inside me, but I forced it back with shaking breaths. "Come on." I took Mom's hand, limp. "We need to go now."

Mom didn't move. She just lay there, her body heaving, gasping for air in a limitless flood of tears.

I tried to loop my arm around her waist and lift her to her feet, but she didn't move.

"Please," I whispered, helpless. "Let's just go home."

There was no reply. It was like she didn't even know I was there. She was making animal noises, raw and desperate, as if the surface of herself had cracked, shattered, leaving nothing but this foreign weeping thing on the floor.

"Mom!" My voice broke. I tried lifting her again, ungainly, not trying to be gentle anymore, but I barely made it a few paces before she slid from my grasp and slowly crumpled back to the ground.

I stood, stranded in the center of the room. The panic was beating down on me now, a thick flock of fear. Voices came from the hall, friendly and carefree, and I listened to them pass, wondering how they could be so close and so far away at the same time: two realities spinning on the same axis, but a thousand miles apart.

A minute passed, the clock on the desk counting past the seconds.

She would stop crying in sixty seconds, I told myself. In forty. Thirty.

Please.

But the countdown ended, and the sobbing didn't stop. I stayed there, paralysed. I didn't know what to do. How could I? Beverly had mentioned psych consults and sedatives, but that would only make it worse, bare our ugly family wreckage to the world. I didn't want Alisha knowing, didn't want the sheriff's sympathies.

Do something. Anything.

I wrenched myself out of indecision, grabbed my phone and dialed.

*

Ethan was there in twenty minutes. I heard a tap, uncertain on the door, then he edged it open.

"Chloe?" He paused there, the question fading on his lips as he looked from me, to my mother, and back again.

"I can't lift her," I said, helpless. "I need to get her home, but she won't move. I can't do it."

Ethan didn't hesitate. He strode over to the corner and crouched down in front of her. "I'm Ethan," he said, his voice clear and even. "I'm a friend of Chloe's. Will you let me help you up?"

Mom slowly opened her eyes. The weeping had stopped, thank God. "Chloe?" she whispered, her eyes darting around.

"I'm right here, Mom." I swallowed back the frustration in my voice and moved to her other side. "We're going to get you home and into bed. Everything will be OK."

Mom paused, then gave a weak nod.

"Hold on around my neck," Ethan instructed her. He put one arm around her waist, and the other under her knees, and lifted her clear off the floor. He straightened up, and I leaped to get the door. I looked behind us, remembering to grab Mom's purse and keys before following them out and down the hallway.

It was quiet, with only a handful of people around to gawk and stare as Ethan strode towards the elevator, me trailing behind. He carried Mom easily. Too easily. Her sleeve fell, loose, and I saw with a pang of guilt how skinny her clothes fitted; a gap at her waist, bony collarbone protruding above her collar.

I hadn't noticed, all this time, the weight dropping off. I'd cleared away her uneaten plates, annoyed at the waste of effort, not seeing her starving herself. I should have noticed. I should have taken better care.

Ethan backed carefully out of the exit doors. His truck was parked up by the sidewalk, and he carefully settled Mom in the front seat.

"I can get her car later." I tried to think of what I might be missing.

"You rode here?" Ethan asked. I nodded over to where I'd left my bike and he swung it into the flatbed with barely a pause for breath.

"I . . ." I felt like I should say something, explain somehow, but nothing came out.

Ethan touched my arm lightly. His eyes were warm. "Let's just get you home."

The sympathy in his voice was too much, and I almost let out a sob, but instead I gave a sharp nod and scrambled up into the front cab on the other side of Mom.

We drove home that way: Ethan at the wheel, Mom between us, and me holding her up, the thin body slumped against me. Now that the immediate crisis was over, I felt a slow flush of shame winding up my spine. I hated that Ethan had seen us like this: Mom, so broken, and me, helpless and weak. He was kind enough to humor us and act as if there was nothing out of the ordinary in picking my mother off the floor like some drunk or homeless woman in the street, but I knew he must be silently judging us with every mile that sped past.

Back at the house, Ethan carried Mom up to the bedroom. I settled her in bed, pulling the covers up around her and drawing the curtains, shadowing her in the dark.

I walked Ethan downstairs, still feeling the flush of humiliation.

"Chloe—" he started, turning to face me by the doorway.

I cut him off. "Thank you. I . . . I don't know what to say. Thanks, I mean it." I opened the door, waiting for him to leave.

Ethan looked at me but, worse than any judgment in his blue eyes, I saw pity instead. "Is there someone you can call?" he asked gently.

I shook my head sharply. "We'll be fine." I lied again.

He paused. "I know it's not my business, but, that, back there? That isn't fine."

"I pushed her too hard," I argued firmly. "She wasn't ready. It was my fault. She just needs more time."

Ethan looked as if he wanted to argue.

"I should get back to her," I said quickly, looking away. "And you're missing work."

Ethan sighed, reluctant. "Call me, if you need anything."

"We'll be fine," I repeated, and again, I was shocked at how sincere my voice sounded, as if I really believed it. Ethan hovered in the doorway a moment more, then awkwardly bobbed in and kissed my cheek.

"Goodbye." He smiled hesitantly, then he walked away.

I shut the door behind him and sank back against it. I could still smell the faint scent of his deodorant or aftershave – something fresh and citrus. I'd noticed it last night, on our date.

Last night . . .

I felt a desperate laugh rise up in my chest. I'd thought I could leave all this behind. It seemed so naive to remember, kicking my feet up on Ethan's dashboard, holding hands like kids in the movie theatre, kissing until midnight.

Now is the time to put away childish things . . .

I didn't know where the saying came from, but it echoed in my head as I walked down the hall and into the small room off the den that Dad had used as an office. It was like the rest of the house now, with half-empty shelves and spaces where he used to be, but I forced myself to go through the box files and drawers in turn, assembling what was left of the paperwork; old bills, receipts and more.

It took me hours to go through it all, sat at the kitchen table, one of my brand-new college-lined notebooks and pens at my side. I'd imagined using them on my first day of classes, away at college, ready to learn. Now I had a different task.

Mortgage statements, bank account balances. Gas and electric, groceries and gas. The neat set of numbers on my notebook grew, frighteningly long with every new expense. I'd never known, the money it took to hold our lives together. We'd never been rich, just comfortable; but with Dad gone ... Mom had taken the house in the settlement, but there was no alimony, no child support since I turned eighteen in the spring. I flipped through the papers, certain I had to be missing something, but it was all there in stark black and white. Mom had been draining her only savings account these past months, trying to keep us afloat. Now that she had no job, there was no way to pay the bills.

We would have nothing.

I looked up from the papers. It was dark outside, and my eyes ached, and that fervent panic had ebbed into something worse, something empty and bleak with resignation.

There was no avoiding it any longer. I'd tried, playing make-believe all summer long, but fall was almost here now, and the truth was beating against my skull in a dull, heavy ache.

I wasn't going anywhere.

THEN

I called Ethan.

It was late. I shouldn't have, but it was the only thing I could think of to keep the future at bay. Not the future I'd dreamed of, bright and full of shimmering possibilities, but this new ugly prison that had suddenly reared up before me, dark enough to block out the sun.

"I'm sorry," I whispered, standing aside to let him in. "I couldn't sleep. I don't want to be alone."

He wrapped his arms around me, like I knew he would. "It's OK," he murmured, gently stroking my hair. I clung to him, my fear mingling with a relief so sweet it made the darkness recede, just a fraction.

I could hold on to him.

Tonight, I could hold him, and I wouldn't be alone.

NOW

I wait for an hour on a hard plastic chair in the hallway, hugging my arms around myself to keep from falling. After the madness of the fighting and the fire, the screams and the sirens, I'm finally alone.

I close my eyes against the cheap fluorescent lights, sinking into the darkness. Safe and still.

But I'm not safe, not yet. He could die.

And if he doesn't . . .

"Chloe!"

I snap my eyes open. Sheriff Weber is sprinting towards me, out of breath. His shirt is buttoned wrong; they must have woken him to get down here. "Jesus, Chloe, are you OK? When I heard on the radio . . ." He reaches out to touch my shoulder, then stops, suddenly unsure. "What happened? They said there was a fire, a boy got stabbed . . .?" He pauses again, catching his breath. "You're bleeding." Weber looks frantically around. "Can we get a nurse over here? Someone!"

I slowly shake my head. I haven't spoken since the 911 call, and now, it takes me a moment to get the words out. "It's not mine," I finally manage to whisper.

"What?" Weber turns back to me.

"The blood." My voice is hoarse, my throat still burning from the smoke. "It's not mine. It's his. I'm OK."

Weber paces back and forth for a moment. "The boy. It was one of the Reznick kids, wasn't it? Where the hell is he?"

"In surgery." I clasp my hands tight. "They say . . . They say he might not make it."

"Christ." Weber swears, and I realize through my daze that it's the first time I've ever heard him curse. The other guys at the station always ran their mouths off, as crude as they came, but the most Weber ever uttered was a pained "Dangit!" when he caught his finger in the desk drawer one time.

Weber stops pacing. "Have you talked to anyone yet?"

I don't reply.

"Chloe?" Weber's voice is careful, but I can hear a thread of uncertainty in his tone. He crouches down in front of me, unwieldy, leaning in so his eyes are level with mine and I can smell the tang of mint on his breath. "This is important, I need you to listen to me. Have you talked to anyone, anyone at all? One of the other deputies?"

I shake my head. "I . . . I haven't said a word," I whisper. "They said I was in shock."

"OK." Weber gives a sharp nod. "You need to think very carefully about what you say. You understand?" His eyes burn into mine, hooded and dark. "What happened in there, I'm on your side. Maybe you were fighting, maybe he tried to push you too far . . . But things like this can get out of control. You need to call someone: your parents, a lawyer. You need someone here to make sure things go right."

I shiver. "I don't understand," I whisper. "It was all a mistake. I never meant—"

"Your parents." Weber cuts me off. "Did you call them?"

I shake my head again. "They won't come. My mom . . ." I stop. "Nobody's coming for me."

Weber exhales in a long breath. He heaves himself up and moves to the seat beside me. "I know a guy, a public defender out in Bloomington. I'll see if he can come down and sit with you for the interviews."

"But . . ." I stop, and try my best to focus. This is all happening too soon; I was supposed to have longer, to think things through. To get my story straight.

"I'm scared," I whisper, feeling the sting of tears in the corner of my eyes.

Weber softens. "It'll be OK," he tells me, and I want to believe him. "Everything's going to be just fine."

We sit there another hour in silence, watching the bustle of activity around us. People go in and out of the double doors, but there's still no word of the surgery, just the smudges of blood, smeared like an accusation on the floor.

Weber doesn't say another word and, as the moments stretch, my panic slowly blooms. He should have questions for me, about what happened tonight, about why someone is laying in surgery with a knife wound torn through his gut. But instead, he just sits there, marking the crossword of the discarded newspaper he found on the waiting-room table. The only time he speaks is to ask me if I want coffee, ambling to the machine down the hall and returning with two cups, hot and bitter.

I accept mine with a faint nod, curling my hands around the polystyrene cup. My eyes stay fixed on those doors to surgery and, every time someone steps through, I brace myself, expecting the worst.

I just don't know what the worst would be.

Finally, the door opens on a face I recognize, the doctor who shocked him back to life. His scrubs are bloodstained, his expression grim.

I don't move. Just like before, the world feels like it's

poised on a knife's edge, ready to tumble either way, depending on the next words out of his mouth.

"He made it." The doctor pulls off his green cap with a weary sigh. "He lost a lot of blood, but we were able to patch the arterial valve and stop the bleeding. He'll pull through."

Weber lets out a breath beside me, but I shiver, anxiety still snaking like ice across my skin. "Is he awake?" I ask quickly. "Can I see him?"

"I'm afraid the surgery was complicated . . ." The doctor pauses. "We were able to stabilize him, but it might be a while before he wakes up."

"But he will wake up?" My voice quavers.

The doctor nods. "Barring any more complications, he should make a full recovery."

I exhale.

"See?" Weber turns to me and I can see the relief on his face. He pats my shoulder, swallowing hard. "Now it's going to be OK. Just a domestic, self-defense." He nods, as if talking to himself. "We see it all the time, they might not even press charges. You'll be fine."

I nod slowly, wanting so desperately to believe him, but knowing all the same that he's wrong. There's still a stormcloud looming, ominous and black, and when I catch a movement out of the corner of my eye and turn to see one of the younger deputies heading towards us, his expression panicked, I know that the storm's touched down.

"Weber?" He pauses a safe distance away and loiters, skittish. "They need you back at the fire."

"What is it?" Weber sounds impatient. "In case you haven't noticed, I'm busy here."

"It's important." The deputy meets my eyes for a second, then whips his gaze away as if he's been burned. "You really need to come now."

Weber sighs. "I don't have time for clean-up. Can't you find someone else to go?"

"It's not just clean-up." The deputy swallows, nervous. He tugs on the collar of his uniform, clears his throat.

I take a slow breath and brace myself, waiting for the next part to begin.

"They found a body."

THE END

"Ethan, please," I beg again. "Don't hurt us."

His eyes come back into focus for a moment, looking at me. They soften, a glimpse of the old Ethan, the boy I used to know.

"Please," I say, desperate. "Just let us go!"

The house is silent around us, thick with paint fumes, plastic still wrapping the furniture; blank picture frames marking places on the walls. Building tools and discarded boxes; candles and champagne.

An unholy mess. The last thing we might ever see.

"Put the knife down,"' Oliver says firmly, edging towards him. "We won't say a word, I promise. We'll go, and this will all be over."

Ethan shakes his head, stumbling back. "You're tricking me. I don't know how, but this is another of your fucked-up games. You're lying. The minute I put this knife down ..."

"Then what?" Oliver finishes for him. Another half-step closer. "You're scaring Chloe. You don't want that, do you? You love her. You would never hurt us."

"No!" Ethan holds out the blade, pointing it directly at him. "No, but you would."

"This is crazy, Ethan." Oliver tries to reason with him. "I'm your brother!"

"You don't care about anyone!" Ethan yells. "You're sick, you always have been!"

Oliver stops moving. Instead, he spreads his arms wide. "Fine, do it then. Kill me. That's what you want, isn't it?"

"Oliver!" I plead with my eyes, but he shakes his head slightly. *Trust me*, his expression seems to say, so I wait, barely breathing. I don't understand him, calling Ethan's bluff like this, it won't work. He's not thinking straight – anything could happen.

"Come on, get it over with," Oliver urges him. "Get rid of me for good, have her all to yourself. I'm right here."

There's silence. Ethan doesn't move.

Oliver snorts. "That's right, I forgot, you never *do* anything. You don't have the guts."

"Shut up!" Ethan snaps, the blade shaking in his hand.

"You just sit around, playing nice with Mommy and Daddy," Oliver continues, relentless. "One happy little suburban family. No ambition or imagination. Even Chloe can't stand it anymore. Why do you think we're here, Ethan? You think there was ever any contest?"

"I said shut up!"

Ethan suddenly swings, knocking Oliver's face back with the hilt side of the knife. I scream. Oliver stumbles back, but right away, he lunges. He grabs Ethan's midriff in a tackle and they go down hard, slamming to the ground, a bloody tangle of punches and gasps. The knife skitters out of Ethan's hand, spinning across the floor.

"Chloe!" Oliver yells, as Ethan rears up, slamming his fist down so hard I hear Oliver's head crack back against the ground. Oh God, he's gasping now, bloodied on the ground. "The knife!"

I scramble for it, my hand closing around the hilt as Oliver rolls on top, choking Ethan, his legs thrashing wildly.

"Chloe," Ethan gasps, clawing blindly at Oliver. He turns his head, his eyes meeting mine in a desperate gaze. "Help me!"

I watch, frozen. They're fighting for their lives because of me. Because of my choices. And I can't go back, I can't change a thing, I just have to decide, right now.

It's me, it's all on me.

So I choose.

THEN (FALL)

I deferred college for a year. It was long, drawn-out process of frustrating phone calls, pleading with distant administrators and wrangling with my dad, who couldn't fathom why I would hit pause on my future for something he described as trivial as Mom's "woe-is-me self-indulgence".

"I don't expect you to understand," I said through gritted teeth, gripping the phone so hard I felt it dig into my palm. He had loved Mom for twenty years then left without a backwards glance; now he was surprised I wouldn't do the same. I swallowed back my anger, doing my best to soften my voice. "Dad, things are really difficult here. Can you maybe send me the money you were going to pay for tuition now, instead?"

"I'm afraid it doesn't work like that." Dad sounded distracted. "That money was tied up in a specific fund, the rules for withdrawal are very particular. And I don't think you should be worrying about things, your mom can look after herself."

"But Dad . . ." I paced in the small storage room, trying to control myself.

"I'm sorry, pumpkin." He had the nerve to use my childhood nickname, as if I was asking for an advance on my allowance to buy a new toy, not keep the electricity turned on. "Things are tight for me too, with the baby coming. If you've made the decision to put off college, that's your decision, but I can't support it, not financially."

I hung up, my heart thundering in my chest, anger still hot in my veins. I should have known better than to expect help from him; still, it surprised me afresh every time he let me down.

He'd left us, and now, every day, he chose to stay gone.

I wouldn't be calling him again.

"There you are." A voice brought me out of my thoughts. I looked up to find Sheriff Weber loitering in the open doorway. "I can't find the incident report sheets; do you know where you keep them now?"

"Sorry!" I exclaimed, tucking my phone away and pasting on a bright smile. "I was just getting more ink for the printer. Be right there!"

"No hurry," Weber added, yawning. "It was just Mrs Farnham's dogs acting up again, Kelly Bates says they went after her cat. Take your time." He shut the door and I was left alone, in the narrow storage closet that housed office supplies and spare uniforms, and all the many reams of paperwork that the Haverford County Sheriff's department required.

This was my new job, my new life now: receptionist, filing clerk, and general errand girl down at the police precinct. It wasn't much, and I'd been lucky to get it at all. With diner traffic slowed to a trickle, Loretta could only offer me weekend shifts, so I asked around town and found they needed someone on the front desk at the station. It was basic work: filing, answering phones, taking lunch orders from the motley crew of local deputies, but I didn't mind the boredom of the work, it left my mind to wander, free to focus on a plan. A plan to keep my sanity intact; a plan to get me through this.

A way to keep hold of normalcy, even with my life slipping further and further out of reach.

It had been a month now since the end of summer, and I'd got us through this far. I used my summer earnings to pay the most overdue bills, and drained the last of Mom's savings account. I rode my bike and took the bus to save on gas money; kept the heat turned off as long as possible, and took home dinner from my shifts at the diner, as many nights as I could. With my new wages at the sheriff's department, and the meager diner tips, I figured, we could just about make it to spring. Mom would be better by then.

She had to be.

I grabbed the box of cartridges and stepped back out into the main floor. The deputies had all abandoned their desks for lunch, but I found Weber by the front reception, regarding the files covering the floor with a twitch of bemusement.

"Sorry." I hurried to explain, hoping I hadn't done the wrong thing. "I know it looks a mess, but I'm reorganizing. Some of the guys were saying they couldn't find a thing."

"Hey, good luck to you." Weber backed away from the mess, as if the avalanche of files teetering precariously on the desk were about to crush him. "The incident paperwork?"

"Right." I looked around, then delved into a blue folder and found the right forms. "And do you need to file a report with Animal Control too?"

Weber sighed. "If I have to. One of these days, someone'll just shoot the damn things, and then where will we be?"

"Filing more paperwork," I replied wryly.

Weber cracked a smile. "You ain't wrong there." He paused, loitering by the desk. "Have you heard from Alisha?"

"Not much this week. Just a couple of emails and texts," I replied, sorting files again. "She said things are still pretty crazy."

Weber nodded. "It's strange to have her gone. Her mom keeps setting an extra place at the table." He gave me a faint smile, almost lost. "We've been calling, but, she's so busy now, with classes . . ." He trailed off.

"It's just the first semester," I offered. "I'm sure once she gets into a routine, she'll have more time."

"I know." Weber gave a nod, then tapped the desk. "OK then, I'll be getting back to work."

He headed to his office, leaving me alone to work through the filing.

Alisha couldn't understand why I stayed. But why would she? I'd never told her what was happening with Mom, so she didn't realize how bad it had become. She departed town in a car packed high with boxes, and I'm sure, she never once looked back. At first, she texted and called every other day. I could hear the uncertainty in her voice as she gossiped nervously about her roommate, and the dizzying size of campus, and how she needed to spend every night in the library, just to catch up. But quickly, the calls dropped off; became shorter and rushed. She found a group of girls to hang out with, and chattered happily about their pizza parties and study nights.

I dreaded and longed for her updates in equal measure.

They were a glimpse of the world still outside my reach, and I couldn't help but imagine myself in the scenes she was painting; where the biggest stress I had to deal with was nerves over a first big term paper, and the frat-boy exploits of the guys down the hall.

Instead, I had filing and telephones, a brown-bag lunch, and Haverford, turning red with fall outside my windows, the same as it had always been.

The department was quiet until after lunch when the younger deputies filed in, still talking smack-talk about a parking-lot pick-up game.

"Blake?" I stopped one of the guys as he passed, a younger guy in his twenties with a blonde crew-cut. "Your mom called for you."

There were whoops and jostling. Blake scowled at me. "What are you trying to say?"

I blinked. "I didn't . . . I mean, your mom really did call." I hurriedly passed him a slip of paper with the scribbled message. "She couldn't reach you on your cell. Says you need to pick up some windshield fluid."

"Sorry." Blake looked sheepish. He crumpled the message in his fist. "I told her not to call here, but she never listens." He sighed. "Can't wait 'til I move out and get my own place."

I looked at him curiously. He'd been a few years ahead of

me in school; a football player, a big-shot as far as Haverford was concerned, which wasn't much. There had been talk of a football scholarship to college, but nothing ever materialized. Now, he was a deputy, swaggering around town with his hand on his gun, writing up tickets for speeding and parking fines.

"So what about you?" he asked, leaning on the counter. "You at home with your folks?"

I nodded.

"Huh, I figured you'd get the hell out of here the first chance you got."

I shrugged, sorting files. Everyone had been surprised by the news I wasn't heading out to Connecticut as planned. I'd brushed off their questions with a wry smile, explaining I wanted to take a year to work and travel first, tuition being what it was. Still, I felt their curiosity, looking me up and down. I was one of the good ones, a decent student, never in trouble. Not the kind to stick around Haverford a moment more than necessary. Yet here I was, a month later. Still in town. "Plans change," I replied lightly.

Blake sighed, restlessly drumming his palms on the counter. "Tell me about it. I'm taking some classes over at Rossmore. Figure it can't hurt."

"Where's that?" I moved a stack of files aside before Blake tipped them.

"Community college, about an hour away." Blake reached for the bowl we kept on the desk, pulling out a Halloween candy. "It's lame, I know, makes me wanna put a bullet through my brain, but hey, the credits are cheap."

"Blake!" A yell came up from the back of the office. Blake sighed. "See ya." He took the balled-up message and arced it into the wastepaper basket on the other side of the room. "And the crowd goes wild," he murmured wistfully as he sauntered away.

I kept filing for another few minutes, but Blake's comment about college jittered in the back of my mind. I put the paperwork aside, took a seat in front of the battered old computer, and clicked through to a search site.

Rossmore College.

Even the website couldn't make it look like much. There were no beaming students studying under verdant trees, like all the glossy prospectuses I'd been browsing this time last year, but I forced myself to check the site, looking at the course catalogue and payment plans. We couldn't afford it, not really, but still, I found myself copying down the details for admissions and financial aid applications. I was grasping at straws here, but even a class or two might be enough; enough to make me feel like my entire life wasn't on hold. That this – this filing and planning and counting every damn dollar in the aisles at the grocery store – was a temporary detour in my future.

Because otherwise ...

I shivered. If this was it for me now, if this town dug its claws into me and never let go, I couldn't bear it.

I didn't know what I would do.

THEN

Ethan came to pick me up as usual after work. I couldn't stop myself from babbling about the college classes all the way home. "I can take them at night, so I don't have to miss shifts, and the credits will all transfer once I start at Mills again," I told him, as we pulled up outside my house.

"I'm glad you're happy," Ethan grinned.

"I'm not happy, I'm ... interested," I corrected him. I hadn't told anyone, not even him, how close we were to the edge financially. He knew the truth about Mom, and that was bad enough, I wasn't about to let him in on the true extent of my desperation. "It'll work out great," I said instead, giving him a quick smile. "As long as the Honda doesn't fall apart on me again."

"I can always give you a ride if you need," Ethan said.

I shifted, uncomfortable. "It's an hour away. I wouldn't ask you to do that."

"Why not? Think about it. I'm always here. And anyway, it would mean more time with you, for this . . ." He leaned in and kissed me slowly until I ducked away.

"I'll be right out."

"Why can't I wait inside?" Ethan sighed. "Come on, I feel like a stalker, loitering out here every night."

I shook my head firmly. "It's too depressing in there. I won't be long."

I scrambled down from the truck and headed up the front path, letting myself in. Today, Mom had made it all the way downstairs: I'd found her in the living room, watching TV in her favorite velour bathrobe.

"How was your day? Did you eat the sandwich I left in the fridge?" I pulled the drapes and straightened up, fluffing up the pillows on the couch, and setting an extra blanket on Mom's lap.

Mom's eyes drifted briefly to me. "Marybeth is out of a coma," she replied, engrossed in the show. "But Gustav kidnapped her baby, and switched it with the kid they found on the church steps."

"Good!" I cheered, my voice bright. "I'm going to heat up that lasagna from last night, I'll just fix your plate."

I went into the kitchen and quickly made up a tray. It had taken a while, but I'd worked out a system to keep Mom fed and washed, at the very least. Breakfast was always a battle, but I refused to leave for work until she managed a few bites of toast. I left a packed lunch in the fridge, fixed us dinner every night. Mom had found a routine too: coming downstairs in time to watch her favorite soaps on TV in the afternoon, even reading a little when I managed to get to the library for the thick romance novels she liked. I could almost tell myself it was good, that we had a pattern to our days now. Routine, stability. It was only when I let myself think about it that the bleak reality seemed so laughable: that Mom managing to take a bath would count as a good day; that any time I came home to find her conscious would be a victory.

"Here you are." I re-emerged into the living room and set the tray on her lap. "I'll be back before midnight, call if you need anything."

"Are you going out with Ethan?" Mom asked, distracted.

"Yes." I bit back my frustration at the same question, every night.

Mom smiled at me. "He's a nice boy. Helpful."

"Yes, Mom." I sighed, making sure she had everything she needed before I went and changed, quickly pulling on jeans and a sweater, and thundering back downstairs. I was back out in Ethan's truck before five minutes had elapsed.

"See?" I said, breathless. "All set."

Ethan gunned the engine but paused. "Are you sure she's OK? We can hang at yours, if you want."

I couldn't find the ways to describe how much I didn't want that. Spending another moment in that house would be more than I could take. It was why I was out with Ethan so much, why his house had become my refuge: warm, and bright, and full of activity, the way a home should be.

"I promised your mom I'd come for dinner," I said instead. "Maybe another night." I waited for us to pull away, but instead, Ethan was waiting. "What?" I asked, still tense. "I'm good to go."

"Just one more thing." Ethan gave me a crooked grin and then leaned over to kiss me.

I relaxed against him, feeling the warmth of his mouth and the gentle curl of his hand against my cheek. I kissed him back, tasting the mint on his breath. This was always the best part of my day.

Ethan pulled back. "Better?" he whispered.

I smiled. "Better."

Ethan put the truck in drive and pulled away. "Now I know why Mom wanted me home on time. She loves you, you know," he said, as we headed through the neighborhood. "It's always Chloe this, and Chloe that, and 'when are we going to see more of her?' " He mimicked his mother's eager voice.

I laughed. "I like her. Both of them. Your parents are great."

Ethan made a face. "I know, it's just ... they're kind of full on. Living at home, working with Dad, it's hard to get any time alone." He gave me a sideways look. "You know, that's another thing about your place." He slid his hand over, across my thigh. "It's practically empty. Private."

I caught his hand, lifting it from my leg and intertwining my fingers through his. "We get plenty of privacy," I reminded him. "And it's just weird for me, having her there. Not exactly romantic."

Ethan sighed, but he didn't press the issue. Since that first night, I'd kept us out of the house. It was a tedious dance, snatching moments between his work and mine; here in the truck, there in his bedroom, his parents downstairs, our music on loud. Sometimes, I wished I could go back, just reset the clock to before I'd asked him to stay, but that wasn't fair. I wanted this too: the way he made me feel, those moments of escape.

"Thank you," I murmured. "For understanding."

"Of course, babe." Ethan gave me a puzzled smile. "Anything for you."

"I'll make it up to you." I lifted his hand to my lips, dropping a kiss on his palm. "I'm sorry if I seemed like a bitch before."

"You could never be a bitch." Ethan smiled at me. "You're too sweet for that. My sweet girl."

We pulled in to the driveway of Ethan's house, a brightly-lit split-level with a neatly-trimmed yard. "Hey?" Ethan called, as he swung open the door. "We're home!"

"Perfect timing." Ethan's mom, Annette, bustled past him, pulling me inside with a hug. "Chloe, so good to see you!"

"Hi, Annette." I smiled shyly, still not used to calling her by her name.

"Sure, ignore me," Ethan teased.

"Oh, hush you." Annette patted his arm affectionately, before turning back to me. Her blue eyes were smiling and she had a streak of flour on her cheek, incongruous against her sleek silk blouse and tailored pants. "I'm breaking the habit of a lifetime and trying my hand at dessert. Come tell me if the fruit is too tart. They said to use two cups of sugar, but surely that must be wrong."

I followed her through the house, savoring the bright, warm rooms and the smell of sugar and vanilla drifting in the air. The Reznick house was like a spread from a magazine; not one of those cold, stark showrooms, but lived in and relaxed: polished wooden floors laid with fluffy rugs, walls covered with family photos and colorful abstract paintings that Annette had collected over the years, overstuffed couches to curl up in front of the fireplace that burned real logs (however much Ethan complained about carrying timber from the shed). I could have happily moved in and left my own cold, dark house behind, pretended as if this family were my own: loud and teasing and good-natured, instead of the fractured broken truth.

"How was work?" Annette chatted, as we reached the kitchen, a blue-tiled haven with acres of countertops now all covered with baking ingredients.

"Fine. Quiet." I slipped on to a stool at the breakfast bar, my usual spot, and watched her stir a pot of something on the stove. She dipped a spoon in, then held it out to me. "Here, try, but watch out, it's hot."

I blew on the sauce, then tasted. "Great. But, maybe more sugar?" I agreed. Annette made a face.

"I'm trying to get the boys to cut down, you should see what they eat all day at work. Nothing but junk."

"And look how it's stunted me!" Ethan sauntered in. He flexed his biceps, grinning. I elbowed him as he passed, and he caught me in a hug, wrapping his arms around me from behind.

"You say that now, but just you wait." Annette looked over, affection clear in her eyes. She scolded Ethan, but it was always good-natured. She couldn't have been prouder of her son if she tried. "Your father was just like you, then he hit middle age and everything changed."

"Then that gives me another twenty years," Ethan laughed.

"It goes sooner than you think," Annette warned him. "Here, Chloe honey, come stir this. I need to get started on the crust."

I helped with the rest of dinner, while Ethan took a shower and changed. We had dinner ready by the time his father arrived home, greeting Annette with his usual kiss.

"Good to see you again, Chloe." Derek Reznick was the older version of Ethan, so much so it was unnerving: the same broad, strapping physique, the same clear blue eyes. Derek's hair was greying from blonde to silver, and his figure was softer and padded with age, but still, there was no mistaking the likeness, a glimpse of what Ethan would look like in another thirty years.

Would we be like this too? I wondered, watching Annette take his coat and shoo him out to set the table. Me in the kitchen when Ethan arrived home from work; the daily pleasantries, the safety of family and home.

The vision should have been a comfort. Instead, I felt a faint shiver. I'd wanted those things too, but after. After life out in the world away from this town, after I'd lived a little, achieved things on my own.

"Can you grab the potatoes?" Annette called back, not even pausing for breath before turning and bellowing, "Ethan! Dinner's ready!"

I shook off the flash of my possible future and brought the serving bowl as instructed, taking my seat next to Ethan's empty chair. He bounded downstairs and slid into it a moment later, dressed in a T-shirt and sweats.

"Couldn't you at least try to dress for dinner?" Annette sighed.

"What, you mean like a suit and tie? C'mon, Mom." Ethan rolled his eyes. He reached for the nearest plate, but Annette made a tsking sound.

"Grace first."

It was the same as always: the rituals and routines that threaded through their every day, like a safety net. Annette made some comment about Ethan's clothes, Derek always said grace before the meal. Ethan always reached across to hold my hand under the table as they all bowed their heads and Derek opened his mouth to speak.

But that night, before he could launch into the short prayer, a noise came from the foyer, the sound of a key in the lock; the door opening.

I caught a flash of something on Annette's face and then a young man arrived in the doorway. He had a shock of golden blonde hair and eyes as clear blue as Ethan's, stubble on his face and a large duffel bag slung over his shoulder that he dropped to the ground with a thump as he took in the frozen tableau. The stranger lifted his eyebrow with an arched smile.

"What, you didn't save a seat for me?"

NOW

From the moment you're born, people start folding you into neat pieces and tucking you inside a box of their own design. No, it starts even before then, the moment the sonogram shows a faded blur. Blue for a boy, tractors and race-cars, big and strong and brave. Pink for a little princess, pretty and sweet. They dress you up in their own expectations, before you even have a chance to understand the constrictions of your fate. That box becomes so cozy and warm, you never really notice that you're bent double, fighting for room to breathe.

I was the good girl. A hardworker, diligent in class. My letters were laborious and perfect; my homework always handed in on time. They told me I was doing it right, rewarded me with cookies and new dolls; bright red 'A' grades and a 3.9 Grade Point Average.

I was the sweet girl. I took care of my mother, and kissed Ethan goodnight. He told me how pretty I was, how special and kind. I felt like I was doing it right, on track, just as I should be.

But Oliver . . .

Oliver didn't fit in a box. He would rather burn the whole world down than spend a moment of his life caving to other people's expectations. He took one look at me, smiling and neat and good, and he knew.

He knew I was pretending, before I even knew it for myself.

Because we were the same.

THEN

There was a split-second silence: the family around me, frozen in prayer, and this newcomer watching us with a smirk. Then Ethan pushed back his seat and greeted him with a hug, slapping his back enthusiastically. "Olly! What are you doing here?"

The stranger laughed. "What, I need a reason to swing home for a visit?"

"Chloe, this is Oliver." Ethan turned back to me, grinning.

I realized who he must be. "The mysterious older brother," I said slowly. I realized I hadn't known what he looked like. He wasn't in any of the family photographs displayed around the house.

"The lovely new girlfriend," Oliver replied, tipping his

head in a nod. His eyes drifted over me, lips curling in a smile. "Well, look at you, guess little brother finally did something right."

I felt myself blush as Oliver grabbed Ethan playfully around the throat, bending him over to ruffle his hair.

"Hey!"

Ethan ducked out of the hold and then they were rough-housing, shoving each other around until their mother's voice broke through in a high-pitched scold. "Boys!"

They broke apart and, for a moment, Ethan looked like a child caught misbehaving. "Sorry," he muttered, sliding back into his seat.

Oliver raised an eyebrow. "What, no welcome home for your prodigal son?" he teased.

Annette caught her breath. "Of course, darling. It's good to see you, you just took us by surprise." She bobbed up to kiss him on the cheek. "There's plenty of food. Why don't you sit down and I'll set you a place?" She darted back to the kitchen with an anxious look on her face.

Oliver shrugged off his coat and took a seat at the head of the table. I watched him, curiously absorbing the fall of his blonde hair, overgrown and scruffy against the crisp white of his Oxford shirt, tucked into slim black jeans. He had something about him, a nonchalant energy that seemed to crackle in the cozy room.

"Why didn't you call?" Derek looked concerned. "We didn't think you'd be back until Thanksgiving."

"It's a long story. Dull, boring, superfluous. That means unnecessary," he added towards Ethan with a conspiratorial whisper.

"Dude, relax." Ethan looked embarrassed. "You're not sucking up to your Ivy League friends now."

"Nope," Oliver laughed, "but I do need to impress your girlfriend with my eloquence." He caught my eye across the table. "What do you say, Chloe? Is it working?"

"Umm, sure," I said, immediately wishing I'd come up with a better response, something witty and sharp. "I mean, maybe."

"Ah, she's withholding judgement!" Oliver announced, dramatic. "That just means I'll have to prove my prowess."

Ethan groaned. "Don't mind him. You can always count on Olly to use five words where one would do."

"And you can count on Ethan here to substitute grunts for actual conversation whenever possible," Oliver replied, as Annette bustled back in with a plate and cutlery, laying them out for him.

"It's good to have you home," she said hurriedly, taking her seat again. "You don't call as often as you should. We missed you."

"Say, Olly, why don't you say grace?" Derek suggested.

I thought I saw a look of amusement on his face, then we all bent our heads again. "Dear Lord," Oliver began, "we thank you for the blessings we enjoy, for the food on this table, so lovingly prepared."

I peeked out from under my eyelashes. He was staring straight at me, his blue eyes burning into mine.

I stared back, caught. "For family, and especially for new friends," Oliver continued, not breaking the gaze. "We thank you. Amen."

Slowly, he winked.

I looked away quickly. The rest of them murmured "amen", and then the moment was broken, and the bustle of cutlery on china and reaching hands quickly filled the strange space our gaze had just occupied.

What was that?

I shivered.

"So what's happening at Yale?" Ethan asked, helping himself to pot roast and passing the plate on. "Do you have a break? I thought they worked you pretty hard."

"I quit." Oliver answered so calmly, it took a moment for the news to sink in. I watched Annette's head jerk up in surprise, as Oliver held a dish across to me. "Potato?" he offered with a smile.

"What do you mean, you quit?" Ethan asked. "Like, you just walked out?"

"Pretty much." Oliver shrugged. He was still holding out the dish, so I took it, trying to ignore the look of panic passing between his parents.

"But I don't understand, sweetheart." Annette blinked at Oliver. "You've been doing so well. You aced all your midterms, and didn't you say you were ranked top in your class?"

"Fifth." Oliver corrected her. "And only because I refused to jump through their stupid hoops. All those lectures and study groups and God-awful group presentations," he added. "Why should I have to tick their stupid boxes? I'm smarter than half my professors, it's a waste of my time."

He sat back, perfectly at ease.

"But honey, you only have another year left." Annette sent a pleading look towards Derek, who cleared his throat uneasily.

"Let's talk about this later, after dinner. I'm sure we'll figure something out. I remember, the stress got to me too, back in the day. Maybe a weekend break away from it all is just what the doctor ordered, eh?" He slapped Oliver on the arm.

"I'm not stressed, I'm bored out of my goddamn mind," Oliver replied evenly. "And now the problem is solved."

"But what will you do?" Annette asked, her voice lifting with concern.

"I don't know." Oliver shrugged. "Maybe I'll stay here for a while, hang out with Dad and Ethan. There is room for me, right?"

Annette blinked. "Of course there is. The guest room is yours, you know that."

"My mother, the perfect hostess." Oliver smiled at her across the table. Annette looked away.

I watched silently, still trying to decipher the scene. Oliver's college bombshell had sent ripples through the cozy room; Annette was fretting, his father confused. Ethan seemed to be the only one unaffected – or oblivious – as he winked at me and dug into the food. But Oliver stayed at the head of the table, chatting about classmates and Christmas vacation plans like nothing was wrong.

"A group of us are thinking about going to Aspen for New Year's," he said, helping himself to more salad. "Someone's family has a cabin there. Although, these guys, a cabin probably means a ski lodge with private chef on call," he added, with a brief flicker of his eyes to the ceiling.

"Are they really that wealthy?" I asked, curious. I didn't think of myself as some naive country kid, but Oliver had been mixing in circles I had never known.

"Disgustingly," Oliver replied cheerfully. "Remember my roommate freshman year?" He nudged Ethan. "The guy was heir to some oil fortune, out in Eastern Europe. I would have hated him for it, except he always picked up the check." Oliver grinned.

I laughed. "Doesn't sound too bad to me."

"It wasn't."

"So why leave now?" Annette spoke up. "Darling, surely if you just finished out the year and graduated . . ."

Oliver's smile slipped. "Mom, please, we've got company. You're making Chloe uncomfortable."

"I'm fine," I said, self-conscious.

"Look, she's practically bolting from the table," Oliver continued.

Annette looked away. "You're right, I'm sorry." She cleared her throat, as if he'd been the one scolding her. "Now, who wants pie?"

After dinner was done, Annette and Derek retreated into the den, leaving "us kids" to clean up while they closed the door on fervent whispers.

"What do you think they'll try this time?" Oliver asked Ethan, lounging back against the kitchen counter as we did the dishes with a practiced rhythm: him washing, me on drier duty. "A new car? Flat-screen TV? My parents are big believers in positive reinforcement," he added, explaining to me. "They prefer to smother you with bribes until you fold."

"Dude, you didn't have to break it like that," Ethan told him, looking up. "Out of nowhere, no warning . . ."

"What kind of warning do they need?" Oliver idly picked at the dessert leftovers. "I'm twenty-one now; it's my life, not theirs."

"It's their tuition check," Ethan pointed out.

"Baby brother doesn't like to disobey," Oliver told me, with a wry look. "He's a people pleaser. But then, you probably knew that already."

Before I could respond, Ethan spoke up. "I told you, don't call me that."

"What, baby brother?" Oliver drawled it with a grin.

"I'm not a kid anymore."

"But you'll always be my baby brother," Oliver said, faux-serious. "We'll be drooling old bachelors on our La-Z boy recliners, and you'll still be younger than me."

"You know what I mean." Ethan turned, his jaw set with frustration.

I quickly stepped between them. "Let's go upstairs," I told Ethan, placing a hand on his arm. "Oliver can finish up here."

"Can I now?" Oliver looked amused.

I tugged gently on Ethan's arm. "Coming?"

"Sure." He hurled the wet dishcloth at Oliver, hitting him squarely in the chest. "All yours, *big brother*."

*

Ethan took the stairs two at a time up to his room. He closed the door behind us and then flopped down on his bed with a sigh.

"So that's Oliver, huh?" I started cautiously.

"Yup." Ethan rolled over to turn his iPod on. A second later, a familiar indie rock song filled the room.

"Is he always this ..." I paused, searching for the right word, but Ethan filled in the blank for me.

"Dramatic? Egotistical? Yup. You'll get used to it." He lay back, folding his arms underneath his head. "I'm surprised it took him this long to quit."

"What do you mean?" I kicked off my shoes and joined him on the bed, scooching back against the wall and curling my legs up beneath me on the quilt.

"Olly can't stick with one thing for long," Ethan explained. "He has the attention span of, like, a gnat. He switched schools every other year, he's always bouncing around the place."

"Still, quitting school is a big deal." I felt a stab of envy. I could barely afford to take a couple of community college classes for credit, let alone go somewhere as prestigious as Yale. "To have that opportunity, and then just walk away?"

My voice must have betrayed me, because Ethan sat up. "Hey, don't let his dumb choices get to you." He reached to slide a hand around my waist. "Oliver is ... his own person.

Believe me, this isn't even the craziest stunt he's pulled."
There was a note of admiration in his voice, so I didn't argue.
Oliver had seemed so cavalier, just announcing his decision
to quit like that, but I didn't know what was really going on
with him. Like he'd said, it was his life.

"Now, how about we stop talking about my brother?"
Ethan suggested with a familiar smile. He pulled me closer,
so I was sitting in his lap, my body pressed against the
warmth of his torso.

"So what should we talk about?" I smiled, relaxing
against him.

"Talking wasn't exactly what I had in mind ..." Ethan
dipped his head and kissed a light trail along my collarbone.
I shivered, pulling his mouth back up to me and kissing him
hard until we were tangled and breathless on the bed. With
the music playing loud, I didn't need to talk, or think, I only
had to feel the race of my heartbeat and his body cradled,
hard between my thighs as his hands hungrily roved across
my body.

"Don't mind me."

I snapped up at the sound. Oliver was standing in the
open doorway, watching us with a smile.

I yelped, rolling out from under Ethan and grabbing for
my sweater. I scrambled to pull it on over my bra as he sauntered into the room.

"You heard of knocking?" Ethan complained, breathing heavily.

"Just be glad I'm not Mom." When I turned back, my sweater securely in place, Oliver was regarding me with amusement. "Does she know you're defiling poor Chloe under her roof?"

I flushed.

"Dude," Ethan said, warning in his voice. "Be cool."

"No judgment." Oliver held his hands up. "I'm all for young love, flowering ye rosebuds etcetera, etcetera. Just saying, you might want to get a lock on that door before things get real embarrassing."

As if they weren't already. I leaped up. "I'll be right back," I said quickly, my cheeks burning as I ducked past Oliver and down the hall to the bathroom.

I shut the door and caught my breath. My expression in the mirror was pink-cheeked, guilty; hair in a mess, my shirt askew. I cringed with embarrassment as I ran cold water over my wrists, trying to collect myself. For the first time, I agreed with Ethan: we needed privacy. Annette and Derek left us to our own devices, but Oliver had strolled in as if the closed door meant nothing. If he'd been even a few minutes later . . .

I remembered the feel of Ethan's hand against my zipper and blushed even harder.

When I got back to Ethan's room, he was sprawled on the

floor beside Oliver, video game consoles in their hands and some kind of violent war scene up on the TV. He was there to stay. I felt a brief stab of annoyance, but then curiosity took over and I scrambled back up on to the bed to watch them.

"You play?" Oliver waved his handset at me.

I shook my head. "Not my thing."

"Shame. It's great to let off a little steam. But then, you already have your ways." Oliver winked.

I hugged my knees to my chest, wishing I could take back the last ten minutes.

"They give you a hard time about the Yale thing?" Ethan asked his brother, his eyes on the screen, absorbed.

Oliver shrugged. "What can they do?"

"You really quit?" I spoke up, watching him. Oliver looked over.

"Yes ma'am. Walked out of an econ lecture and never looked back."

I shouldn't have pressed, but I couldn't help it. "What about a job? Won't you need a degree? And what will you tell people, when they ask why you didn't finish?"

Oliver tilted his head at me, assessing. "I'll tell them whatever I want. Maybe I got recruited by a top-secret government agency, or left to start up my own billion-dollar tech firm."

"But that's not true."

"Don't you know? There's no such thing as the truth." Oliver yawned. "We all walk around trapped in our own subjective consciousness, experiencing the same events through a totally different lens."

I blinked at him, thrown.

"Dude, enough of that philosophy bullshit." Ethan kicked at Oliver's outstretched legs. "True fact: I'm whipping your ass right now."

"Dream on."

The boys went back to their game, but Oliver's words lingered. He was right; hadn't I thought it often enough this year, that me, Mom, and my dad were all living completely different versions of the same events? To Dad, he was the hero in his story, "doing the right thing" despite the wreckage it left in his wake. Wreckage I was left to clear up, every single day.

"So what's your story?" Oliver's voice came over the din of explosions on-screen, and when I looked up again, he was watching me with that cool blue gaze.

"What do you mean?" I avoided his eyes, watching the two fighters moving through a bombed-out village, peppering machine-gun fire through the smoke and fire.

"Why haven't you gotten the hell out of this one-horse town? Don't get me wrong, it's very charming, in the whole Norman Rockwell picket fence way, but I wouldn't have thought it was your scene." Oliver jerked his console and a line of villagers were mowed down.

"You're meant to be saving the civilians, not smoking them." Ethan laughed.

"My bad." Oliver glanced up, meeting my eyes with an arch of his eyebrow. "Well?"

I rested my cheek against my knees, not sure how to reply. He already thought he knew who I was: he'd put me in a box in his mind, and I couldn't help but wonder what that was.

"Chloe's helping out at home," Ethan answered for me, reaching up to pat my legs. "Her mom's sick, so she's waiting for a while before college."

I felt a flicker of irritation, like he'd shared a secret he shouldn't have. But that was wrong. It was hardly a secret if everyone in town knew.

"Why?" Oliver asked again.

"Why what?" I said slowly.

"Why should you have to look after her?"

I paused. "She's my mom."

"And?" Oliver prompted.

"And nothing." I clenched my jaw to keep from snapping.

"Easy there, tiger." Oliver's lips curled in a smile. "I'm just saying, our Aunt Glenda broke her leg last year, but that didn't mean I had to put my whole life on hold to go help her to the bathroom."

"That's different," I argued. I felt my irritation growing, an inexplicable burn. "She's my mom. I'm supposed to look out for her."

"Only if you choose. Obligation is a two-way street," Oliver said, turning back to the game. "Doesn't work unless you agree to play. But hey, leaving home can be a scary thing. Ethan here never managed it. Maybe it's good you have an excuse to stay."

"Bro . . ." Ethan warned. "Drop it."

"No!" I spoke over him, scrambling to my feet in a flash of anger. A month of stress and constant anxiety suddenly reared up inside me. "You don't get to say that," I accused him. "You think this my choice, to stay here, instead of starting my actual life? You think I want to be stuck working crappy temp jobs trying to pay the bills?" My voice came, loud. "That I'm using the fact my mom had a nervous breakdown as some kind of *excuse*?"

Ethan was on his feet in an instant. "Hey, it's OK," he tried to calm me. "Olly didn't mean that, did you?" He turned to Oliver, who was still sprawled on the floor.

Oliver held up his hands, his face innocent. "I was just asking."

"See?" Ethan soothed me. "You took it wrong."

It didn't feel that way to me, but just as soon as it had boiled up, my anger deserted me. I stood there, heart pounding, feeling foolish at my outburst. "I think I should go now," I muttered.

"No, stay." Oliver put the console aside and got to his feet. "I'm leaving. See? You guys can get back to ... well, whatever you were doing." He slapped Ethan on the back, but that was even worse.

"It's late," I said. "I have to get back. Ethan?"

"Sure, I'll take you." Ethan looked for his shoes, but I was already heading for the door.

"Nice meeting you, Chloe." Oliver's voice followed me out into the hall. "See you soon!"

I headed blindly downstairs, trying to pull myself together. I'd overreacted, I knew that already, but still, I couldn't help it.

"Don't let him push your buttons," Ethan said, catching up in the foyer. "It's what he does, you'll get used to it."

I turned away. "I'm fine." I grabbed my coat from the hall and pulled it on. "Ready to go?"

"All set." Ethan held the door open, waiting until I'd stepped out into the cold night air before following after me.

We walked slowly away from the house. "You didn't say you were paying the bills," Ethan said quietly. "I thought you were saving for tuition, travel."

My stomach lurched. "I am." I managed a bright reply. "I just meant, it's a lot of responsibility, that's all."

"I know." He reached over and took my hand, pulling me to a stop. He looked down at me, reaching to tuck a strand of hair behind my ear. "I think you're amazing," Ethan said quietly, looking almost shy for a moment. "What you're doing, taking care of her."

I looked away, self-conscious. "It's not a big deal."

"It is." Ethan corrected me. "I'll talk to Olly, he shouldn't have pushed you like that. He's just making trouble."

"Don't." I could see Oliver's eyes on me, whenever Ethan answered for me or reached to pat my legs. Like I was some kind of helpless girl in need of protection. "It's fine, really. I don't care," I said again. "But maybe you should get that lock for the door."

Ethan chuckled. "First thing tomorrow. Anyway, I'm sure he's got better things to do than hang around here. I'll make sure he doesn't bother us again."

NOW

I watch him through the window of the ICU, laying so pale and still. My fingers itch to push his hair back out of his eyes, trace the contours of his face the way I used to, late at night.

I swear, I know his body by heart.

It shocked me, just how easily he tore apart under that blade: skin slicing open, the fibers of his form splitting apart, gaping red and angry inside. He was always so solid to me, from the moment he first sauntered into my life: every limb and sinew flowing together in an indivisible whole; the smile and the walk and the absent-minded gestures. He was a presence, complete.

Necessary.

I never thought about the cells and cables strung just

below the surface, the clockwork pieces ticking to keep his body in time. The things that could be pulled apart and, in a heartbeat, make him less than the sum total of himself.

There are wires trailing over his body, machines that beep in a low hum. Glass walls divide us, keeping me from him.

I watch, and I wait, and I wonder.

Did they find the other body too soon?

THEN

The week passed, day by dreary day. Ethan didn't mention Oliver again, so I didn't ask. Instead, I threw myself into applications for classes at Rossmore, navigating the process of getting my transfer approved in between my shifts at the sheriff's department and late nights working at the diner. I had a glimpse of light, some way to make sure this time wasn't wasted in vain, and I was determined to make it work. When Mom was better, when I was back in college again ... The promises I made to myself seemed distant and wispy, but they were all I had.

"So if I get my credits, I could start as a sophomore next year," I explained to Alisha on our Friday night call, taking a break from my shift at the diner. "I wouldn't miss a thing."

"Uh-huh, that's great." Alisha paused. "And Ethan's good?"

"Yup. Work's fine too," I offered, wishing I had something more exciting to share. "Crazy Mrs Wellstone is fighting with her neighbor over the land division again; she kept lighting garbage on fire and throwing it over the fence. They had to send two deputies to calm her down."

"Wow, scandal in Haverford, it never stops." Alisha's voice was teasing, but it made me regret saying anything at all.

We fell silent. I could hear noise in the background on her side of the call, laughter and loud music. "Sounds like a party," I offered quietly, feeling a sting of envy as I looked around the diner. It was after ten now, just a few customers lingering over late-night fries and pie.

"What was that?" Alisha asked, sounding distracted.

"I said ... Never mind," I sighed.

"Oh, wait, did I tell you, I saw Jace Dade the other day?" Alisha asks, naming a boy who'd been the year above us in school. "He's at college out here too, it was totally random – I bumped into him at this party thing by a guy in my calculus class. We talked about you," she added. "He couldn't believe you're still in town. He said you were like the girl least likely to stay in Haverford."

She laughed, but I felt the words like a blow.

"I mean it though, Chloe." Alisha's voice dropped. "You

need to figure this out, it doesn't make any sense for you to be stuck back there, not after everything we went through to get into college in the first place." There was muffled conversation for a moment, and then Alisha's voice came again. "Look, I've got to go. Things are crazy here. Say 'hi' to my dad, OK?"

"OK," I replied, but she'd already hung up; back to the party of her new life, while I wiped down tables and refilled ketchup bottles.

I didn't know if I could take talking to her anymore. Every call reminded me of what I was missing out on, how small and mundane my life had become. She was my last remaining friend, save Ethan – the rest of my high school classmates had drifted away in a clutter of online updates and laughing photos – but I could sense Alisha's reluctance every time she answered my calls, hear the faked enthusiasm in her voice when she quizzed me about my boring jobs and everyday life.

We'd always been glued together by ambition: to get into a good college, out of Indiana, to have *more* than the pedestrian lives we saw played out every day around us. "Eyes on the prize" we'd tell each other, as much a comfort when we were passed over for dates and party invites as a motivation. Alisha was the sheriff's daughter, sure, but her good-girl status ran deeper than that, a fear of winding up no better than her cousin – a cautionary tale who fooled around with her boyfriend and wound up pregnant at sixteen, taking night classes at the community college and grappling for her diploma.

"She was stupid," Alisha would say scornfully. "Mess around like that, there's always consequences."

I believed it too. If you followed the rules, if you were careful and hardworking, you would get what you wanted in the end.

But I was beginning to see how naïve that was. I'd always done the right thing, but there I was on a Friday night, pouring soda refills, while people who worked half as hard, sacrificed half as much, were living it up in a world I could only imagine.

By eleven, there was only one other person left in the diner. Crystal was sprawled in a back booth, showing no signs of leaving. She'd been there for hours now, dressed in a pair of tight black jeans and a leather jacket, eking out a side of fries and a single Coke.

"We're closing." I loitered by her table, eyeing the check she'd left untouched.

She glanced at her phone and sighed. "My ride is late. Can I hang out until he shows?"

"I guess …" I looked around, but there was nobody to see either way. "I mean, sure."

I finished sweeping up, and began turning over chairs and pushing the tables back. Crystal didn't move from the booth, she was poring over a local newspaper with a red pen bit between her teeth. It was the classifieds, I could see.

"You're looking for a job?" I asked.

She looked up. "Yeah. My new boss at the Quick-stop is a total ass, he keeps brushing up against me. Accidentally." Her voice dripped with scorn.

I wandered closer, curious.

"Any luck?" I nodded at the paper.

She shook her head. "Nothing yet."

"I'll keep an eye out at the sheriff's office," I offered. "People are posting ads on the bulletin board all the time."

"Thanks." Crystal blinked. She looked at me from under her choppy bleached bangs. "How do you like it there?"

"Fine." I shrugged. "I mean, it's a job."

"Tell me about it," she sighed. "You get benefits?"

"In another month." I was counting the days until they came through and I could afford to take Mom to the doctor, maybe find her some medication.

"I bet it's hard keeping a straight face with those guys," Crystal added, rummaging in her purse. She pulled out a compact mirror and makeup bag. "They think they're such big-shots, walking around town with their badges and guns. But hey, bet you get out of speeding tickets easy."

"I don't know." I watched her apply another layer of liner, smudging the kohl black around her eyes. "I never tried."

"You should. Minimum wage is shitty enough, you've got to take the perks where you can." Crystal looked up at me, and cocked her head. "You should wear lipstick sometime, stop you looking all washed out."

From any other girl, it would have been a catty insult, but Crystal sounded friendlier than I'd ever heard before.

I propped the broom against the wall and slid into the booth. Crystal passed me a lipstick. "Try this one."

I thought a moment about hygiene, then immediately felt bad about it. The shade was a deep pink, one I'd never buy for myself. I never really wore much makeup, aside from a dab of lipgloss and mascara sometimes, but watching Crystal carefully paint her face, I saw that it was more than vanity. A mask, taking her normal expression and making it bold and edgy.

"You ever think about leaving?" I asked curiously. "Or do you think you'll settle here for good?"

"Are you kidding?" Crystal snorted. "I can't wait to get the hell out of this place. The day I get enough saved, I'm gone."

"Where will you go?" I asked.

"Anywhere but here. I don't know, LA maybe?"

"Sunshine and palm trees." I thought of the post-cards my dad sent, back when he was pretending to care at all.

"Sounds good to me. I figure, another six months maybe, then I'll have enough." Determination skittered across her face. "Even if I don't, I'm getting out of here, I don't care if I have to hitch-hike the whole way."

I knew how she felt, but my baggage wasn't so easily hauled around.

I finished the lipstick and looked at myself in the mirror. It was different. Bold.

"Hot." Crystal nodded with approval. "Your guy will flip. You're still with that Ethan guy, right?"

I nodded.

"And he's got a brother too, what's his name?"

"Oliver." I blinked. "How do you know him?"

"Saw him around at some bar. Good genes in that family." She waggled her eyebrows suggestively and I had to smile.

"Pretty good," I agreed.

Crystal's phone sounded with a message. She checked it and rose to her feet.

"Your ride's here?" I asked, feeling a pang of disappointment.

"On his way. You know, you guys should come to this party tonight," she suggested. "Out at the McNally farm, you know, past the highway? Just a kegger, the usual crowd, but it should be fun."

"I don't know . . ." I demurred, thinking of the beer and

smoke, and the guys who worked out at the quarry: stained ball-caps and plaid shirts. "It's not really my scene."

"Swing by, check it out," she pressed.

I shook my head. "No, thanks. I don't think so."

Crystal looked amused. "You know, you should quit pretending like you're above it all. You're not better than us, not anymore. High school's long gone. We're all the same now." She gave me a rueful shrug and then walked away, the door closing behind her with a jangle.

When I arrived at the precinct for work the next morning, something was wrong, I could tell. The main floor was hushed, the phones ringing, unanswered, while the deputies clustered in a tight knot by the coffee machine. They were eying the back interview room, talking in low voices.

"What happened?" I slung my jacket over my chair and walked over. "Anyone going to pick up a call?"

One of the deputies looked up. "You didn't hear?"

"Hear about what?" I started to pour myself a cup of coffee.

"There was a crash last night, out past the highway."

I stopped, remembering the last time it happened, the sad wilted flowers on the side of the road. For weeks, I'd been filing paperwork about parking tickets and land disputes, but this was real. "Is everyone alright?" I asked.

He shook his head. "It was Blake, riding with some girl. He's real shaken up. Sheriff's interviewing him now."

I looked over to the closed door.

"I don't know why they've got him in there like some criminal." One of the other guys spoke up. "I bet it was her fault all along. Everyone knows those roads are dangerous."

"Chief's just doing his job," another argued.

"But Blake's one of us, it's not right."

The phone started ringing again, and I could see the switchboard at my desk lit up on every line. "I'd better get that," I told them, backing away. They shrugged, turning back to the coffee machine.

"Hello, sheriff's depart—" I barely got the words out before the voice on the other end of the line started demanding answers. What had happened? Was Blake driving drunk on duty? Were we pressing charges? A concerned citizen, they needed to know. I put her on hold, but the other lines were the same, all morning.

I scribbled the messages and then headed back. The interview room door was shut, but I could hear voices inside, Blake, muffled but angry. "I wasn't drunk, it was just a couple of beers. It was the ice!"

"You blew point zero nine," Weber's voice came. "Kid, I'm trying to help you here."

"Come on, Weber." Another voice spoke up. "That breathalyzer was a joke. Your guy here couldn't administer one to save his life."

I cautiously tapped on the door.

"Yes?" Weber's voice came.

I pushed it open. He was sitting across from Blake and a man in a sharp-looking suit. Blake looked like hell, slouched in his seat in an oversized sweatshirt, red-eyed, like he'd been crying all night.

"I'm sorry, but the phones won't stop." I waved the messages. "And there's a guy from the District Attorney's office on the line too . . ."

"Already?" Weber hit pause on the recorder on the desk. "OK, we'll take a break for now."

"Actually, I think we're done here." The man in the suit stood up and nodded for Blake to follow.

"Now, wait a minute . . ." Weber protested, but the man just took out a business card.

"Either charge him, or call to set up another interview. Come on, Blake." He steered him out.

Weber watched them go, clearly frustrated, but saying nothing.

"I'm sorry." I lingered in the doorway, feeling awkward. "I can come back."

"No, it's fine." Weber waved me in, so I brought him the

batch of messages. He stared at them, sighing. "What a god-damn mess."

"What happened?" I asked, cautious.

"A party out at the McNally farm," he sighs. "There was a keg, kids blowing off some steam, then Blake's car winds up wrapped around a tree. He had his belt on, but the girl ..." Weber stopped and gave a slow shake of his head. It wasn't good.

"So what happens now?" I asked.

"Who knows?" Weber stared at the stack of messages. "He wasn't on duty. I can suspend him, book him for reckless driving, try to get the DUI charge to stick ... But they've got that lawyer from the city now." He shook his head too, looking regretful. "He's a good kid, too. Good family. "

I turned to leave him, but something stopped me. The one thing nobody had mentioned all morning. "Who was the girl?" I asked quietly.

He looked up blankly.

"The girl, the one who got hurt. Is she from here?"

Weber nodded. "Crystal Keller. Doctors say it doesn't look good."

I called the hospital for an update. The nurse wouldn't talk, but when I said I was from the sheriff's department, she relented. There was no change. Head trauma, blood loss. Crystal was in a coma.

I sat behind the front desk, frozen, and thought back to last night: doing makeup in the diner, and the look on Crystal's face when she talked about getting to California someday. She'd been kind to even invite me to that party, a brief flash of friendship in my lonely day. It was only a few hours ago; a few drinks, a few hairpin curves in the road.

The nurse said they didn't know if she would wake up.

It felt wrong for the world to somehow keep spinning, but it did. The deputies needed their lunch orders phoned in; people came to complain about parking tickets and the neighbor's overflowing trash. In the end, it was almost a relief that the calls kept coming, occupying my thoughts. By afternoon the calls had slowed, and I had time to even think again, snatching time for a sandwich at my desk.

The front doors swung open. I braced myself for a parent or pissed-off deputy, but instead, it was a familiar face.

Oliver.

I tensed. "What do you want?" I asked, putting down my lunch.

He sauntered closer. I hadn't seen him in a week; he was cleanly-shaven and had a haircut now, but was wearing the same outfit as before: slim-cut dark jeans and a white shirt under his coat, blonde hair falling over his angular face. He hugged his arms around himself, exaggerating a shiver.

"Brrr. Is it just the icy reception, or is it cold in here?"

I paused. I'd been the one to overreact before, making a scene out of nothing. And besides, he was Ethan's brother. I pasted on a smile. "Sorry, it's been a weird day. Can I help you with anything?"

"Yes, you can." Oliver planted his hands on the front desk and smiled across at me. "I came to make amends."

I blinked, surprised. "You did?"

"Ethan explained about how much stress you're under." Oliver's eyes swept around the room, taking it all in. "He wants us to be friends, so I'm here to let bygones be bygones. What do you say?"

He turned back to me and gave a wide smile, but it wasn't open and guileless like Ethan's; there was something more, almost amusement in his eyes.

"Sure," I said slowly. "We're fine. No problem."

"Good. Then let me take you out for a drink," Oliver announced.

I paused. "I'm underage," I said carefully.

"You can drink things other than alcohol, can't you?" Oliver's lips quirked at the edges. "Coffee, tea, a nice refreshing lemonade ... What time do you get off work? We can drive into town, have some dinner even."

I stared at him, thrown. It sounded like he was asking me out on a date. But of course, that was impossible. My mind raced. "Sure," I replied at last, deciding to act oblivious. "Sounds good. Ethan's picking me up, so we can all go together."

Oliver looked amused. "That's not exactly what I had in mind."

"Oh?" I made my eyes wide and confused, tidying some paperwork on the desk. "What did you mean?"

Oliver's hand shot out suddenly, grabbing mine. I froze, shocked at the touch. He was studying me, those blue eyes narrowed and quizzical.

"You shouldn't play dumb," he murmured. "You're better than that."

I stared back, my heart racing. Then he slowly released my hand.

"Another time then." He smiled, nodding. "Tell baby brother I said hi."

I watched him saunter out, still reeling. What had just happened made no sense: for him to ask me out like that, and then ...?

You're better than that.

I cradled my hand to my chest, still feeling where he'd held it. I stood there, dazed, until the phone started ringing again and I went back to work, but all afternoon I couldn't shake the memory of him watching me, his lips curled in that curious smile: as if he was in on a private joke. As if he knew something about me I didn't.

*

I was still on edge when Ethan picked me up from my house after work. I'd deliberated over telling him about Oliver, but any way I framed it, it all came together wrong. He'd come to apologize and invite me for a friendly drink – on the surface, it was all too innocent to matter.

Better not to say anything at all.

"You hear about the crash?" Ethan asked, right away. "Did you know her – Crystal?"

"No, not really. It's been non-stop at the office," I said quickly. "Can we just not talk about it?"

"Oh." Ethan paused. "Sure, whatever. Want to go back to mine?" He leaned over to kiss me.

I shook my head. Oliver was the last person I wanted to see. "No, it's too crowded there. Let's go somewhere we can be alone."

Ethan grinned. "I like the sound of that."

He drove us out past town, around the lake to his dad's construction site. Our headlights cut through the dark woods, the trees bare now, the ground littered with dead damp leaves.

I wondered if Crystal had driven on these roads. If she'd seen it coming. If she'd been scared at all.

I'd thought about stopping by the hospital, but I knew I'd just be in the way. I wasn't close friends with her, after all, and it would be wrong to linger there as if my concern was any use at all.

"... Chloe?"

"What?" I snapped my head around. Ethan was waiting on me.

"I said, did you hear anything back about those classes?"

"Oh, yes." I shook away the darkness. "I signed up for a couple of credits. English and modern history."

"What? That's awesome!" Ethan exclaimed. "Why didn't you tell me?"

"I ... I forgot." I shrugged. "I'll start next week, it's not a big deal."

"It is to me." Ethan reached across and took my hand, bringing it to his lips. "I got a good one." He smiled. "Pretty and smart."

Soon, we were turning on to the construction site, the security lights set up around the buildings, pale in the night. Ethan helped me down from the truck and across the muddy ground to the bare bones of the development. I'd seen it before, back when it was all bare ground and wire markers, but now it was taking shape: the foundations laid, concrete blocks, with steel girders and wooden beams making the framework of the houses.

"They're going to look so good when they're done." Ethan used a flashlight to guide us past the construction. "I want a place like this one day. Imagine, drinking your morning coffee, looking out over the lake." He grinned over at me, and I wondered if I was in that picture with him.

"You see yourself living here then?" I asked. "For good, I mean."

"Here, or someplace like it." Ethan nodded. "Small, friendly. Someplace you can get to know your neighbors, you know. A good place to raise kids."

He smiled at me again and I thought I saw a flash of hope in his eyes. Did he see me in his future? Did I want to be there?

I shook off the thought, following him to the cabin they were using as a base camp for the construction. Inside, there were lights and an electric heater. Ethan spread the blanket he'd brought on the floor, and we settled in the corner, huddled close to keep warm. "I know how to show a girl a good time," Ethan joked, pulling me closer for a kiss.

I smiled and kissed him back, trying to lose myself in his warmth and the feel of his body under mine. Usually, I could count on him making the world go away, but something wasn't right. I felt a restless ache that wouldn't quiet, not for all Ethan's sweet kisses and grasping touch.

I pulled away and caught my breath. "Oliver came to see me," I started, watching Ethan's expression. "He said you talked to him."

"About the other week? Yeah." Ethan nodded, leaning back. He traced idle circles along my ribcage, and I felt his touch, shivering through my shirt. "I told you, he can be annoying sometimes. Did he apologize?"

"Kind of," I replied, wondering how much Oliver had told him.

"Let me guess, it didn't sound much like an apology?" Ethan rolled his eyes. "Sorry, he can be a dick about that stuff."

"It's fine." I paused, sitting up. "So, is he going to be sticking around? What happened about college?"

"He won't go into it, says he's done." Ethan shrugged, his fingers slipping up higher under my shirt.

"You guys aren't close." It was a statement, not a question. I watched him carefully, catching the flicker of tension in his jaw and the way he dropped his hand from my body.

"I guess." Ethan looked evasive. "I mean, he was older and always off at school."

They were so different, I couldn't imagine how they'd both grown up in the same home.

"He was in boarding schools, right?" I pressed. "Why didn't you go too?"

"There wasn't the money." Ethan sat up then. "He was the smart one," he explained, matter of fact. "Mom was always going on about his potential, how he needed to be challenged, so they found a way for him to go."

I could tell he didn't want to talk about it, but still, that didn't stop me. "It must have been weird, watching him get all the attention."

Ethan shrugged again, looking away. "I don't know, I got the easier break, Mom was so overprotective of him. He was her favorite," he added. "She wouldn't let him out of her sight when we were kids. I just got to do my own thing."

"Still, having him back must be strange," I said, trying to picture them as kids. Ethan was easy, he would have been happy and easily entertained, but I couldn't see Oliver. That careful, knowing gaze didn't belong in a child's eyes; even now, it seemed years too old for him. "Are you closer now?"

"I guess. I don't know. Why are we even talking about him?" Ethan looked confused.

"Because he's your family," I laughed. "And we've done enough talking about mine to last a lifetime."

"So don't talk." Ethan gripped my hips, suddenly rolling me beneath him. I caught my breath at the movement, reaching up for more, but instead, he propped himself on his arms, waiting above me, his lips inches from mine.

"Are you telling me to shut up?" I teased.

"No ma'am," Ethan smiled softly, brushing back my hair. "I'd never do that."

He kissed me softly. Too soft. I could feel the pull of lust again, snaking through my body, mingling with the deep, aching sadness I'd been battling all day. I could tell him about Crystal – he would listen, and murmur sympathy, and say all the right things. But that wasn't what I wanted; I wanted to feel something. Anything but this ... defeat.

Frustration rose in my chest. I wrapped my arms around him, pulling him down to me, hungry, needing something more. Ethan tried to hold back, but I didn't let him, demanding, and soon he was caught up again in tongues and hands and grinding bodies.

I reached between us for his belt.

"Here?" Ethan tried to detangle himself. He was breathless, his body hard against me, but still, he tried to hold back. "It's OK, we don't have to."

"I know." I reached for him again. "I just want to be close to you."

Ethan smiled, relaxing against me. "If you're sure ..." He kissed me again, slow. Sweet. Like he meant it.

When I closed my eyes again, I saw Oliver staring back at me.

THEN

Crystal Keller died at eight thirty-two p.m., six days after the crash. She'd been non-responsive since they brought her in; her brain activity was negligible, she showed no signs of breathing on her own.

Her mom turned off the ventilator.

I heard the news just before my first class at Rossmore College; I was already seated in the cramped, windowless room when the call came in. I'd asked the nurse on duty to keep me updated, and now I was stuck, sitting at the tiny half-desk in a room full of students as the professor began his introductory talk, writing his name up in big letters on the board.

"Call me Ashton," he joked. "Not Ishmael."

There were a few low titters, but most of the class didn't understand what he meant.

Crystal was dead.

I stared blankly at my notebook, tuning out the professor's voice. It didn't make any sense to me, that she was here, and then, gone.

No more late-night eyeliner and stops at the diner. No new job, or first apartment; no husband or kids one day. No getting to California, getting out of this town at all.

She was just gone.

I didn't notice class was over until the scrape of chairs and sound of chatter broke through my thoughts. I looked up; the room was emptying fast, and there were notes on the board: our first assignment. I quickly scribbled it down, grabbing my things and joining the exodus to the front of the room.

My classes ran two nights a week, and I'd managed to get a financial aid package that dulled the cost. Still, it hurt. While my old classmates posted photos of freshman parties and excited status updates about lectures and trips, I would be driving an hour on the freeway after work, to go and sit in a cramped room in an anonymous concrete block and take notes from an ancient projector; the other students dozing, bored, around me.

Still, I told myself, I was lucky to be there.

Lucky to be alive at all.

"Excuse me." I lingered at the front of the room as it emptied. The professor, Ashton, turned. He was young, early thirties maybe, with neatly-gelled black hair and wire-rimmed glasses.

"What can I do for you?" He smiled at me.

I shifted my books in my arms. "I was wondering, if you had any more reading lists, ones that were, um ..." I tried to think of a way to phrase it without seeming rude. "More advanced?"

His eyes swept over me a split-second. "Sure, I can dig something out. You are ...?"

"Chloe. Chloe Bennett."

He paused a moment, then brightened. "Oh, right, I saw your transcripts. You know, we don't usually let people start mid-semester, but I figured someone like you would be able to catch up."

"Oh, thanks." I blushed.

"If you hang on a minute, I could grab you something now?" he checked.

I nodded. "I'm not in a hurry."

"Great." Ashton finished tidying his papers into a leather messenger bag, which he slung across his body. "I can print you some of the next-level assignment lists. I figured I should start these guys off easy," he added with a rueful look. "You wouldn't believe how many of them drop out after just a few weeks of study."

He ushered me out of the room and turned off the lights behind us. "Teacher lounge is – that way," he decided after a moment, pointing down the empty, after-hours hallway. "Sorry, I'm still figuring my way around. It's kind of a maze here. You deferred for a year, right?" he asked.

"Yes. I have … family commitments," I answered carefully. "I'm needed at home right now."

"Tough break," he said, sympathetic. "I'm kind of in the same boat. I was all lined up for an adjunct position in Philadelphia, but it fell through. My girlfriend's got family here, so …"

He opened the door to the lounge, set with a few faded armchairs and bookcases. He went over to the huge printer in the corner and pulled a laptop from his bag, clicking through until the printer whirred to life.

"You know, I can email, if it's easier," he offered.

I shook my head. "Our internet's been acting up," I lied. The truth was, we didn't have internet anymore – it was an unnecessary expense when I could check email at the sherriff's office.

"No problem." Ashton drummed his fingers against the table as the printer sounded in fits and starts. "Jesus, when was this thing made – the eighties?" He met my eyes. "Not exactly the Ivy League, huh?"

"Not exactly," I agreed.

"So are you planning on an English major?" Ashton asked, bending to click some more files on his computer. "Because I teach a Wednesday morning American Lit class – you might like it. More discussion, a lot of the classics, but new stuff too. Franzen, Lorrie Moore, Updike."

"Sounds great," I replied, with a pang of regret. "But, I have a full-time job. Night school is the only way I could make this work."

"Too bad," Ashton said. "Well, I'll throw in the syllabus for that one too, in case you change your mind. And if you feel like tackling any of the assignments, just send them my way, and I'll take a look."

"Thanks," I replied, surprised. "You don't have to do that."

"Hey, it's my job, isn't it? Instilling a love of literature in the youth of America," Ashton joked. "Besides, between you and me, you've shown more interest in the last five minutes than ninety percent of my students here. Community college isn't really a hive of academic ambition."

He finished printing the reading lists for me then walked me out. It was dark and the parking lot was empty – everyone else long gone. Ashton looked around and frowned. "Do you have a ride coming? This is a pretty sketchy neighborhood after dark."

"No, I drove. Thanks for this though." I stuffed the papers in my bag. "I really appreciate it."

"Anytime. See you next week!"

I hurried to my car and threw my books inside. Ashton tooted his horn and waved as he drove past, turning out of the lot towards the highway.

I got inside and slammed the door, shivering but upbeat. I hadn't known whether Rossmore would be worth it, if I was just kidding myself that I could stay on track for college; but today had been a pleasant surprise. Ashton seemed like a good teacher: engaged, and willing to help me out.

Maybe it wasn't such a loss after all.

I turned the ignition.

Nothing.

I tried again. There was a sputtering sound, the faint hope of life, and then it faded away – along with all happy traces of my brief good mood.

"Fuck!" I slammed the steering wheel. The parking lot was deserted, empty in the dark. Anger suddenly welled up in my chest, sharp and hopeless. "Fucking piece of shit!"

It had been on the brink of quitting on me for weeks, but I didn't want to take it in to a mechanic, we didn't have the money. And now I was stuck, way too late for the bus, or any way home.

I fumbled in my bag for my cellphone, and hit redial on the only number I ever used these days.

"Hello?"

"The car gave out on me," I sighed, slumping back in the driver's seat. "I'm stuck at Rossmore. Can you come get me?"

"Sure thing, sweetheart."

I sat up. It wasn't Ethan's voice on the other end of the line.

"Oliver?" I asked slowly.

"That's right." His amused drawl came, clear. "You've got yourself in quite a pickle, haven't you?"

I caught my breath. "Where's Ethan?"

"He had to overnight with Dad, they're looking at land down south. Didn't he call you? Oh, that's right, he left his phone behind."

I clenched my jaw. "Fine. Sorry I bothered you."

Oliver sighed. "Look, I'll come get you. Where did you say you are?"

"No thanks," I replied shortly.

"Seriously?" Oliver laughed. "What are you going to do, walk home? Come on, don't be like this. Baby brother would never forgive me if I left his girl all alone in the dark."

I hesitated. I didn't want to see him, or worse still, owe him, but I didn't have a choice.

"Fine," I replied at last. I gave him my address and hung up, snuggling deeper in my jacket as I settled in the cold car to wait. I had nothing else to do, so I found my notes from class and the assignment for next week. I had the book with me, so I read through the first chapters, making notes as I went, until lights shone through the night. The Reznicks' black BMW cruised slowly around the parking lot and came to a stop in front of me, engine running. The window lowered, Oliver leaned out.

"Come along, Chloe," he called, beckoning. "Time to stop playing damsel in distress."

I grabbed my bag and locked up the car; hurrying over to slide into the passenger seat. I hoped that Oliver would give his usual acerbic wit a break, but instead, he regarded me with amusement. "Your chariot awaits. Just call me your knight in shining armor."

"Thanks," I said, reluctant.

"Don't go crazy with gratitude," Oliver smirked. He drove away, turning down the dark streets towards the highway. "And what did we learn today?"

"Just leave it," I replied, gazing out at the lights blurring by.

"Leave what?"

"This. The smirky comments, and all your bullshit. Not tonight, OK?"

There was a pause.

"What happened?" Oliver's voice was quiet. I glanced over. His expression was open, no sarcasm in sight, and despite myself, I felt my defenses slip.

I swallowed, feeling it all well up again. "A girl died. A friend of mine. No," I corrected myself. "We weren't friends, but I knew her. She was getting out of this place, she didn't deserve ... She didn't deserve to just be gone. She was a good person. And I know you're about to say there's no such thing as good, or evil," I added fiercely. "But there is. Crystal never hurt anyone, she deserved better than this."

There was silence for a moment, then Oliver's voice came, clear beside me. "Aren't you good too?"

I stopped for a moment, weighing the question. What I should say? Ethan thought I was good. He told me all the time, how kind I was, how sweet. "I've got a good one," he'd say, like I was a prize he'd won at ring-toss at the county fair. The truth was, his compliments just made me feel guilty, like he was blind to the flashes of anger and bitterness that rose to the surface, too often these days.

"No," I admitted quietly, resignation ringing hollow in my chest. "No, I'm not."

I braced myself, waiting for a glib response, but Oliver

didn't reply. The miles slipped past, until he turned in at a rest stop gas station. "Wait here," he told me, stopping the car.

I watched him walk up to the store, a dark figure in the neon lights. He went to the counter inside and chatted with the clerk for a moment before emerging with a brown paper sack. He passed it to me and started the engine again.

I looked inside. A six-pack of imported beer and a bottle of whiskey.

"I don't drink," I told him, confused.

"You don't, or you haven't?" Oliver countered. "Pass me the M&Ms."

I did as he asked and he ripped open the packet with his teeth, driving again, too fast, out on highway back roads until I didn't know where we were anymore.

I didn't care. Home was nothing but a new bundle of frustrations. The further we went, the less I had to think about: cocooned in the warm car with the headlights cutting through the night, the music playing something dark and sweet. Oliver didn't ask me anything, didn't make a single demand, just stayed there, silent in the driver's seat, taking me away from everything.

At last, he turned on to a gravel road, slowing to ease the car over the bumpy ground. He drove a while, snaking through shadows and vast piles of rubble, until finally he came to a stop at the edge of a huge quarry.

"What is this place?" I asked.

He shrugged. "Does it matter?" Oliver reached over and took the bag from me, then got out, walking around to hitch himself up on the hood of the car.

I paused a moment, watching as he took a swig from the whiskey bottle. I got out too.

The night was clear and crisp, my breath fogging in the air. The quarry stretched in front of us, several football fields in size, the carved edges disappearing down who knew how far into the dark. There were some buildings visible on the far side, with lights shining weakly in the dark, but, aside from their pale glow and the distant flash of cars on the free-way, we were completely alone.

I took a deep breath, feeling the cold chill me from the inside out.

I climbed up on the hood next to him and held my hand out. Oliver raised an eyebrow again in that now-familiar smirk, but he passed the bottle.

I took a sip, almost choking, but forcing the burning liquid down. "Why do you drink this?" I spluttered.

"Wait for it," Oliver told me, and a moment later, I felt the warmth slipping through my bloodstream, the deep burn.

I took another sip.

The silence stretched. I snuck a sideways look at him.

Oliver was leaning back on his elbows, looking at the stars. His coat had fallen open, revealing a thin white T-shirt and his usual skinny black jeans. He wore dress shoes, I noticed, and a leather-banded wristwatch. He wasn't as built as Ethan, who had broad shoulders and a solid, muscular torso; Oliver was tauter, lithe.

He turned his head and caught me watching him. I glanced away and took another drink.

Oliver sat up. "Chloe, Chloe ..." He said it sing-song and my skin prickled. I didn't like the way I was on edge with him, not knowing what he thought, or how he felt.

"Quit that," I told him, tensing.

"What?" Oliver sounded innocent.

"You know what." I stared out at the dark quarry, the endless black night. A whole world out there and I was still right here. "Why did you come back?" I asked him. "You could be anywhere, doing anything. Why would you choose this?"

"I'm not here to stay." Oliver took the bottle back from me, and lifted it to his lips in a long swig. He wiped his mouth with the back of his hand. "Just a month or two, I'll figure something out."

I paused. "You don't know how lucky you are."

There was silence for a moment and then Oliver's voice came, clear in the night. "You don't belong here."

I turned. His eyes were on me, sharp and blue. I looked away.

"You don't even know me."

"I know everything about you, sweetheart," Oliver's voice was matter of fact. "And I know you're better than this. Than anyone in this town."

I swallowed, my skin prickling with awareness. "Your family's here," I pointed out, trying to deflect his laser-sharp attention.

Oliver chuckled. "Yes, they are."

Silence.

My pulse kicked. I didn't know why, but I wanted desperately to believe him. That I had something special inside me, more than Haverford could contain. That I could be more than this.

Tears stung, sudden in my throat. I slid down from the hood. "I should be getting home," I mumbled, not meeting his eyes.

Oliver didn't object.

We drove back in silence, but this time, I couldn't shake my awareness of him, inches away in the dark car. My head was spinning, just a little, from the whiskey and the day, too long. Work, and Crystal, and school, and the quarry all blurring into one.

Just one day, but it felt like something had shifted, split open inside me. I felt raw, the many weeks of holding it all together catching up all at once, too messy and too damn sharp to keep contained in such a small body. I clenched my fists at my sides, digging my nails into my palms, counting the breaths until Oliver pulled into my driveway and turned off the engine.

"Thanks," I muttered, grabbing my bag. "For the ride. And . . ." I stopped.

"Anytime," Oliver replied lightly.

I opened the door and bolted up to my front porch, scrabbling for my keys. I'd left the light off and now I felt blindly around in my bag for the touch of metal.

"Chloe." Oliver's voice rang out.

I turned. He was sauntering towards me, unhurried, his face cloaked in shadow. "Did I forget . . . ?"

My words died in my throat as he kept on walking, straight up to me, backing me up against the door without breaking stride and taking my face in his hands.

He kissed me hard, before I had time to think. Before I had time to even breathe; his tongue demanding, his body pressing into me, hands trapping me in place with no space to resist as he branded me with his mouth, biting down on my lower lip hard enough to make me flinch.

He stepped back, leaving me gasping.

"Good night." Oliver's smile was almost cruel as he turned and walked back to the car; starting the engine, sweeping back out on to the street and away, the noise receding in the night.

I stood there, shaking, my heart racing, my body weak.

What the hell was I supposed to do now?

NOW

I'm used to secrets.

This year, I became an expert, accumulating them like rare butterflies in a delicate glass case. Mom's illness; the money; Dad's betrayal; my own illicit desires. I tucked each one away in turn and locked the door tight, hidden and silent, as secrets should be.

Now, they're all escaping. Sharp wings and an angry flutter, beating louder in the silence of the empty hospital hallways. A crescendo, building to the most terrible truth of all.

The body I left in the burning building. The boy I didn't love enough to save.

The wingbeats stalk me with every step. *Soon*, they promise.

Soon, you'll have to tell.

THEN

I didn't tell Ethan about the kiss. I couldn't. What would I say? He'd think it was my fault somehow, that I'd led Oliver on. He was his brother, after all, I was just the girlfriend. It was no contest whose story he'd believe, and then where would I be left?

Alone.

I'd be all alone in this town, with nothing to take me out of that house, alleviate the dark lonely drudgery that my life had become. Without Ethan, there would be no warmth, no fun, no laughter between work, and Mom, and the quiet glare of the television, night after night after night.

I couldn't take it. I wouldn't make it through.

So I said nothing and waited, anxious, for a change in Ethan. Any sign that Oliver might have told. He wouldn't, I told myself, what reason would he have to hurt his brother like that?

But what reason did he have to kiss me in the first place?

Ethan was busy, thankfully, with work at the construction site and commuting out to the new development, so I was able to avoid the Reznick house for weeks. Guilty, I did my best to be the perfect girlfriend: calling him every night, responding to his texts right away. I even invited him for dinner at my house and cooked his favorite lasagna, painfully aware of my mom, sitting in front of the TV in the next room, even as Ethan slid his hands around my waist and nuzzled my neck from behind.

"Did I tell you you're, like, the best girlfriend ever?" he murmured, lips against my throat. I stepped away, pivoting across the kitchen to grab some milk for the white sauce.

"Don't distract me," I protested, trying to sound normal. "I want to get the recipe right."

"Whatever you do will be great." Ethan lounged back against the countertops, smiling at me. His hair was getting longer, a ruffled mess. "You're the sweetest."

"I'm not." I concentrated on stirring.

"You are," Ethan insisted. "I can't believe you're doing all this for me."

"It's nothing." I felt my cheeks flush, guilty. "You've

been working hard all week, that's all. I wanted to do something nice."

"Well, this is perfect. I'm just happy we get to spend some time together." Ethan reached out and caught me against him again, arms settling loosely around my waist. "I've missed you."

His eyes were warm and honest as he smiled at me. I looked away.

"I missed you too," I murmured. I moved to step away, but instead of letting me go, he tilted my chin up to him and found my lips in a slow kiss.

I swayed against him, feeling the warmth of his mouth, and the slide of his hands, bringing me closer, but when I closed my eyes, all I could think about was Oliver's lips, not his. Oliver's body, hard against mine.

It had been intoxicating.

That was the source of my secret shame, the reason I was running in circles trying to make it up to Ethan. Not just that it had happened, although the simple fact of my betrayal was bad enough to make me sick with guilt. But worse still, worse than anything, was the fact I had liked it.

God, I'd loved it.

When Oliver had kissed me, there had been no hesitation or sweet, eager fumbling. His lips had been ruthless, possessive, hard on mine with a stony intent. I'd never been kissed like that before, taken so completely, and even now, with Ethan's arms around me, I felt the imprint Oliver had left, shame mingling with desire in my bloodstream, glittering and dark.

"Oh, I'm sorry." My mom's voice came, and I broke away to find her in the doorway, dressed in sweats and a dressing gown. "I didn't mean to interrupt."

"That's OK!" I exclaimed quickly. "We're fine. What's up?"

"The bulb went out in my craft room," Mom explained. "I was looking for that step ladder."

"I'll get it." I made to move, but Ethan quickly cut me off.

"Who needs a ladder? I'll take care of it."

"Are you sure?" Mom asked. "I don't want to be any trouble."

"No trouble at all." Ethan grinned.

"I'll go get the bulb then," Mom said. "It's just upstairs."

She left and Ethan turned to me with a smile. "Craft room?"

"It's her new thing," I sighed. "I cleared Dad's files out of the study and put the old TV in there with her knitting stuff. She never leaves. Just watches old movies and crochets these terrible sweaters all day long."

"It must be helping her," he said. "She seems much better. Hey, maybe she'll be back at work soon."

"Uh-huh," I nodded brightly. "Maybe."

He exited the kitchen and I took a breath. It wasn't the knitting helping Mom, it was two hundred and forty milligrams of anti-depressants daily, but even that wasn't enough to get her out of the house. She'd fought it, I knew she would, but I'd managed to get her to the doctor, and we'd tag-teamed her with the hard-sell. Just a few pills and she'd be right as rain. Wouldn't that be nice? Didn't she want to feel better? She'd relented, but still, progress was incremental. Sitting up all day instead of lying in bed; knitting for hours instead of staring blankly at the wall.

Small, expensive victories.

I turned back to the stove, checking the food. I'd asked Annette for her recipe, Ethan's favorite, and baked garlic bread too. He'd been so surprised at the invitation, but I was wondering how much longer I could keep up the charade. How much longer I would be paying penance for my crimes. Maybe Oliver would go back to school, or take off on one of his trips soon, I thought with desperate hope. Then, everything could go back to the way it was, before.

The sound of the doorbell came.

"I'll get it," Ethan's voice called. I quickly grabbed a towel to wipe my hands, emerging from the kitchen with it still damp in my hands.

"Mmm. Something smells good."

I froze.

It was Oliver, of course it was. Taking off his coat and hanging it in the hallway, like he was supposed to be here.

"But . . . Why . . .?" I stuttered, painfully aware of my hair in a mess and the stained apron tied around my waist. "I mean, what are you doing here?"

"Baby brother said you were cooking." Oliver sauntered towards me, an unreadable smile on his face. "I couldn't resist. I know, I'm gatecrashing, but look, I brought gifts!" He held up a bottle of wine, and a six-pack of beers. "I'll put them in the fridge, OK?"

He brushed past me, leaving me with Ethan in the hall. "Sorry," he said, rueful. "I didn't know he was coming. I could ask him to go, if you want?"

I caught my breath. For a moment, I was tempted to tell him yes, make Oliver leave, but that was impossible. I had no reason not to want him here, at least, none I could explain out loud.

"What are you talking about? It's fine." I tried to pull myself together. "There's plenty of food. The more the merrier, right?" I pasted on a smile.

Ethan kissed my forehead as he passed. "Thanks, babe. You're the best."

I stayed there a moment, alone in the hallway, panic taking flight in my chest. Why would he come here? Was he going to make a scene of it, let something slip?

No. I forced myself to take a breath. He wouldn't do that, surely. This must be him trying to smooth over what had happened and act as if nothing had changed. And if he could do it, then I would too: pretend, the way I had been doing for weeks.

Simple.

When I joined them in the kitchen, Oliver was uncorking the wine with swift, expert movements. "Do you like red?" he asked, looking up. "I got a great Pinot."

"I ... don't really know anything about wines," I replied. My voice came out forced, too high, and I blushed, feeling like our betrayal was written all over my face. But Ethan didn't notice anything was wrong, he just helped himself to some chips and dip I'd left out on the countertop.

"No?" Oliver raised an eyebrow. "What a shame. Well, no better time to start than now. You'll love this, I promise." He poured into wine glasses I didn't even know we had, holding one out to me.

"I don't know ..." I tried to avoid his gaze, busying myself with fetching silverware and plates.

"I insist." Oliver closed the distance between us, and I felt his hand on my arm. I froze, flinching back from his touch. "Sorry, I didn't mean to startle you." His lips curled with amusement as he pressed the glass into my hand. "Here, try it."

I took it, caught in his gaze. His eyes watched me, clear

and blue, and I remembered the look in them as he'd strode towards me on the front porch, just outside. Full of intent.

"Thanks," I managed. His fingers brushed mine and I fumbled. The glass slipped, shattering to the floor.

"Are you OK?" Ethan sprang up.

"Yes, fine," I said quickly, stepping back. The wine pooled, dark as blood on the floor, glass shards scattered everywhere. "Just clumsy, that's all."

"You should be more careful," Oliver said calmly. He stepped over the mess to the sink to grab the roll of paper towels. "You could hurt yourself."

"Here, I've got it." Ethan found the broom and swept the glass into the dustbin. "I'll put it straight in the trash, you might cut yourself."

He opened the kitchen door and headed out, into the dark of the backyard.

We were alone.

I waited for Oliver to say something, but there was silence. When I looked over, he was sipping his wine, gazing at the photos and books around the room, utterly at ease.

The moment stretched and, all the while, my pulse raced. "Why did you come here?" I finally blurted.

Oliver slowly turned, raising his eyebrows inquisitively. Immediately, I regretted saying anything. "I told you, I'm a sucker for a home-cooked meal."

"That's not what I'm talking about," I replied, swallowing.

"No?" Oliver watched me, his expression even. "Let's not beat around the bush. Why don't you say what you really mean?"

I opened my mouth, but there was only air. I couldn't. Not with Ethan just outside, and the truth so confusing. What could I say?

Oliver chuckled, as if he'd known I wouldn't be able to manage the words. "I wonder . . ." He took a step closer, his expression suddenly serious. "Do you even know you're lying to yourself? Or have you been pretending so long, you don't even know the difference anymore?"

I stared back, caught. There were a few feet of kitchen floor between us, but I could swear, I felt his hands on me again, the way they had been that night; the burn of his lips on mine.

More real and vivid than anything I'd felt before.

Oliver's eyes seemed to look straight through me. "Don't you see, Chloe? Life can be a whole lot more interesting, if you'd just be honest about what you want. *Who* you want," he added in a low voice, just as the door opened again, and the kitchen was flooded with a blast of cold air.

"All set." Ethan came in. "Wow, that smells amazing, babe. I can't wait."

I didn't speak for a moment, still caught in Oliver's innocent smile and the slippery accusation hidden in his words.

Ethan looked between us. "What did I miss?"

"Nothing much," Oliver answered smoothly. He grabbed a beer and sent it sliding down the kitchen island to Ethan, like a bartender in an old saloon. "Chloe here was just quizzing me about ideas for your birthday. It's coming up pretty soon."

"Aww, you don't have to make a big deal." Ethan looked bashful. "I don't like to do anything."

"Everybody likes birthdays," Oliver protested. "Every year he's the same," he added in my direction, with a theatrical roll of his eyes. "He refuses to do anything fun at all, takes all the joy out of it. Maybe between us, we can convince him this time around."

"I don't know," I said hurriedly, still thrown by the sudden switch in mood. "If you don't want to celebrate, you shouldn't feel any pressure."

Ethan shrugged. "I could do something. It would be fun, the three of us."

"See?" Oliver raised his glass. "That's more like it. Look at you, loosening up, baby brother. I can tell, this one's a good influence."

Ethan chuckled. "Yeah, she's pretty great." He kissed the

side of my head, hugging me against him. I felt the guilt burn, hot and accusing.

"Too bad you already snapped her up," Oliver remarked. "Hey, Chloe, you got any friends you can set me up with?"

Slowly, he winked at me.

I stared back, my head spinning. What was he thinking, taunting me like this with Ethan standing right there? Didn't he know what he was risking? Didn't he care?

Oliver sipped his wine, idly leaning back against the counter. He had a curious expression on his face and it took me a moment before I realized where I'd seen it before: Sheriff Weber, with his crossword puzzles. Studying the clues, figuring out the right word to fit – the brief smile of satisfaction as he wrote the letters into place.

He was enjoying this.

The realization hit me all at once, and with it, I finally understood. Oliver *wanted* me to be unsettled, he liked watching me flustered and unsure. Maybe that was what he'd planned all along: asking me out, kissing me, showing up here to disrupt our evening and make me uncomfortable in my own home ... It was a game to him.

I should have been angry, and I was – furious – but more than that, I felt a hot rush of embarrassment flood through me.

I'd been so stupid! Oliver had said I was better than

this, better than the rest of them, but instead, I'd been reeling with panic all week, acting desperate and guilty and weak.

I met his eyes across the kitchen. He was watching me, smiling, but now I could see the challenge in his gaze.

This was a test. He wanted to know what I would do.

I would show him, I wasn't so easily beaten.

This was all just a game. Well, I could play too.

I forced myself to take deep, even breaths. "Olly, can you pour me another glass of that wine?" I asked casually. I opened the oven, and lifted out the lasagna dish. "And Ethan, maybe set the table? We're nearly ready to eat."

"Yes ma'am," Oliver saluted me. He sauntered over, offering another drink, and this time I took the glass without flinching, meeting his stare dead on. I lifted it to my lips and took a long sip, tasting the dark, rich liquid, the slight bitterness and tang. "Well?" he asked, waiting.

"It's OK." I shrugged. "Not my thing."

I caught a flash of amusement on Oliver's face. He raised his glass to mine in a toast. "To new experiences," he drawled.

I felt a thrill, unfamiliar in my veins. The crackle of challenge. "New experiences," I echoed, smiling. "And new friends."

*

We ate at the formal dining table, Ethan and I on opposite sides of the table, Oliver seated between us, at the head. I was still on edge, hyper-aware of every word and movement Oliver made, but this time, my heartbeat was racing from anticipation, not fear, as I forced myself to try and figure him out.

What was he playing at?

"So why are you still single?" I asked Oliver, a teasing note in my voice. "Weren't those Yale girls throwing themselves at your feet?"

He grinned, his eyes bright. "Constantly. I couldn't walk around campus without tripping all over them."

"Sounds like a safety hazard. You should come with warning signs," I replied, my voice arch. There, I wanted to tell him, I could keep up.

He grinned. "It was a liability, certainly. I drove the staff mad."

"Olly doesn't do girlfriends." Ethan spoke up, his mouth full. "He keeps dating these amazing girls and then it's all over. Who was that one I met freshman year? Lucy?"

"Lucinda," Oliver corrected him.

"She was the best," Ethan told me. "Pretty, smart, the sweetest girl, totally in love with him. And he turns around and dumps her in, like, five minutes flat."

"What was wrong with her?" I watched Oliver, his unruffled confidence as he reached to help himself to more garlic bread.

"I got bored." Oliver sounded unconcerned. "Most people bore me. Haven't you noticed, the world is made up of spectacularly uninteresting people."

"I don't know about that," I laughed, still playing casual, but he fixed me with a penetrating stare.

"No? You don't think so too?" he challenged. "You don't spend your life, day in and day out, dealing with tedious small-talk and mindless bullshit, about last night's reality TV, or what that slut of a pop star wore this time around. Mediocre people leading mediocre lives, acting like it's the only option until you'd rather just blow your brains out than pretend it matters anymore?"

There was silence. Ethan gave an awkward laugh. "Way to be creepy, bro."

I laughed along, but inside, I felt a chill. Of course I'd thought that, it rattled in my head louder every day. Even with Ethan, I found myself biting my tongue, having the same conversations about nothing, or worse still, not wanting to talk at all.

"Why settle?" Oliver asked, as if hearing the truth behind my silence. "Why waste my time on someone who doesn't intrigue me, or challenge me? People are so ... limited. What's wrong with wanting more than that?"

I blinked. "I don't know," I said quietly, looking down. "Maybe more doesn't exist."

"You really think that?" Oliver pressed. "Or is that just what you tell yourself, as an excuse for putting up with so much less? Playing it safe," he added, his voice mocking. "Following the rules like a good little girl."

"Hey, dude." Ethan spoke up, but I didn't want him defending me, not this time.

"Don't," I told him, before turning back to Oliver. I drew myself up, glaring at him. "Where do you get off, acting like everyone is beneath you?" I demanded. "Just because you don't want something, doesn't mean that it's 'less'. Maybe they're not the boring ones, maybe you're the one with the problem instead. You're the one who can't keep up a real relationship, after all."

"Chloe!" This time it was Ethan objecting to me. He frowned at me. "You don't have to get personal."

"It's OK." Oliver smiled, and I realized with a sinking heart that I'd done it again: let him wind me up, press all my buttons so I couldn't help but lash out. "Maybe she's right," he added. "Maybe I should just try and find a nice girl like Chloe. You seem happy together, after all." He looked at me, taunting. "The perfect match."

"Yes, we are," I said firmly, reaching for Ethan across the table. "Very happy." I brought his hand to my lips and kissed his knuckles, my gaze never leaving Oliver's.

Don't mess with me, I tried to tell him silently. I wouldn't be dancing at the end of his strings any more, I wasn't so weak as that.

Oliver just smiled knowingly. "You're right, there's nobody quite like her. What do you say, baby brother?" he said lightly. "I could fight you for her."

Ethan laughed. "Over my dead body."

THE END

I watch, still paralyzed, as the boys grapple on the bare concrete ground. The empty house around us makes it feel staged, like scenery waiting for the cameras to start rolling, but this isn't pretend, playful wrestling, it's elbows and teeth and vicious angry hands, choking for air. Pure fury. Murder in their eyes.

"Stop it!" I cry. But they don't even pause for breath. It's like I'm not even here. "Stop it, both of you, please!"

I finally break out of my shock and grip the knife harder. The handle fits in my palm so smoothly, it could have been made for me: a steady weight, the sharp edge of the blade. I scramble to my feet and stand there, shaking, as they grab and hit. Oliver's face is bloodied, Ethan lets out a low grunt as he slams his elbow into Oliver's ribs.

"Stop!" I scream at the top of my lungs. There's nothing I can do, no way to break their fury. Except . . .

I hold one arm out, pull the shirt-sleeve back, hold the blade to my skin. "Stop, or I'll hurt myself!"

Ethan surfaces from his violent haze. He sees me and his face goes slack. "Chloe! What are you doing?"

"Let him go." My voice shakes, but my hand is steady. I press down, feeling the sharp bite of metal. A thin thread of blood appears, trailing down my wrist. I press harder. "I mean it, let him go. Both of you, get back."

Ethan scrambles up right away, his hands out, his face a mask of fear. "Be careful," he begs me, "you don't know what you're doing."

"Oh, she does." Oliver rolls over and spits a mouthful of blood on the ground. He takes a breath, labored, then heaves himself to his feet. "Bravo." He grins at me through the red, a gruesome smile. "Well played."

"This isn't a game!" I yell, fear mingling with anger, hot in my veins.

Oliver looks at me curiously. "Of course it is, sweetheart. And you've got the trump card. So, what are you going to do now?"

I swallow. "We're leaving," I say, gripping on to the hope with everything I have. "You and me, Ethan," I say, fixing my gaze on him. I lower my voice, soothing, pleading.

"We just walk out of here and it's over. Nobody has to get hurt."

"You and me?" Ethan blinks, looking desperate. He has hope too, I realize. He just wants this to be over as well.

"Yes, of course. You and me," I promise him, managing a smile. "Everything will be OK."

I lower the knife, trembling, and start to edge across the room. Ethan takes a breath, and then his body relaxes. I reach him, and take his hand. "We'll be OK," I promise him again. "Everything will be OK."

I send a look back to Oliver, warning him. Let this go. Ethan is calming now, but his temper is still a hair-trigger, we're not out of danger yet.

I gently tug on Ethan's hand. "Let's go home," I tell him softly. "It's late. We can just crash out and sleep tonight."

His eyes flicker over mine, searching. I hold his gaze, barely breathing. I'm close, so close to getting out of here, and I know, Ethan wants to believe me.

He always did.

"You're hurt," I add softly, reaching up with a shaking hand to touch a cut on his neck. "Let's get you cleaned up. It'll all be better in the morning."

Ethan nods, a jerk of his head. "I'm sorry," he whispers, broken. "I didn't mean to hurt you."

"It's OK," I soothe him again. "I know, it all just got out of hand. We'll be OK."

I take a step towards the door, and then another, still holding my breath. There's a beat, and then Ethan follows me, holding my hand tight.

It's over.

Blood pounds in my ears, I'm dizzy with relief.

I reach the door, already thinking fast, ahead to what's to come. If I just get Ethan home, he'll calm down. Back in his house, away from Oliver, I can talk him down. The fight has drained from him, I can see it in his eyes. It was a moment of madness, but it's over now.

I'm safe. We're all safe now.

"Not so fast, baby brother." Oliver's voice comes.

I spin in time to see him wielding a length of copper pipe. It cracks against Ethan's back. He goes down, sprawling on the ground.

Oliver stands over him, blood dripping from his mouth, a furious glint in his eyes.

"We're not done yet."

THEN

Oliver was sitting on the Reznick front porch with a shotgun.

I stopped, halfway to the house.

"No need to be scared, this isn't for you." Oliver looked up. He finished polishing the barrel and held it up, checking the frame. "I've got bigger prey in mind."

I exhaled, closing the final distance to the steps. Snow had been falling all week until a blanket of white covered the town, but their path was shoveled clean. Ethan's work, I knew. "I thought you were off in Aspen. Or, Miami." I shrugged, as if I wasn't tracking his every move.

"What? And miss baby brother's birthday?" Oliver smiled. "Never." He paused, meeting my eyes with a teasing smile. "How have you been? Read any good books recently?"

I flushed.

The text messages had started the day after the infamous dinner. An unknown number, a single line:

Man is the only creature who refuses to be what he is. – Camus

I knew immediately it was Oliver, so I didn't reply, but that night I stopped by the library under the pretext of collecting more romance novels for Mom. I found the slim volume tucked in the classic literature section, the pages dog-eared and yellowed with age. I checked it out, feeling like a thief, and read it cover to cover, late into the night.

The next day, it was a quote from Nietzsche. Then Bret Easton Ellis. Each time, I refused to respond, but still, I tracked down the books, wondering what Oliver was trying to tell me – if he was trying to tell me anything at all. I read each page, searching for the meaning, and although I didn't see him for weeks, it felt as if he was there in the room with me every night.

Watching me.

And now he knew it too – he'd known I would run right off to follow his notes. "Nothing much." I feigned casualness, still trying my hardest to beat him in this twisted, curious game. "Why, you have any recommendations?"

Oliver smirked. "Ethan!" he bellowed. "The light of your life is here!"

Ethan came out, dressed in warm winter wear: boots, a turtleneck sweater, a thick jacket, and more. "Hey!" He lit up at the sight of me, sweeping me off the top step and into a hug. "I thought you were working!"

"I took the afternoon off sick." I kissed him, my lips cold against his. "I wanted to surprise you."

"You did, this is awesome." Ethan beamed. "Now you can come too!"

"Come where?"

"Hunting," Oliver replied. He stood up, slinging the shotgun over his shoulder. In his navy wool coat, he looked like a Revolutionary War soldier, deadly and uncomfortably dashing. "The eternal struggle: man against beast. Or, woman," he added with a smirk.

I shook my head. "It's OK, you guys go ahead. I can meet you after to celebrate."

"No, you have to come," Ethan protested. "I promise, it'll be fun."

"I would just be in the way." I shot a glance at Oliver, but he was wrapping a dark red scarf around his neck and checking his bag for ammunition.

"But you're already out here. Please?" Ethan asked, taking my hands. He made a puppy-dog face at me, all wide eyes and hopeful innocence. "It'll be a blast, I promise."

"Quite literally," Oliver spoke up.

"It's my birthday, right?" Ethan added. "That means you have to do what I say."

"Is that how it works?" I joked, my mind racing. I met Oliver's eyes over Ethan's shoulder and, despite myself, my pulse kicked. I knew I should leave, that I should keep my distance, but something inside me was restless. Work had been dragging for weeks now, and the classes at Rossmore were barely a relief – exchanging one fluorescent-lit room for another, one set of paperwork for textbooks and class assignments. Now that winter had arrived, my life seemed colored with grey, the color of melting snow, dirtied and worn.

The Reznick brothers were the only flash of life and color I had now. This, if nothing else, wouldn't be dull.

Besides, part of me was dying to know: what would Oliver do next?

"Fine," I told Ethan, dragging my eyes back. "But I'm not really dressed for the woods."

"You can borrow Mom's boots," Ethan grinned, kissing me on the cheek. "We've got a ton of jackets hanging around. Come on, I'll show you." He led me inside.

"Don't take too long!" Oliver's voice echoed after us. "We don't want to waste daylight."

We set out into the woods bordering the back of their property. Ethan and Oliver had shotguns and hunting packs, but my hands were free, a bag with an extra sweater and Thermos of hot coffee slung over my back. The snow crunched underfoot, the trees were bare around us and the sky an icy blue above as we followed a barely-visible trail deeper away from civilization.

"Are you sure you know where you're going?" I asked, looking around for signs of the route. I was used to running in the woods, but with the snow, everything looked different. "It's been snowing pretty hard."

"Relax," Ethan reassured me, reaching to take my hand. We fell behind Oliver. "You can't get lost out here."

"We'll loop up by the lake," Oliver announced, checking a map on his phone. "The guy at the store said they've seen plenty of bucks up there this week."

"Great," Ethan agreed. I looked over.

"You didn't say you hunted."

"Not much, usually I just go out with Dad or Olly," he explained. "He's the real hunter. You should see the trophies he's got, it's like a gift."

Oliver turned. "Speaking of gifts, why don't you show Chloe your new toy?"

"Oh, yeah!" Ethan opened his bag and pulled out a large hunting knife, sheathed in a leather case. "Look what Olly got me." He slid the cover off, showing me the blade, eight or nine inches long. "Isn't it great? I can use it for stuff at work too, we're always unloading materials and dealing with all that plastic wrap."

"Great," I echoed quietly. The blade glinted in the sun, silver and sharp, and before I even thought about it, I found myself reaching for the knife. I sliced an arc through the air, feeling the weight of it in my hand, and how the hilt curved against my palm.

"You like it."

I looked up. Oliver was watching me. "Oh, yeah, it's great," I said, handing it back. "I left my gift in the car," I told Ethan quickly. "I'll give it to you later."

"You didn't need to get me anything," Ethan grinned.

"Yes, I did."

"Aww, you're too sweet." Ethan tugged me closer, kissing me on the lips. I kissed him back, my mind alert and acutely aware of Oliver, only a few paces away. The knowledge made me guilty, but there was a thrill there too. The risk. A challenge.

"Enough of you lovebirds," Oliver's voice came, but I kept hold of Ethan's jacket, kissing him longer before finally breaking away.

Oliver's gaze was on me, amused. "This way." He nodded to a fork in the trail. "And keep it down, unless you want to broadcast our arrival to the entire herd. Deer may be stupid animals, but they are at least smart enough to run away when danger comes their way."

His eyes lingered on me, and I wondered if that was a message. Was he danger? Was I supposed to run?

I wasn't afraid.

"Lead on," I told him, striding ahead into the snowy wilderness. Oliver chuckled, and kept walking.

Oliver followed some tracks out to a spot by the lake, then had us settle in behind a scree of brush and trees. He watched the water through military-style binoculars, while I snuggled up to Ethan and passed the coffee and snacks.

"So now we just sit around, waiting?" I asked.

Oliver chuckled, his eyes still fixed out on the scene. "Didn't your mother ever teach you: good things come to those who wait."

"Good things like pneumonia and chilblains?" I shivered.

"Hey, you cold?" Ethan immediately unwrapped his scarf and looped it around my neck.

"I'm good." I smiled at him. "It's nice to be out, I've been trapped behind that desk all week, fielding calls."

"Better than laying cement," Ethan countered, laughing.

"True."

"Hey, did they ever charge that driver?" Oliver spoke up. "The one who killed your friend."

My heart clenched at the mention of Crystal. I'd gone to the funeral, a useless gesture, but I needed to be there, to see them lower the box into the cold ground, adorned with a single white rose.

"Not yet," I managed to reply. "There's a whole load of legal back and forth. Blake's parents got this big-shot lawyer in, talking about police incompetence and tainted evidence."

"The Haverford sheriff's department? I'd never believe it." Oliver's tone was light.

"They never even arrested him," I said bitterly.

"So he'll get away with it?" Oliver turned.

I shrugged, even as my blood itched with the injustice. "I don't know. Sheriff Weber says the guilt will stay with him for ever."

"Yes, but that's not justice," Oliver said, as if reading my mind.

I swallowed back the sharpness rising in my chest. "I know. But, what can you do? Some people just get away with it. Wrecking lives, and then moving on. They never miss a beat."

"It's OK, babe, we don't have to talk about it." Ethan hugged an arm around me and I caught the warning look he sent to Oliver. "I'm sure it'll all work out in the end."

"I was just asking." Oliver turned back to the lake.

"Let's talk about something less depressing," Ethan announced. "Like what we're going to do with this deer when we get it."

"That's not depressing?" I laughed, glad of the change of subject. "And who says you'll get anything?"

"We always do," Ethan told me. "Believe me, Olly won't go home empty-handed."

"I always get what I want, even if it takes all night." Oliver gave me a smile that sent shivers down my spine. "Ethan will bring the truck round, isn't that right? We're not more than half a mile from the road now."

"And then you'll what, mount its head on the basement wall?" I was intrigued by their casual confidence, talking about a dead animal like it was nothing. I'd grown up around hunting – this was wild country, after all – but I'd never been this close to the action: fascinated and repulsed in equal measures.

"No." Oliver's voice dropped, serious. "You don't fuck around like that. You have to eat the meat, bury the bones. Honor the life you're taking."

"Oh." I blinked, thrown. "Sure, I mean, that makes sense. In a twisted sort of way," I added.

"What's twisted about it?" Oliver tilted his head, watching me now instead of the lake. "You eat meat, don't you?"

"Yes, but that's different."

"How?" Oliver countered. "It comes from an animal, it all does. In fact, this is far more humane a way of dying than all those abattoirs serving up your Big Mac and Whoppers. As long as man existed, we've hunted: it's primal, deep in our DNA." Oliver smiled. "Survival of the fittest."

Ethan leaned in. "Don't get him started, he'll be on about this for days. Man's essential nature, all that crap."

"I forgot," Oliver chuckled, "you *essentially* want to watch football and drink beer."

"Nothing wrong with that!" Ethan laughed as a ringing noise came, muffled.

Oliver sighed. "What did I say about noise?"

"Sorry, dude." Ethan fished his phone out of his pocket. "It's the site." He made a face, then retreated a little way into the woods, out of earshot.

"Come look." Oliver held the binoculars out to me.

I hesitated a moment, then got up, moving to join him at the edge of the undergrowth. I held the viewer to my eyes, adjusting to the clarity, magnifying even the smallest clump of weeds with perfect vision. "Wow, these are strong," I exclaimed.

"Military-grade," Oliver replied. "My shells are too. I get all kinds of things online."

I watched through the snow, Oliver standing beside me, his breath fogging the air.

"You think about what I said?" he said quietly.

"You say so much, it's hard to keep track," I replied glibly.

"About being honest with yourself." Oliver's hand closed over mine on the binoculars, and even through the thick knit of my mittens, I could feel his heat.

I slowly lowered the viewfinder. "I thought about it," I admitted, meeting his eyes. My heart shivered in my chest, but I forced myself to stay calm.

"And?" Oliver arched an eyebrow.

"And, I wonder why you even care." I gave a careless shrug. "We're all beneath you, after all. Little chess pieces in your game." My eyes narrowed, determined, expecting another sarcastic comment, an ironic quirk of those eyebrows.

Instead, Oliver looked away.

"I guess I hoped you were different," he whispered, as Ethan came trampling back loudly through the snow.

I took a half-step back.

"Bad news." He sighed. "They need me on-site; someone delivered the wrong kind of insulation, and I have to go sort it out."

"But it's your birthday!" I protested.

"It's OK," Ethan said. "I won't be more than a couple of hours, we can still go out for dinner like we planned."

I made to grab my backpack, but he waved me off. "No, you guys stay here, you're all set up."

"No way, I'm coming with you," I protested, but Ethan was firm.

"I have to head straight to the site, you'd be hanging around for nothing." He kissed me on the forehead and grabbed his gun. "Stay, watch Olly in action. It'll be fun."

I paused, glancing back at Oliver. He smiled. "You're welcome to stay, you could learn something."

My pulse kicked. Staying out here, alone in the snow with Oliver ... It was dangerous. Reckless. I'd spent weeks keeping my distance, trying to focus on the good with Ethan, but now, the opportunity to spend time with him all alone suddenly seemed thrilling.

Hadn't he said, the deer knew better than to stay when they smelled trouble?

I didn't know what his next move would be, but that was the point. In the long stretch of sameness, he was the live wire. Unpredictable. His eyes glittering bright in the sun, waiting for my response.

"I'll stay."

THEN

I watched Ethan wave goodbye, turning to tramp back through the snow on the path we'd taken. His bright blue jacket weaved through the trees, getting smaller and darker. I could have changed my mind and run to catch up with him, but instead, I just watched him walk away, until finally he was gone and I was left alone with Oliver.

"Well, aren't you just full of surprises."

Oliver's voice wasn't arch this time. Instead, he sounded almost impressed.

I smiled to myself, glad that I'd managed to do something unexpected. That was what I wanted, wasn't it? To get under his skin and figure him out. It was why I'd stayed.

I turned back to him. He was drinking from the Thermos

of coffee, leaning back against the frozen bark of a tree in a casual pose, all angles and cool assessing gaze.

I raised my eyebrows. "I thought you were never surprised. People are so dull and uninteresting, remember?"

Oliver smiled. "Why does it make you so angry that I say the things you already know are true?"

I felt an automatic spark of protest, but I fought to stay in control. "I'm not angry," I said lightly. I knelt down by our stack of bags and supplies and found the water, but when I straightened up again, he was still watching with a thoughtful look on his face.

"I didn't realize you cared so much about what people thought of you."

I blinked. The way he said it, I knew it wasn't a compliment. "What makes you say that?"

"Oh, I don't know." Oliver straightened up, taking a few paces, kicking at the powdery snow. "How about the way you smile, and act so sweet and innocent with Ethan all the time?" He looked up, his eyes cutting through me. "You tie yourself up in knots to avoid showing any real emotion; I'm surprised you can function at all."

I shivered. He was doing it again: seeing all the things I thought I'd kept so well hidden, saying my secrets out loud as if they meant nothing at all. "Don't we all do that?" I shrugged. "Everyone pretends to be something they're not. Even you."

"No. I don't." Oliver looked certain, but I laughed.

"Sure you do. You play at being so nonchalant, but you care what people think too. Your family, Ethan . . . Imagine if he knew what you were doing," I added meaningfully. "What you did."

"What *we* did." Oliver corrected me with a smile. "And no, I don't care. I'm not his keeper, his life is his choice. And mine is mine."

It sounded glib, like the kind of platitudes we all said, but when I looked closer, I realized that he meant it, every single word.

He really didn't care about the consequences, or about betraying Ethan. He didn't care about his parents' plans for him, or their pressure to finish school. And he didn't care what I said or did next, if I judged him for his beliefs. In fact, I realized, with a shock of clarity, I could do anything right now. Say anything. It wouldn't affect him at all.

My heartbeat quickened. There was something terrifying and liberating about that kind of freedom, after months of play-acting. And to live your whole life that way like Oliver claimed . . . ? I couldn't even imagine it.

I stared at him, fascinated.

"Who *are* you?"

The words left my mouth before I could think them through.

I'd never met anyone like him before. Every rule I'd ever learned, he was breaking; everything I'd been taught to hide away, he announced it out loud.

I envied him. To be so bold and reckless, to care only about his own needs ... My life was full of worries about other people: my mom, Ethan, the guys at the station. All my responsibilities and the obligation to keep their lives running smoothly. Keep *them* happy.

But Oliver? He only worried about himself.

As if he'd seen something in my expression, Oliver took a step towards me, and then another, until he was standing just inches away.

My pulse kicked.

I could feel the warmth of his breath in the air between us, and when he reached to touch my cheek, the leather of his gloves was cold against my skin.

Still, I didn't flinch away.

"Who are you?" I asked again, a note of urgency creeping into my tone. Suddenly, I didn't just want to know his secrets; I needed to, desperately.

I needed to find a way to be so free.

"I'm the only person who will tell you the truth, the real truth," he murmured, leaning closer, until his lips were barely brushing my skin. "Not just all the pretty lies you want to hear."

I swayed towards him. This was different to that night at the house. Then, I'd been taken by surprise, my mind scattered, powerless under his will.

Now, I felt desire twisting through me, waking every sense in my body. The icy air was sharp in my lungs, my body prickling with heat under the layers of sweaters and scarves. I saw the blue of Oliver's eyes up close; not clouded with hues of grey like Ethan's, but startlingly bright, like the harsh winter skies.

My eyes drifted shut, my breath caught, waiting for his kiss.

There was a noise, a rustling in the bushes near the lake. I felt the warmth of Oliver's body leave mine a split-second before my eyes flew open. He was already back by the scree, reaching for the binoculars.

"Look," he whispered, a note of excitement in his voice. "It's here."

I caught my breath, my heart still racing. I quickly crouched down beside him, peering through the undergrowth.

It was a deer, tripping delicately towards the water. She leaned down, her long neck stretching to take in the drink.

"What happens now?" I whispered, feeling a shiver of fear. "Do you take your shot?"

"Not yet. It's too easy." Oliver shifted his weight, passing me the binoculars.

"I don't understand." I frowned. "I thought the point of hunting was to kill something."

Oliver turned his head. "The point is the hunt. You think I'm here just to blow that thing away?" He was scornful. "I could walk out there, let off a couple of rounds, and she'd go down. Where's the fun in that?"

I paused. "Fun," I echoed, uncertain.

"You have to get to know her first," Oliver explained. His voice was low, still just a whisper, but there was something hypnotic about it, and the intensity of his gaze. "See what kind of beast you're dealing with. No two animals are alike; they all have their habits and foibles, and until you get a glimpse of their true nature, you won't be able to beat it."

"Just like people," I noted wryly.

Oliver let out a chuckle. "Just like people."

We waited, watching from our hidden spot in the undergrowth for ten long minutes as the deer drank from the lake and then grazed around, nudging under bushes for grass that hadn't been covered with the snow. Oliver barely moved a muscle, his focus entirely on his prey; every muscle tense and alert, while I tried my best not to fidget and shift my weight.

Oliver watched the deer, and I watched him.

He was so still. Ethan was like that, but his was a different kind of stillness: calm and relaxed, not this poised, precise energy. Oliver's focus was absolute, and after a few minutes without a word, I wondered if he'd forgotten I was there at all.

"You're bored." Oliver's voice came, but he didn't look around.

"No," I protested quickly. "I guess I'm just trying to understand."

"She doesn't realize it yet, but these are her last few moments on this earth." Oliver did look at me, nodding for me to study the deer again. "This is the last drink she'll ever take. The last meal she'll eat. You'd rather rush it, and take all of that away from her?"

I frowned. "Does it matter? You're going to kill her in the end, either way."

There was a flash of motion, a bird landing by the lake. The deer skittered slightly at the movement, retreating a few paces into the woods. She looked around, and then slowly turned and began walking away.

"Finally," Oliver murmured. "Come on."

He didn't wait for me to reply before setting off, footsteps light in the snow. He kept his distance, using trees and brush for cover, never losing sight of the deer as she meandered through the woods. His movements were swift, his body lithe, the gun slung across his back, the wooden barrel polished to a dull sheen.

I scrambled after him, trying my best to mimic his silent

steps. I kept completely silent, watching every move ahead of me, my pulse thundering loudly in my ears. It was thrilling, like an adult game of hide-and-seek; waiting until the deer moved far enough ahead before slipping through the trees, my heart in my throat. I knew the smallest noise would spook her, so I made every step as delicate as I could, barely breathing to keep from making a sound.

We followed her deeper into the woods, before she stopped, nuzzling around the base of a tree that had sheltered the ground from the worst of the snow. Oliver held up his hand, signaling for me to wait. The woods around us were hushed, blanketed in white, as I crept up beside him, hidden back behind some trees.

Oliver took the shotgun down and lifted it into position; resting over his shoulder, his head cocked to view through the sight. "See," he whispered, "you hold it, just like this. Support the weight, here."

He moved then, swiftly turning and placing the gun in my hands.

My heart caught in my chest. "I can't ... I mean, I've never used one of these."

"That's why I'm teaching you." Oliver stood behind me, wrapping his arms around my shoulders. I could feel the heat of his body, solid against my back as he moved the gun into position, angling my arms and hands until I was holding it correctly, supporting the weight. I felt a thrill, awareness shivering through me to have him so close.

"Now, line up the sight," he murmured, his breath whispering against my ear.

I could see the deer through the rifle, the crosshairs of the barrel wavering with every breath I took.

"Easy," he breathed against me. "Now get your weight behind it."

His hands dropped to my hips. He moved them, shifting my stance, then lingering, slipping around to the front of my body. My jacket and jumper had risen up, just an inch by the waistband of my jeans. I could feel the touch of his hand, a tiny sliver of ice against my stomach.

Desire curled, tighter.

"You only get two shots." Oliver's voice was still low in my ear.

"Not one?" I turned my head, so our lips were almost touching. When he spoke, I felt his words whispered, as much as I heard them.

"Two." Oliver corrected me. "One to wound her, the second, to down her, once she tries to run. So think about it," he breathed. "Where will she go when she hears the first shot? Which way will she bolt?"

I forced myself to turn back to the deer, trying to see it the way he did, to get inside her mind. She'd skittered left, back at the lake when she'd seen the bird landing. And now, foraging in the undergrowth, I could see her head lift, tilting to check her right-hand side when she thought she heard a sound.

"Left," I whispered. "She favors her left."

"Good. So when you aim, aim where you think she'll be, not where she is. Cut her off before she has a chance to run."

Oliver moved my hands more firmly on the trigger. I felt the resistance of the metal beneath my forefinger and it hit me for the first time just what I was about to do.

The weapon in my hand could kill.

The rounds in the chamber would damage and destroy.

That deer was a living thing, and I was about to take all that away.

"Oliver," I whispered, suddenly scared.

"This is how it was always meant to be," Oliver murmured quietly. "Man and beast. Remember?"

"Still . . ." I couldn't move, torn between his certainty, and the sight of the deer, so oblivious to her fate.

"Ask yourself." Oliver's lips brushed my ear. I shuddered as his hands slid higher, until his palm was resting on the bare skin of my stomach, burning under his touch. I couldn't move, flooded with the sensation of him against me, holding me in place. "Are you hesitating because you want to, or because you think you should?"

His question rattled in my mind.

"What would you do if nobody was watching?" Oliver continued. "If nobody would ever know?"

My breath caught.

Who was I when nobody was looking? Without judgment, without expectations. Without somebody to please. That was why he'd brought me, I realized; that was why Oliver had put the gun in my hands and pointed me here. To see who I was, away from it all.

To know the real me.

I raised the rifle.

Oliver's breath quickened. I felt his body tense with expectation. I lined up the sight, carefully, carefully, holding my breath until the crosshairs were perfectly aligned on her chest.

The deer looked up, straight towards me. Our eyes met.

I fired.

The recoil shocked through me, but Oliver was holding me tight. The deer stumbled, hit, then bolted left, just the way I knew she would. I fired again.

She went down.

Victory coursed through me. Oliver released me, whooping. "You got her!"

I reeled back, gasping. The gun was heavy, too heavy in my hands, and I quickly threw it down.

I'd done it. I'd killed her.

Oliver grabbed his pack and took off, loping through the trees until he reached the body. I stumbled after him, my heart pounding. Just a few seconds, just one split-second choice, and now I couldn't take it back.

When I reached them, the deer was writhing on the ground. Blood was blossoming, a dark stain on the snow.

I stared, hypnotized.

I'd done this.

"She's in too much pain." Oliver was on his knees beside her. "You need to finish it."

"What? How?" I asked. I glanced back at our makeshift camp where I'd left the gun, but Oliver opened his pack and brought out a knife. Ethan's knife, I recognized, the one I'd sliced through the air just an hour ago, admiring the weight of it.

I hadn't thought for a moment about its real purpose.

Oliver unsheathed it and held it out to me, the blade glinting in the setting sun.

I looked from the blade to the deer and back again. "I can't."

An impatient look skittered across his face. "Finish what you started," he told me, but I couldn't do it, not with the deer wheezing and kicking limply on the ground. There had been space between us with the gun; I'd pulled the trigger, it had gone down. Neat and simple. Remote. But this, this was bloody and gruesome and real.

"No, please." I swallowed. "Just put her out of her misery, Oliver, please!"

Oliver turned back to the deer. He took hold of her jaw from behind, pulling her head back against him, and then drew the knife across her throat in one swift stroke.

Blood spurted from the wound. I watched it flow, red streams in the snow. Then the deer's motions faded; the kicking stopped, the breathing stilled. I watched life slowly drain from her body, until Oliver slowly placed her head back on the ground, and she was silent.

Dead.

I exhaled the breath I didn't even know I'd been holding. It was over.

He straightened up. "Congratulations," Oliver smiled. "Twenty pounds of meat, a nice hide." He circled her, assessing. "You bagged a good one."

I shivered, turning away. He was talking so impersonally, as if moments ago this hadn't been a living, breathing being.

A life I took, for no reason except to know that I could.

"Don't." Oliver's voice was sharp.

"Don't what?" I asked.

"Don't quit on me now and go spiraling back into your little 'what have I done?' pity party," Oliver replied. He took my arm in a firm grip, pulling me back around to look at the body, at all the blood.

"Don't," I murmured weakly, but Oliver held firm.

"You can't play that innocent act with me now, I was there, remember?" His eyes drilled into me. "I watched you take the shot. I felt your heart race as you pulled the trigger. It was your choice. You did this. So own it. There's nothing wrong with it."

Nothing wrong.

I took a breath, steeling myself. "I did this," I echoed, still staring at the wreckage, getting more real by the minute. All year, I'd been cleaning up other people's messes, but this damage? It was all mine.

I swallowed, the sick guilt receding, replaced with a curious glow. It took me a moment to figure out what it was I was feeling, it had been so long since I'd felt the sensation: a boldness, a sharp victory that made me clench my fists at my sides.

Power.

I'd done this. I'd pulled the trigger. I'd taken this life, because I wanted to.

"Welcome to natural selection," Oliver told me, his lips curving in a conspiratorial smile. "The strongest survive, the weak are culled from the pack. It's all just a part of this beautiful thing we call life."

I looked at him, my heart pounding. I wanted to be like him, so sure of himself, somebody who made the decisions and left other people to deal with the fallout. I wanted to be reckless and brave, the way I felt I was, deep down inside.

I took two quick steps towards him and reached up to take his collar.

"Easy, tiger," Oliver smirked, stepping back.

I stumbled, off-balance, but he caught me, his hands closing around my wrists. I felt a damp stickiness and, when I looked down, I saw the blood on his hands.

He released me. "Your first kill," he murmured. He pressed his fingertip against my mouth and I felt the smear of blood, wet on my lip.

A shudder of revulsion trembled through my body, but then his mouth was on me, capturing my lips in a kiss, pulling me closer, tight against his body. I tasted metal, and him, and then there was nothing left in my mind but the dark heat, and the bright, cold snow, and the feeling that I could do anything, anything at all.

NOW

Annette and Derek Reznick arrive at the hospital in a fluster of thick winter coats and panic.

"Chloe? Chloe, thank God!" Derek races down the hallway, grabbing onto both my arms. "What happened? They said there was a fire. Where is he?"

Annette hangs back, her eyes flicking to the deputies Weber left waiting in the hall with me. He's gone for now, out to examine the wreckage now that it's not just a fire site, but a crime scene too.

I don't need the official report, I already know what they'll find.

How much is left? I wonder. What could be standing now, after the flames? The fire was raging by the time I dragged his body out; the fire crew might have doused the flames, but by now, there would be nothing but charred remains of the brother I'd left behind.

Would there be enough to identify him? To tell what we'd done?

"Chloe?" Derek's voice is hoarse with fear. "Where's our boy?"

I snap out of it. "He's just out of surgery," I manage to reply. "They operated, I don't know what exactly, but it seemed to go OK."

"Dear God," Annette breathes, and then her legs give way and she slumps against the wall. Derek goes to her immediately, steering her into a waiting-room chair. Annette's shoulders shake. "I thought..." she stutters, hysterical. "I thought..."

"Shh... shh... Everything's going to be alright." Derek soothes her. At last, her sobs fade. He looks up again to where I'm standing, stranded.

"You're sure he'll be fine? The doctors said so?"

I nod. "He lost a lot of blood, but, they think he'll make a full recovery." I pause. "We just don't know when he'll wake up."

Derek closes his eyes a moment, his lips moving in a silent prayer. "I'm going to try Oliver again," he tells Annette. He pulls out his cellphone. "I don't know why he's not picking up. I've left half a dozen messages."

They don't know.

My heart catches. *Oh God*, they don't know.

I wait there, my mind racing as Derek makes the call.

"Son, I don't know what you're playing at, but this isn't the time to go off the grid. You need to call me back, as soon as you get this." He paces back and forth on the faded linoleum floor, leaving another message that will never be received. "We're at Hartford Memorial, third floor."

He hangs up with an exasperated sigh. "What's the name of the boys he was staying with?" he asks Annette. "Maybe we could find a direct number."

"I don't know." Annette glances over at me, and I quickly look away.

There's silence.

When I look back, she's still watching me, but this time I'm caught in her gaze, guilt flushing on my face.

Her eyes suddenly widen, flickering with realization. She knows, Oliver's not staying with friends. She knows, he was a part of this too.

I'm sorry, I want to tell her. *I'm so, so sorry*.

"I should get out to the site," Derek says, still pacing. "Insurance will want to know what happened. I don't understand, Chloe, was it a gas leak, do you think? Or were you playing around with candles. You can tell me, I won't be angry, I promise," he adds, looking haggard. "I'm just glad everyone's safe."

I close my eyes. Not everyone.

"Honey." Annette finally reaches out, and tugs on Derek's arm. He stops pacing.

"What is it?"

She looks at me. "Tell us, Chloe," she whispers. "Who do they have in surgery?"

"What are you talking about?" Derek looks between us.

"She didn't tell us," Annette says, her voice rising, high and desperate. "She didn't say who they brought in. Is it Ethan or Oliver?"

I can't say it. I look down, clutching my hands together. I'm still wearing the ring Ethan gave me, the silver promise band, and I twist it on my finger, over and over.

"Chloe!" Derek's voice rises. "What happened? Where are they? Who was in the house with you?"

"Yes, Chloe, tell us." Another voice enters the fray. Sheriff Weber is coming back down the hallway, brushing the rain off his coat. There's no sympathy on his face now, only suspicion.

Fear clenches in my chest, sharp as ice.

Weber comes to a stop in front of me, eye to eye. "We found a body," he says quietly. "We haven't identified him yet, but you know who it is, don't you?"

I nod. A sob rises in my throat and I feel tears, hot on my cheeks.

"There's a body?" I hear Derek let out his breath in a whoosh. Annette reaches for him, trembling.

"Oh God. Who is it, Chloe? Tell us. Please."

I force myself to look at them. They deserve that much.

"Chloe." Weber prompts me, warning.

I can't hide it anymore. They need to know. The dominoes falling, click, click, click.

"Ethan," I tell them, my voice breaking. "Ethan's safe. But Oliver . . . He didn't make it."

THE END

"What are you doing?" I gasp in shock at Oliver. Ethan is crumpled on the ground between us, groaning from the blow. "It was under control! I talked him down, he was letting us go!"

Oliver tosses the pipe aside and shakes his head at me. "That's not how this plays out, sweet Chloe. You don't get off so easy."

"I don't understand!" I back away, grasping hold of the wall for balance. Oliver has a wild glint in his eyes, something that chills me to the core.

"I think you do." Oliver grins. He's still got blood dripping from his mouth from Ethan's blows, a terrifying scarlet smile. "I think you know just how this has to end."

I shake my head, trembling. "Let's go, right now. Get in the car and drive like we planned. He won't hurt us now!" My voice twists, pleading.

Oliver tuts. "That's not the Chloe I know and love. What happened to the wild Chloe, the one who would happily take another life?"

"No, Oliver." I shake my head. "That was different! That was just an animal!"

"I thought you were done pretending." Oliver baits me. "Isn't that why we're here at all? You did this, Chloe. You. And now you need to finish the job."

Finish . . .

I stare at him, finally realizing what he means. He set this up, this whole pretty scene. He lured Ethan here tonight, so I would have to face him. It was all part of his game, moving the chess pieces around.

Our pieces. Our lives.

"You thought about it, didn't you?" Oliver adds softly. "All those nights he was pawing at you, smothering. Didn't you just want to make him stop? Now's your chance, Chloe. End it for good."

Ethan crawls to his knees, blocking me from Oliver. "Don't listen to him." He looks at up at me, plaintive. "This isn't you, you're not like him."

"Don't tell her who she is." Oliver cuts him off, scathing.

"She's not your toy, to pat on the head and fucking smother with all your listless suburban bullshit. Chloe ..." He turns back to me. "You can do this. You want to do it."

I shake my head slowly. I can't think, not with them both so loud. Not with the knife, still curved, glinting in my hand. "This wasn't the plan," I protest weakly, "Oliver ... You promised. You said nobody would get hurt!"

"It's too late for that." Oliver takes a step towards me.

"Hey!" Ethan tenses. "Don't touch her!"

Oliver's lips curl into a smile. "You see that, Chloe? Even after everything, he still thinks he needs to protect you. That you're so helpless, you need protecting."

"Don't let him get in your head, Chloe," Ethan warns me. "It's what he does, he's sick, you know that!"

"Stop it!" I cry. "Both of you, please!"

They stop.

There's silence, nothing but the sound of our breath, and my heartbeat, skittering so loud I think it might drown me for ever. "I can't," I whisper, turning helplessly to Oliver.

His eyes fix on me, fervent and blue. "I know you," he tells me softly. "I've seen it, all the dark places inside you, everything you are. I don't care. You don't have to hide it any more, Chloe. You can be free."

Free ...

That's all I ever wanted, to be gone from this place for

ever. Away from the pity and the struggle, and all the dreary days I somehow stumbled into. A life I never meant to be mine.

"You can be so much more. The two of us, together," Oliver whispers, and the words shiver through me, bright with possibility.

Ethan catches his breath, seeing my face change. "No, Chloe, you can't. Please." His voice twists with fear and my resolve wavers again.

He was always the good one, better than I ever deserved. Surely, he doesn't deserve this.

"Do it," Oliver orders. "Chloe, I'm warning you. If you don't, I will."

NOW

"He was protecting me. He didn't have a choice!"

We sit in an empty hospital room. Two chairs, an empty bed. Sheriff Weber and I.

Ethan's parents are visiting him in the ICU now. I wanted to go, but I know, they won't want me anywhere near them, not after the news I just delivered.

Their boy, gone for ever.

Derek broke down into loud, messy sobs, but Annette just stood there, her hands folded, her expression blank. And her eyes, burning into me, full of accusation.

She knows.

But of course she doesn't, I tell myself, trying to stay calm. She can't. Even Weber here doesn't know where to begin, pacing back and forth and clearing his throat, wanting to demand answers, but still, not able to forget the good girl I've been. The times I've brought him coffee and pie; the months I've taken his phone messages; the years I slept over with Alisha at his house.

"Tell me from the beginning."

"You said, we should wait." I swallow, nervous. "For that lawyer to get here ..."

"We can't wait around. Not now that – that we've found ..." Weber stops. "He's dead, Chloe. Dead. They'll be all over this come morning, you understand? Cops, journalists ... This is serious."

"I know." My voice twists. Of course I know, I was there, in the midst of everything. The blood and the fear and the cold, sharp truth.

"I should have you back at the station now," Weber adds, pleading. "You should be in interrogation, with a tape recorder running. My guys are already asking questions."

I nod again. "I'm sorry," I whisper, still twisting Ethan's ring. "I want to help. I'll tell you whatever I can, I promise."

Oliver, laying there on the floor; Ethan prone on the gurney. Their features blur in my mind, blonde hair and brown. Two bodies, two sets of clear blue eyes.

One survivor. One way out of this.

History is told by those who win.

"It was Oliver's fault." I take a deep breath, meeting his eyes. "He called me, saying to meet him at the lake house; he said it was important."

Weber starts taking notes.

"I thought it was kind of weird," I lie, my voice growing stronger. "I was running errands, so I stopped by. But when I got there, he was acting crazy."

Weber looks up. "What do you mean, crazy?"

I brace myself. "He was obsessed with me," I tell him, spinning the story that will set all of this to rest. "He'd been asking me out for months, showing up when I was working, sending me texts, calling all the time."

I can feel Weber's eyes on me, studying.

"It was my fault too," I admit. "I kissed him, just once," I lie quickly. "He was so charming and interesting and ... But I stopped it, I told him; but he wouldn't listen. When I got to the house, he was saying how we could run away together, get out of town. He had the knife."

"What kind of knife?"

"Ethan's hunting knife," I whisper. "Oliver got it for him, for his birthday. I was scared, and then Ethan showed up. That's when things got crazy. Oliver was ranting, angry, saying how we had to get rid of Ethan, so we could be together." I shudder. "He wanted me to hurt him, hurt Ethan, but I wouldn't. I would never hurt him. Then Ethan lunged and they were fighting. It all happened so fast." My voice shakes. "They were on the ground, and Ethan was hurt, and then Oliver dropped the knife . . ."

I shudder, remembering the glint of light on steel. The weight of the blade in my hand.

Weber paces, absently rubbing his bald spot. "So it was self-defense?" There's a note of hope in his voice. "Oliver stabbed Ethan, and he killed him in self-defense."

"Yes!" I cry. "Ethan didn't have a choice. He would never hurt him, but Oliver came at him, and then . . . then I couldn't tell what happened, they struggled, and there was all the blood . . . Oliver went down and . . . he didn't get up."

My voice breaks on the final word and I reach for the end of the bed to hold myself up. Oliver, lifeless on the ground. The flames swallowing his body.

An ending. His life, done.

Weber stops pacing. He looks like he's aged ten years tonight, everything about his face haggard and worn out. "Was he dead when you left him?" he asks slowly.

"I don't know. He wasn't moving, but there wasn't time to check. I was so scared," I add. "It all happened so fast, and then there was fire, and Ethan was bleeding . . ." I stop, choking back a sob. "I thought we were all going to die!"

It sounds true, because it is. Fragments of fact, pieces of what happened, stitched together in a new shape. Weber could never understand what led us to that moment, so I don't even try to explain. It's already too late. What happened in that house is only blood and ashes now; telling the truth won't bring Oliver back, heal the wounds on Ethan's body, or wipe the last eight months from my mind.

All that matters now is assigning the blame.

"It was Oliver," I say again. "It's all Oliver's fault. He was dangerous, I just didn't realize until it was too late."

THEN

After the hunting trip, I couldn't think about anything but him. We didn't spend a moment alone together, but somehow, that didn't matter. It was the guilt and anticipation; the delicious adrenalin rush I felt meeting his eyes across the room, even with Ethan's arm slung around my shoulder.

It was a fever dream, and I couldn't get enough.

I was on edge, wound tight with wanting him. Every time the front doors of the sheriff's department swung open, I expected to see him there, sauntering in to lounge by my desk and remind me just what I'd done out there in the woods with him.

"Hey, babe."

My heart caught in my chest, but it was just Ethan,

smiling as he held the door open for someone on their way out of the station. He came over and kissed me on the cheek, his skin chilled and his ears tipped with red from the cold.

"Hey." I pulled away, confused. "Did we have plans? I checked my phone, but—"

"I need an excuse to come visit my beautiful girlfriend?" Ethan asked. "No, we're stuck waiting on some deliveries, so I figured I'd drop by. I'm sorry I've been so busy with work," he added, taking my hand. "I'll make it up to you."

"No, it's fine, you haven't," I protested.

"I have," Ethan argued. "Olly even said I'd been neglecting you."

I froze. Oliver?

"He did?" I asked carefully.

"Yup, gave me a whole lecture, said I shouldn't be taking you for granted," Ethan grinned. "Except he used a bunch more words and, like, five different metaphors."

"Right." I forced a smile. "Sounds like him."

My mind raced. Oliver sent him over here, but why? To remind me what I'd betrayed with Ethan and keep me on edge? I'd been pulling away from Ethan all week, guiltily laying the groundwork to break up with him, but now I wondered if Oliver really wanted to be with me, or just liked the thrill of this, the chase. Another game.

And if he did, that meant it was my move.

"So, you coming for lunch?" Ethan asked.

"I can't," I told him, relieved it wasn't just an excuse. "I have to stay on the desk. Weber asked me to edit his statements too, and I have all these computer records to update ..."

"But they'll all still be waiting when you get back." Ethan captured my hand again, tugging lightly, a charming smile on his face. "C'mon ... I'll treat you to shakes at the diner. No one will mind."

"I said no." I pulled my hand back, feeling a flash of irritation at how oblivious he was. "I'm sorry, but I can't just leave. I need this job, remember? I'm not the boss's son."

Ethan's smile dropped. "That's not fair."

"I'm just saying, I don't get to waltz off anytime I like."

"And I was just trying to do something nice for you, that's all." Ethan looked confused. "You've been so distant lately, you're under so much stress ... Don't be mad at me for trying to help."

I exhaled. "Of course, you're right." He always was. "It was sweet of you to think of me, but I really can't leave."

"Then how about dinner?" Ethan suggested hopefully. "Come over to the house. Mom says she hasn't seen you in ages."

"I don't know ..." I hesitated, still not wanting to lead him on any more. It seemed wrong to keep agreeing to dates when Oliver's name was the only one that whispered in my mind.

"They're going into the city, so it'll just be the two of us," Ethan added, suggestive. "And Olly too, but he promises to stay out of the way."

Oliver.

My stomach kicked with the thought of him. "Sure," I heard myself agreeing. "I guess I could come over."

Ethan grinned. "Perfect. I'll pick you up, it'll be a break, I promise. You won't have to lift a finger."

"Ethan . . ." I protested.

"I mean it," he laughed. "I'll feed you grapes and give you a foot rub. You deserve it. You really are the best, you know." He leaned in and dipped a kiss on my lips.

"See you tonight."

I spent the rest of the afternoon watching the clock, willing time to pass quicker so I could see Oliver again. All I needed was a sign from him and I would end it with Ethan for good. My guilt faded; betrayal was just a word, flimsy in comparison to the breathless memory of his lips and hands, and – worst of all – the race of power thundering in my bloodstream, my first kill laying beside us on the snow.

I was sick. It was wrong. But I couldn't stop the memories, even if I tried. Something was awake in me now;

Oliver had showed me a glimpse of what it felt like to be invincible, *alive*, and as much as it terrified me, I craved another taste. I knew that I should push it down and bite my tongue, fold myself neatly back into the box I'd been living in: good girlfriend, dutiful daughter, but I couldn't. I didn't want to any more. Everything seemed duller now, faded and grimy against the vivid hues of the white snow and Oliver's bright blue eyes, sharp and watching in the back of my mind.

I didn't know what would happen next and, God, it thrilled me.

Finally, my shift was over. I set the voicemail on and grabbed the statements for Weber, heading across the floor to his office.

"Hi." I tapped quickly and then pushed the door wider. Weber was on a call, but he gestured for me to wait.

"No," he said, "no charges. As far as we're concerned, the case is closed. Uh-huh . . ." He listened a moment longer, then finished up. "I know. Thanks, Bob, you say hi to Kathy."

He hung up and gestured me in. "Thanks for doing this. I know it's not exactly part of your job description."

"It's fine." I shrugged. "I'm just heading out now."

"Have a good night."

I paused in the doorway. I should be leaving, but I

couldn't ignore what I'd heard on the call. "Was that about Crystal?" I asked.

Weber looked blank.

"The crash," I explained.

"Oh, yeah, it was. We're wrapping it up," Weber explained, checking through paperwork. "It's not fair to keep dragging it out."

Something hardened in my chest. "He just gets away with it?" My voice rose; I stared at Weber in disbelief. "Blake was drunk-driving!"

Weber shook his head. 'We don't know that. The breathalyzer's inadmissible and Blake swears he didn't touch a drop. He's a good kid."

I didn't understand. "But didn't he say so, in the interview?" I asked. "I came in with the messages and I thought I heard him. He said he'd had a couple of beers."

Weber shook his head. "I don't remember that. We went over the tapes, there's nothing there. I'm sorry," he added, giving me a quiet smile. "I know she was a friend of yours."

"Right," I nodded slowly. "Sorry to bother you."

"No bother at all," Weber reassured me. "This has been hard on everyone. Maybe now it's all over, people will be able to move on."

Weber smiled. "You have a good night now."

I headed back to my desk to grab my coat and bag, confusion still lingering in my mind. I could have sworn I'd heard Blake talk about drinking, but that day was a jumble; the shock and grief had blurred it all together; the only moment in sharp relief was later, with Oliver. His kiss.

I felt a shiver of anticipation. Not long now.

"Hey, Chloe, did you get those tickets I needed?" Blake stopped me on my way out.

I stared at him, a chill settling over me. He was back from suspension, looking just the same as he always had. It had been barely a slap on the wrist, a couple of weeks' lost wages.

Crystal had lost everything because of him.

"I'm just on my way out," I replied, icy.

"I know." He gave me a pleading look. "But I'm on speeding duty tonight, Weber wants me out by the highway."

"They're in the lock-up, third shelf from the back," I told him, edging away.

"Please?" Blake sighed. "I can never find a thing in that place. You're an angel," he wheedled, and I realized he wouldn't stop until I did what he wanted.

"Fine."

I hurried around the corner to the evidence lock-up, pulling out my keys. But the door was unlocked, and when

I swung it open, I found Weber pulling out a carton from the bottom shelf.

He startled, straightening up and banging his head against the shelves.

"Sorry!" I cried.

"No, it's fine, you just surprised me." Weber rubbed his head. I quickly found the ticket books and grabbed one for Blake, holding it up.

"You need to run some kind of induction," I told him. "They come crying to me every time they need something."

"Right. Sure." Weber coughed, looking uncomfortable.

"Anyway, good night. Again." I headed back out, tossing the ticket book to Blake as I passed.

"Wait, I still need—"

"Too late!" I called back. I wasn't going to spend another moment in the station, not with Oliver waiting for me.

Oliver and Ethan.

I arrived at the Reznick house early, there was no reason to linger at my own. Mom was still knitting by the spool, wool trailing across her makeshift craft room as the needles clicked faster, her attention focussed on the TV. I fixed her dinner and then drove over, checking my reflection in the rear-view mirror before eagerly hurrying up the front path.

"You look nice." Ethan greeted me with a long kiss. I'd spent a little longer at my dresser picking out an outfit and doing my hair – but it was all for Oliver, not him.

"Thanks." I pulled back, surreptitiously looking around. The house was quiet.

"C'mon." Ethan took my hand. "I've got chips and pizza and instant streaming. I meant it when I said, you're going to relax."

I followed him to the den. He had the table laid out with food and soda, everything we needed for a quiet evening in. He began scrolling through the movie options on the TV and I took a bite, forcing myself to go another ten seconds before asking. "So where's Oliver?"

"He went out." Ethan didn't look up.

My heart fell. "Oh?"

"Yeah, he met some friends to go drinking. Said we could have the place to ourselves."

Disappointment was a bitter itch in my veins. I'd been looking forward to seeing him all day and now I felt like a foolish kid, getting my hopes up for nothing. "I didn't know he had any friends in town," I said lightly, concentrating on the cheese strings twisting from my slice.

"You know Olly." Ethan gave me a look. "He can make friends with anyone. Mr Popularity."

"Right."

"I'm glad you guys are getting on better," he added. "It means a lot to me that you're trying."

The pizza turned to cardboard in my mouth.

"Oh. It's fine." I choked the mouthful down.

"No, I know you didn't get off on the best foot," Ethan argued, "but the hunting trip helped, right? He said you guys had fun."

Fun wasn't the word. Not for something so bright and reckless, but Ethan couldn't understand that if he tried. "Sure," I agreed quietly. "Oliver's not so bad, I just needed to get to know him, that's all."

"Well, he'll be out of our hair soon." Ethan stretched, reaching for another slice of pizza.

"What do you mean?" I felt a tremble of panic. "Is he going back to college?"

Ethan shook his head. "Some buddy of his says he can fix him with a job out in New York. Some start-up, technology or something. He's the geek, and he needs someone to schmooze investors and be the face of it. Right up Oliver's alley, don't you think?"

I nodded, but my heart was pounding with dread.

He was leaving. Oliver, just like the rest of them. All of this with me was just a momentary distraction for him, a way to kill time amusing himself before he left.

The realization of what I'd been about to do crashed

through me. I would have ended things with Ethan for him; torn apart the one good thing in my life for nothing.

I would have been all alone.

Relief came, sharp and swift. I would have destroyed everything, but Ethan didn't know. He didn't know anything.

I leaned across and kissed him, taking him by surprise. "Thank you," I whispered, my heart still pounding in my ears. "For doing this tonight, for everything. You're the best."

Ethan flushed, smiling. "What did I do to deserve you?"

It was the kind of thing he said all the time, but now it made me cringe, knowing how close I'd come to ruining everything. "Don't." I shook my head.

"I know you don't like all that sappy stuff," he insisted, "but you have to know, you're everything to me."

I stopped.

"I mean it," Ethan said, still serious. "I've never felt this way about anyone before. Olly probably told you, I never really dated much." He looked bashful. "But that's because I was waiting for someone like you. I don't know what I'd do without you, Chloe, I can't even imagine it."

"Ethan . . ." I struggled to find the words, guilt and relief twisting in my stomach. I wanted to stop him, but part of me held back. What was I supposed to say, with him looking at me so adoringly, like he'd do anything for me?

"I love you."

My mouth dropped open.

Ethan grinned. "You don't have to say anything, I know you have enough to be dealing with. I just, wanted you to know. You should know you're loved."

He pulled something from his pocket, a small box, and for a moment, panic sliced through me.

"I wanted to give you this." He passed it, awkward. "It's a promise ring. To show you how much you mean to me."

I exhaled in a shaky breath, slowly opening the box. The slim silver ring had a heart etched on the inside of the band. It was sweet, the kind of thing you found in a mall store, with a stuffed teddy-bear and a display of red roses.

Pedestrian. Cliché.

I blocked out Oliver's whisper in the back of my mind and forced a bright smile. "I love it," I said loudly, sliding it on to the middle finger of my right hand. "Thank you."

Ethan moved closer to wrap his arms around me. I tucked against his body, fitting just right. He held me there and something welled up inside, an ache of longing. I'd felt so alone, not just since Dad had left, but for years now; it felt like loneliness was my default setting. I'd never fitted in quite right with the girls at school, not even Alisha. Despite the time we spent together, ours was an alliance of convenience. No matter how many afternoon study sessions or lunches we shared, there was a part of me I knew she would never understand. I'd always felt drifting, untethered on the edges of the crowd. They didn't know me, I wondered sometimes if I would always be alone.

I'd never belonged to anyone, had something all my own.

"I'm sorry," I whispered, hugging him tight, as if I could erase the last few weeks of madness, all the shame of my betrayal.

"What for?" Ethan stroked my hair.

"Just, I don't deserve you."

"Bullshit," he said tenderly. "You're the sweetest girl in the world."

I wasn't. I was all wrong inside, but for a moment, I just wanted to be that girl he saw, the good one, the best.

The one who was happy here, with her boyfriend, and nothing more.

"Can we just sit here for a while?" I asked quietly. "No movie or anything."

"Whatever you want," Ethan murmured. I shifted, so I was sitting with my back against him, in the V space between his legs. I let my head fall back against his chest and watched the fire dance in the grate. We stayed like that for hours, quiet and holding, as if nothing was wrong.

I told myself I was done with Oliver now. I had to be.

THEN

For all my promises to myself, I didn't sleep. Ethan lay, unconscious beside me, his arm flung heavy across my stomach. I'd given up on moving him, he always wound up splayed back across the middle of the bed, reaching for me in his sleep, as if I was his comforter, to tuck against his side.

I stared at the dark ceiling, silently counting the minutes pass. The sweetness of the evening had drifted away and now I felt restless in my own skin again, my body still humming. Unfulfilled. For all his eager touching, the methodical effort of his hands and mouth and body, Ethan could never pull me over the edge. He tried, so sweet and tender, but that was almost worse. It was my failure, my fault that I stayed in my own mind, absent and detached, part of me guiltily waiting for him to be finished, willing him to just be done.

At last, I heard the distant sound of the front door closing shut.

Oliver was home.

I lay there another moment, holding on tight to Ethan. I should stay there with him, fall asleep in his arms. I shouldn't feel the pull downstairs, like a dark kind of gravity, calling me out.

I should, I should, I should.

But temptation won, of course it did. I gently lifted Ethan's arm and slid out from underneath. I was wearing an old T-shirt of his, naked beneath the XL football emblem, and I tugged it down over my bare thighs as I tiptoed to the door and waited there, holding my breath, listening to the steady rise and fall of Ethan's chest.

No change.

I slowly turned the handle and stepped out into the dark hallway, shutting the door behind me with a faint click. The carpet was soft under my bare feet as I crept silently around the corner and down the stairs, the cold air whispering along my skin.

My pulse was racing, every sense alive as I walked slowly towards the light, a low glow coming under the kitchen door.

I pushed it ajar.

"Miss me?" Oliver was by the refrigerator, drinking juice straight from the carton. He met my eyes with a knowing stare and, right away, I knew, I'd come too soon. I should have waited, let him wonder. I shouldn't have scampered down like an eager puppy to his master.

"I didn't know you were back. I couldn't sleep." I feigned a casual tone, padding across the cool tiles. I reached past him and opened the freezer, looking for the tub of ice cream Ethan and I had left unfinished.

"Liar." Oliver whispered, turning so that his body was flush against mine, his lips brushing my ear.

A shiver rolled down my body, every hair standing on end.

"You missed a fun night," I told him, turning around to meet his eyes. "Ethan and I had a great time."

Oliver's lips curled in a smile. "Trying to make me jealous?" he drawled slowly.

I held his gaze. "Are you?"

Oliver's face remained impassive, but then I lifted the ice cream out of the fridge and his gaze settled on the promise ring. The tendon in his jaw flickered, just a moment, taut with tension. "Is that new?" he asked, his voice still casual.

"Ethan gave it to me." I felt a rush of victory. "Tonight."

Oliver scowled. He took a step closer. "Did you fuck him?"

My blood rushed in a shock as he watched, smiling. "None of your business," I managed to reply.

Oliver just took another step, backing me up against the kitchen cabinet. "Do you think of me, when he touches you?" he demanded, reaching out to trail a fingertip down my cheek, and along the line of my throat.

I shivered, caught in his gaze. "No," I lied.

"Liar." Oliver's finger trailed lower, over my collarbone, down over the swell of my breast. "I think you fucked him and thought of me. I think you imagined me, every minute he was inside you."

I couldn't believe he was saying those things. Worse still, they were true. Oliver's eyes flashed and then suddenly his other hand was on my waist, gripping me hard, shoving me back in place as he pulled up the hem of Ethan's shirt.

My breath caught in my throat. I couldn't look away, not with his eyes still fixed on mine, intent and victorious. This wasn't like Ethan, fumbling and eager; Oliver touched me with precision, detached and remote, watching my every response. I tried to stay unmoved, meeting his control with my own, but he was good, too good, his fingers sliding cool on my hot skin until I broke, gasping against him, the roar of blood in my ears.

A noise came from down the hallway.

Oliver stepped away from me, sliding smoothly around

the kitchen island so that when the door swung open, he was sitting on the other side of the room to me.

"There you are." Ethan looked surprised. "I was worried."

"I . . . I'm fine." I caught my breath, my cheeks burning, my blood still shimmering from release. "I couldn't sleep."

"Hey, dude." Ethan nodded at Oliver as he crossed the kitchen towards me. "Good night?"

"It was . . . eventful." Oliver smiled, his eyes on me.

I looked away.

"You're all red." Ethan frowned, looking down at me. He reached to press the back of his hand against my forehead. "And you're burning up. Do you think you're getting sick?"

"Maybe." I inhaled quickly and grabbed a glass from the counter, running the faucet cold. "I haven't been feeling so good. I probably just need some rest, is all."

"Aww, come back to bed," Ethan told me. "I'll take care of you."

I nodded, my eyes cast down as I passed Oliver. I could still feel the imprint of his touch on my body, my pulse racing in my veins; the remnants of desire.

"Yes, don't worry," Oliver added, his voice following me out. "You'll be in good hands."

NOW

I know, you're judging me – and I would too.

We all pretend to be so much better than we are, but if you're really honest with yourself, you've felt it. Laying there, silently willing their hands lower, their touch harder. Wishing you could tell them just what you need, but finding you have no voice, no words to sound.

Nobody's told you how to say those things. Nobody said you ever could. So you stay silent, and restless, and guilty.

Bad, for wanting so much more.

Bad, for not appreciating everything they give.

Bad, for all the dark places inside your soul you try so hard to hide.

And so it goes, day after day. Every sharp word and every

angry, impure thought. You press them down, pretending they're not a part of who you really are – the sweet, good girl, the smiling, happy person – but the truth is, that anger is more real than anything. It burns and blooms and blossoms, twisting tighter with every faked smile until you wonder, what would it be like to just let it free?

Stop pretending. Stop hiding. Stop being the girl they all said you should be.

Imagine that freedom. God, can't you feel it?

What harm could it do?

THEN

They dropped all charges against Blake. No DUI charge, no manslaughter trial, not even a ticket for reckless driving. The statement said there was no evidence of wrong-doing. It was time to draw a line under the tragedy and let the community heal.

A pipe burst along the east wall of the sheriff's department, flooding the evidence lock-up. Two crates were destroyed, including the interview tapes from the night Blake was brought in.

Weber. The evidence room. The tapes. Blake's testimony.

I could have said something, I know. Crystal was gone and they were sweeping it aside, like her death meant nothing, not compared to loyalty among officers. A couple of beers might not have made any difference in the end, but it was a lie.

A lie I could have exposed.

But I did nothing. I turned my head away and bit back my suspicions, and told myself that they were right, it was time to move on. The truth was, I didn't have room in me to rail at Crystal's injustice; I didn't have the energy for her fight, not with my own underway. I had bigger things to worry about.

Mom had stopped taking her medication.

I didn't notice at first, I was too intoxicated by Oliver, I didn't know how long she'd been slipping back into her old depression. I only realized when I came home from work early on Friday night and found the stench of urine, thick in the air.

She'd wet herself.

A grown woman, sitting in her own filth. Crying quietly with the TV on, as if she couldn't even find the effort to get up.

"Mom!" I pulled her to her feet. The smell was terrible and I tried not to gag. "Jesus, Mom, what happened?"

"Did you see?" she hiccupped, pointing at the TV. "Those poor babies."

It was some news report about an orphanage in Asia. I

quickly shut it off, then tried to coax her upstairs to the bath-room. "It's OK," I told her, over and over. "Everything's going to be OK."

I helped her strip off her soiled nightgown and get into the shower. She stood there, shivering like a child under the jets.

"I'm sorry," she whimpered. "I'm trying, I really am."

"I don't understand, you were doing so well." My voice twists. I thought we had it figured out, I thought all this was under control. And now, now it was threatening to fall apart again. Panic rose up in me, sharp and swift. I couldn't do this, not again, not from scratch for month after anxious month.

"We'll go back to Dr Mayhew," I told her, fighting to stay calm. "Your dosage must be wrong. We'll try new meds, we'll figure this out."

I left her cleaning off and went into her bedroom, hunt-ing for fresh clothes and towels. Her pill bottle was standing on the bedside table and I paused. The last time I checked, weeks ago, it was about half full. When I lifted it again, I real-ized: it still was.

Anger flared.

"Mom!" I strode back into the bathroom. I yanked the shower curtain aside, holding the bottle up. "What the hell is this? You've stopped taking them. I can't believe you've stopped taking them!"

"I don't like it," Mom mumbled. She turned her head away. "They make me feel like someone else. It's not right."

"Not right . . . ?" I gasped for air, drowning in the rage that flooded through me, the harsh blow of frustration. "Not right is me running around after you, having to make sure that you dress yourself, and wash yourself, and don't piss your pants on the fucking couch!"

I grabbed her arm and pulled her roughly out of the shower. She protested but I ignored her, shoving a clean robe at her and pushing her out into the bedroom. "I'm sorry," she whimpered again, tying the robe around herself with shaking hands.

"Don't just say that, do something about it!" I took the pill bottle and shook two onto my palm. I held them out to her. "Take them."

Mom shook her head. "I can't."

"Take them!"

My voice echoed, a furious scream.

Mom cringed back, her eyes widening with fear, but I didn't care. "Take them, or I'll drive you to the ER right this minute," I ordered her, my blood pounding in my ears. "I'll tell them you tried to kill yourself, that you're a danger to yourself and others, and they need to commit you."

She gaped at me in crumpled disbelief. "You wouldn't."

"I will," I promised her and, God, I meant it. "And if you

think these drugs are bad, just wait and see what they put you on in there. Have you seen the psych ward?" I demanded, moving closer. "Have you? They'll strap you down in an empty room and leave you there alone to rot."

"Don't!" She broke into sobs, her body shaking. "Please, Chloe ..."

"There won't be fluffy pillows!" I yelled, hurling one from the bed. "There won't be cooking shows, and knitting, and a nice dinner every night. I'll leave you there, and I won't ever come back!"

"Please!" She sank to the floor, weeping. "Please, don't leave me, Chloe, you're all I've got."

Her words tried to wrap around me, suffocating, squeezing tight, but I fought them back, determined. I was done with hesitance and panic and creeping around in the dark. I had the upper hand now, I knew how to keep her in line. "So you'll take the meds?"

She nodded.

"Promise me, you have to take them. Otherwise ..." I let the words hang in the air.

"I will!" Mom gasped eagerly. "I promise, I'll be good."

She reached for the pills, quickly gulping them down dry. "See?" She managed a quaking smile. "It's OK, sweetie, I'll be better." She tried to hug me, but I stood back. I couldn't look at her like this, not another second longer.

"I'm going to class. I want you in bed by the time I'm back."

I turned it over in my mind, all through Ashton's lecture at Rossmore that night. What to do, what to do? Every step I thought we were progressing, Mom would back-slide at a moment's notice – and now I had to accept for the first time, that she might never get any better. I'd been hanging on the hope that recovery was just around the corner: that with enough time and the right meds and careful, nudging support, she would crawl herself out of the darkness of her own mind and somehow shed this helpless, weary skin, becoming the person she used to be again.

Now, I realized, that was just a childish dream.

There was no getting "back to normal". There was no magical solution, no pill that would wipe the slate clean. Any recovery would be hard-fought, day by day, with relapse and breakdowns and a dozen other awful failures along the way.

It could take her years like this. Years of my life, right here.

The longer I sat staring at my blank notepad, the teacher's voice drifting just out of reach, the more I felt something harden inside me, an angry resignation. Part of me wanted to just follow through on my threat: hand her over to be somebody else's problem, wash my hands of her for good . . . but what would that make me? I tried to tell myself I owed her more than that, but I knew that obligation was wearing thinner by the day, strained to breaking point after months of her helpless collapse.

I was her daughter, I told myself, over and over, even as I dreamed of escape. That had to mean something.

I was no closer to a solution when the chairs scraped back around me. Class was ending in a bustle and rush. I packed my things away, untouched, and followed the crowd towards the exit.

"I know this stuff isn't exactly riveting, but could you try and pretend like you're listening?"

I turned. Ashton was wiping down the board. He gave me a wry look from behind his square-rimmed glasses.

"I'm sorry." I swallowed. "Was it that obvious?"

"Not as much as the guy snoring beside you, but yes. It's OK," he added, sighing. "I'd zone out too. God, this place is depressing." He finished cleaning up, looking around the windowless room with an expression I recognized as pure resentment.

I felt a surge of empathy. He'd had other plans too, I remembered: tenure in a city somewhere, another life away from here.

"I thought you were supposed to give us inspirational

speeches," I replied lightly. "About how this is the first step in the great adventure of our lives."

He snorted. "Please. We both know, you don't make it out of a place like this."

"I can see it on the prospectus now," I joked darkly. "Rossmore, where dreams go to die."

Ashton laughed. "Walk you out?" he offered.

"Sure." I hitched my bag up. He shut off the lights and we walked down the empty hallways, our footsteps echoing on the scuffed floor.

"I read your paper," he said. "I'll have it back with the rest of them next week."

"What did you think?" I asked, nervous. I'd taken a shot at one of the assignments for Ashton's American Lit class; I hadn't been in the classes, but I'd done the reading, and tried to follow the outlines he'd suggested.

"You're getting there," he started, sounding encouraging. "It had some good arguments, but you need to watch your structure. You go off on tangents sometimes, and it dilutes the central thesis. Believe it or not, less is sometimes more."

His criticism stung a little. "I'll remember that," I said quickly.

"But don't be discouraged." Ashton had clearly seen the disappointment on my face, because he stopped, turning to me with a reassuring look. "You have a nice style, clean, unsentimental. You've got potential, you're just starting to get the hang of this."

I nodded. "OK. Thanks."

We got outside. Ashton looked around. "Any wild plans?" he asked, joking.

"Sure." I gave a wry laugh. "This place is party central."

Ashton made a face. "Tell me about it. They say it's so great out of the city, less pollution, all this nature. But I can't sleep at night, it's so fucking quiet."

There was an edge to his voice, I recognized it well: a discontented hum, vibrating under the surface. I'd noticed the change in him in class too – he'd been buoyant at the start of semester, full of enthusiasm, but it had been draining away in the face of the general apathy of the students, who seemed to doze their way through the session.

"Still, it's just the year, right?" I said, reminding myself, as much as him.

He nodded, giving me a brief smile. "I can make it if you can."

"Deal."

I said my goodbyes and headed over to my car, sending up my usual prayer that she would keep going just a few miles more. But when I turned the ignition, the engine started, spluttered briefly, and then died.

Again.

I sank back in the freezing seat, too worn out to even be mad. Another trip to the mechanic to fix the engine that was already past its use. Another three hundred dollars we didn't have, another call for Ethan to come rescue me, because that's all he ever did these days.

Goddamn.

I saw a pair of headlights light up on the other side of the parking lot. Ashton.

My spirits lifted. I quickly grabbed my bag and got out of the car.

"Hey!" I waved him down as he slowly drove towards the exit. He pulled up alongside me, rolling the window down. "I'm sorry," I apologized. "But my stupid car died again. I'm totally stranded."

I waited hopefully. Sure enough, Ashton waved me around. "I can give you a ride."

"Are you sure?" I checked. "I don't want to be any trouble."

"It's no problem, get on in."

I went around and slid into the passenger seat. It was warm inside, the radio playing some talk show about politics. "You're a regular knight in shining armor," I told him, relieved to be out of the cold. "I swear, I'll pay more attention in class next week. I'll even ask questions."

Ashton laughed, putting the car back in drive. "Hey, no need to go overboard."

He drove away from the college, making the turns towards the highway. I watched the darkness blur outside the window.

"So, tell me, how am I stacking up?"

I turned. Ashton was looking at me expectantly. "School gossip, behind the scenes. C'mon, I want to know."

"That's confidential, *sir*," I joked, as if I was party to any of the gossip around college.

"Aww, I told you, it's Ashton. And I'm serious, what are my feedback sheets going to look like at the end of the semester? Do I need to brace myself for zeros?"

"You know you don't." I stretched, getting comfortable. "Now, Mr Yi might be giving you a run for the money in the 'hottest teacher' department . . ."

Ashton laughed. Mr Yi was pushing seventy, and shuffled around college with a cane. "Damn, I thought I had that one locked down."

"Maybe next semester," I joked. "He might not last long."

Ashton smiled. "Any way at all you can take that Wednesday class? You're screwing up the grading curve for this session."

"I can't," I sighed, "I work full-time."

"What if I wrote your boss a note?" Ashton said, still playful. "Dear . . ."

"Weber."

"Dear Mr Weber," he continued. "Please excuse Chloe on Wednesdays, I urgently need her to brighten up my classroom. I will be bereft without her."

I laughed. "Cut it out."

"What? I mean it." Ashton glanced over. "You're the only one of those kids who gives a damn."

"I'm not a kid," I answered automatically. There was a pause, Ashton glanced over, his lips curling in a smile.

"No, you're not." He paused. "You know, my place isn't far. I could swing by and pick up some of the books on the list, if you'd like to borrow them. I know the cost can add up," he added, sympathetic.

I looked over. "Sure, if you don't mind. I mean, that would be great."

"It's no problem at all. Anything for my favorite student," he said with a smile.

Ashton drove another couple of miles, then took an exit, heading through a more suburban area filled with construction and half-built houses. He slowed, turning on to a cul-de-sac lined with identical red-brick buildings and streetlights, bright over the silent sidewalks.

"Have you lived out here long?" I asked, watching the front-yard pass. It was all brand new, like something from a movie set, and for some reason it wasn't what I'd expected

Ashton's neighborhood to be. He looked like he should be hanging out in a loft somewhere downtown, across from a dive bar and record store, not here, among the swing sets and mini-vans.

"About six months now," Ashton replied. "My girlfriend picked it. Great schools," he added, but there was a note of tension in his tone.

"It's nice," I said quickly. "Safe."

He pulled into the drive of a semi-detached house near the end of the street. "Most of my stuff is still in boxes," he apologized. "It'll take a minute to dig everything out."

"That's fine, I don't mind," I said, pulling out my phone to pass the time.

He laughed. "You can't wait out here. Come on in. I warn you, the place is still a work-in-progress," he added, closing the door behind him. I paused, then grabbed my purse and climbed out, following him to the door. "It's always the way, right?" he said, opening up and turning on the lights. "You unpack just enough to make the place livable, and then leave everything stacked in the closet until you move again."

"I don't know." I felt self-conscious as I stepped inside and looked around. "I've never moved anywhere before."

The house was open-plan and box-fresh, the walls still plain white; the furniture stranded in the middle of the living room in front of a flat-screen TV.

"Well, you will," Ashton declared. "And when you do, remember: labels are your friend. The first night, we spent hours opening every damn box trying to find the clean sheets."

I took another few steps inside, drifting to the huge bookcases that spanned the far wall. They were the most lived-in part of the place: packed with old cloth-bound hardbacks and dog-eared novels, cluttered with photos and mementos. I paused over a framed photograph of Ashton with a smiling blonde woman. He looked younger. Happier.

"Is this your girlfriend?" I asked.

He looked up, rifling through a box in the corner. "Yeah, that's Bree. She's visiting friends in Fort Wayne. Some bachelorette girls' thing." He straightened up. "I know it was here somewhere ..." he said, surveying the boxes with a frown.

"It's OK," I said quickly. "I don't need them right away."

"No, no I've got this." He left the room and I turned back to the bookcase, tracing the spines. He'd travelled all over, I could see from the flyers and maps lodged between the covers. I felt an ache of longing.

One day, I would get the hell out of this town. One day.

Music came from the speakers in the corner. "You like the Original Riot?"

I startled, turning. Ashton was leaning against the door to the kitchen, pouring a glass of wine.

"What?"

"This band, I saw them play a couple of years ago," he explained, watching me. "They're great live."

"I don't know them," I said quickly. "You know, thanks for looking for those books, but I really have to get back."

"You've got time for a quick drink." Ashton held the glass out, offering it to me.

"No, thanks." I shook my head.

He laughed. "You can relax, we're not in school now. I promise, I won't tell."

"It's fine." I moved towards the door. "My mom's waiting up for me. She gets worried if I'm late."

"So call, tell her you'll be a while." Ashton took a sip of the wine, still watching me with a lazy smile. "We can get to know each other a little better."

My heart began to beat a little faster, adrenalin skittering in my veins.

We were alone in the house.

"You know what, I'll just call my boyfriend and have him come and pick me up," I said, picking my purse up from where I'd set it on the table by the door. I fumbled with the strap, trying to find my cell, trying even harder to stay casual, seeming relaxed. "You don't need to go out of your way for me."

"It's no trouble." Ashton put his wine glass down and moved closer to me, looming just a few inches away. "Stay, have a drink, then I'll run you back home."

"No, I have to go," I said again, pulling out my cell. Before I could dial, he took it from my hand.

"What is this thing, a relic from the nineties?" he laughed, examining the case. He juggled it from one hand to the other, teasing. "Do you have to tap out a message in Morse Code?"

I froze, my heart racing. "Can I have that back?" I asked. I tried not to panic, there was nothing wrong. He was just kidding around. "Ashton?" I asked again, reaching for my phone. He ducked back, out of my grasp. "Please, Mr Davis, stop it."

I hoped using his formal name would remind him he was my teacher, but instead, Ashton just laughed. "I've told you, we're out of the classroom. You can cut that student-teacher bullshit now." He dangled the phone in front of me, then pulled it away again when I reached.

I swallowed back my fear, giving a weak laugh. "Come on, that's not fair. Give it back."

Ashton tilted his head, his eyes travelling over me. His gaze lingered on my body, hungry in a way that made my blood chill in my veins.

"Make me."

THEN

I swallowed back a surge of fear. "Fine," I said firmly. "I'll use your line."

I walked over to the phone, mounted on the wall by the kitchen, and lifted the handset. My heart was racing, counting through all the stupid risks I'd taken. I was in his house, away from anything, with no way of leaving on my own.

Nobody knew I was there.

"Aww, don't be like that. I was just playing around." Ashton sighed. He tossed the phone back at me, and I scrambled to catch it, feeling a shock of relief. I was overreacting, he was playing around, that was all.

"You know, I'm just going to wait outside." I clutched my phone to my chest. Ashton was standing in front of the door, but there was no other way out. I took a hesitant few steps towards him.

He didn't move. "What's wrong?" he asked. "I'm not that terrible a host, am I?"

I tried to fake another smile. "No, no," I stuttered, taking another step. "I just, want some privacy to call, that's all."

Ashton looked at me, his eyes narrowing behind his spectacles. "You could always take it in the bedroom," he suggested. "It's just through there."

I froze. "No. Thanks."

I wanted to run. To bolt past him and disappear out into the night. But I had to force myself to stay calm. There was still the hope that this was all a misunderstanding, that he was being inappropriate, sure, but not anything worse. We were balanced on a razor's edge here, and I could only pray that if I smiled and played nice I would be fine.

I took another step, and then another. As I reached the door, Ashton finally stood aside.

I exhaled in a shaking breath of relief. "Thanks for the ride, this far." I made my voice bright and cheery as I turned to say goodbye. "I really appreciate it."

I didn't have time to react before his hands were on my waist and his lips came down hard on mine.

I panicked, shoving with both hands at his chest and trying to turn my head away, but he pushed me back against the door, his tongue plunging in my mouth, his hand groping at my ass.

I struggled, my protests muffled under his kiss. His body was crushing me, too heavy to move, and I reached desperately, shoving at his chest, his shoulders, anything to push him back. Finally, he came up for air. "Hold still," Ashton breathed, stroking my cheek. "It's OK, just relax."

"No!" I cried, struggling. Fear was thick around me. "Let me go!"

"Come on, you don't have to play the good girl with me." Ashton groped at my chest, his breath catching in his throat. "I know you want this. You've been panting after me since the start of school."

He dipped his head to kiss at my neck. Bile rose in my throat.

"No!" I tried pushing him away again, but I was trapped against the door. I had no room to move, no room to breathe.

Desperate, I turned my head, reaching, stretching to bite down hard on his ear.

"Fuck!" Ashton lurched back, clutching the side of his head. He brought his hand away. Blood. He stared at me in shock. "What the fuck did you do that for?"

"I told you, no!" I scrabbled at the lock, but it was a chain fastening, and I couldn't get it right. "I don't want this, I never did!"

"So it was all a game to you, leading me on?" His jaw clenched, eyes flashing dark with anger. "You're a fucking tease."

He moved towards me again.

"Don't touch me!" The chain was still caught. I couldn't get out. My heart raced, blood pounding in my ears as I stared at him. "I'm warning you . . ."

"What?" Ashton gave me a cruel grin. "If I were you, I'd be a little nicer. I still determine your grade, remember?"

"I don't care if I fail." I glared at him.

Ashton made a tutting sound. "I can call any college you apply to, and tell them what a disappointment you are."

I froze. "You wouldn't," I whispered.

"I will." Ashton's expression was harsh. "I'll tell them all about how you disrupted class, and cheated on your tests, and didn't show your teacher the proper respect. "Unless . . . you make it up to me. Show me your respect," he breathed.

He stroked my cheek again and this time I couldn't flinch away. I felt sick, but I couldn't move. He had the power, he had the rest of my fucking life in his hands.

I stood there, motionless, hating myself as his finger trailed lower, lower, to the neckline of my shirt and under the edge.

"Good girl." Ashton smiled in victory. His hand closed around my breast, squeezing.

I shuddered, but I didn't move.

His hand slid lower, to the waistband of my jeans. "You don't have to be scared," he murmured, leaning closer. "You'll like it, I promise."

His lips came down on my neck again, kissing hard as he fumbled with his zipper.

This was how it went, I thought numbly. A busted engine; a car ride; his girlfriend out of town. Another choice that wasn't mine. Because what I wanted never mattered, not anymore. Fury rose up inside me, breaking through the fear.

No way. No fucking way.

I reached out blindly grasping on the hall table for something, anything I could use. My hand closed around a smooth, round shape; a handle. It was a travel Thermos, something for his morning coffee. I had a brief flash of his girlfriend filling it for him today, sending him off with a wave and a goodbye kiss.

And here he was, raping me anyway.

I swung it with everything I had, slamming the metal against the back of his head. Ashton let out a pained grunt, his body sagging against mine. I shoved him back, swinging the flask again. It slammed against his forehead this time and he fell backwards to the floor.

He rolled, groaning, struggling to his hands and knees.

"Bitch," he cursed, gasping. "What the fuck . . .?"

He was coming up again, reaching towards me, so I lunged first: grabbing the back of his head and slamming my knee into his face in a sickening crunch.

Blood pounded in my ears. None of this would be happening if I had just got the hell out of this town. If I didn't have to play nice to get what I needed, if I didn't *need* so damn much at all.

"What about what I want?" I screamed at his limp body. I grabbed his hair again, yanking his head up and slamming it back against the wall. "Do you even care? No! Because I'm nothing to you, just another stupid girl!"

My blood ran hot with fury. I slammed again, caught up in the whirlwind of red. Again, again, until my hands were shaking and blood ran, dark down the pale wood, sticky on my hands.

I released him, gasping. There was silence, not one movement. Not a sound.

Oh God.

I backed away, fumbling with the door again until the chain finally clicked into place. I grabbed my purse, closing the door behind me and stumbling outside. I made it three steps on the dark front drive before my legs crumpled beneath me, sending me crawling in the sharp gravel. I gasped for air, scrambling until finally I was on my feet and running, running down the street with nothing but my heartbeat pounding in my ears and the sound of my own ragged breath for company.

What had I done?

My lungs burned and my limbs ached by the time I reached the main road. There were no cars around, just rows of empty houses, dark and still. Nobody there to see what I'd done.

Silence.

My hands shook as I pulled out my cellphone, trembling too hard to dial. It took four tries before I finally found the station number and could click through to call.

"Sheriff's department." The voice came, drawling, steady, bored. It was Blake, I recognized over the thunder of my heartbeat, and in my mind I could see him, reaching for a slice of pizza, his boots kicked up on the desk, leaving smudges I'd have to clean come Monday. "What can I do you for?"

I opened my mouth, but my breath rasped in my throat. I couldn't make a sound. I could still see the way I'd left him, Ashton, crumpled in a bloody heap on the floor.

I didn't know how many times I'd hit him, how much damage I'd done.

I wavered, sick with the realization. He could be dead. I could have killed him. What would happen when they found him? Would they believe me if I tried?

"Hello?" Blake asked again, bored. "Hello?"

I hung up, my cellphone falling down by my side. I saw headlights on the road ahead and quickly leaped back into the shadows of the trees. My mind was racing now, my desperate panic spinning into something else, fear and doubt and terror taking an iron grip of my mind.

I could hear them already, what they'd all say.

I'd gotten in the car with him, hadn't I? I'd followed him inside the house. Maybe I'd liked it. Maybe I hadn't had to fight back so hard.

Maybe I'd lied.

Bile rose up in my throat and I stumbled to the edge of the road, retching violently, again and again, collapsing on to my knees as the world spun, dark shadows everywhere as I pressed my eyes shut fast and gripped the wet grass and desperately prayed for it all to be over, *please just be over*, please let this be done.

I wasn't sure how long it was until the world steadied and I slowly rose to my feet again. I breathed deep, searching in the dark until I found my cellphone. It was muddy but unharmed. I scrolled through my contacts until I found the name I needed, the one person who would know what to do.

Oliver.

THEN

He came without questions, not a single word, just a sideways glance from the driver's seat as I fumbled with the door and threw myself into the car.

"Please," I managed, my hands still shaking, "just drive."

Oliver pulled away, our headlights cutting through the dark in bright, sure swathes. Here, inside, I was safe, I told myself over and over again, as we sped further away from the suburbs. The warm air blasting from the dashboard, the talk radio show murmuring on low, the casual way Oliver leaned back, hand resting on the steering wheel even though he must have been going twenty over the limit by then. I was safe now.

But I knew that was a lie.

He was back there, somewhere. Hurt. Bleeding. Furious.

What would he do now?

Oliver made a turn and then there were lights, blaring neon and bold. I blinked, looking around. We were at a drive-through, on one of those rest-stops off the highway. Oliver pulled up to the speaker and looked over.

"What do you want?"

I stared back, dazed. I couldn't have eaten now if I'd tried. My stomach was still churning, my whole body sick with tension.

"I ... nothing." My voice shook, and I hugged myself harder, trying to keep it together. "Oliver ..."

"Sure?" Oliver smiled at me. "I'm buying. Go crazy."

"Please," I heard the note of begging in my voice, "I just want to go home."

Oliver ignored me, winding down the window and leaning out. "Yeah, I'll get a burger deluxe, two portions of fries ... Oh, and a milkshake. Chocolate."

I looked at him in disbelief. I'd called him to come pick me up in the middle of nowhere, barely able to speak, and he was ordering fast food like nothing was wrong.

"There's a sweater in the back," Oliver said, glancing over again.

"What?" I didn't understand.

"You're a mess," Oliver said calmly. "The sweater. Put it on."

I did as I was told, pulling the oversized blue sweatshirt over my bloodstained clothes. I slouched lower in the seat, trying to disappear into the soft folds of fabric as he drove up to the window and paid, chatting nonchalantly to the cashier about the weather and the late shift. Then, when I almost couldn't take it anymore, he pulled into a space in the far corner of the parking lot and turned the engine off.

"Here," he offered, holding out a bag of fries. "I knew you'd only steal mine."

The smell hit me, grease and starch, and I gagged. I quickly threw open the car door and leaned out, waiting until the rush left my bloodstream before slowly sitting upright again.

Oliver was eating his burger, licking sauce off his fingers.

"So," he began, looking at me again with those clear blue eyes. "What do I need to know?"

I shivered. Already, the scene in Ashton's house seemed like a dream, a terrible nightmare. Here, with the lights, and the buzz of traffic audible and Oliver so casually ripping open a ketchup packet and smearing the sauce on his cardboard carton lid, I could almost tell myself it wasn't real.

Then I felt the imprint of his touch, burning on my body, and I was right back there again. Screaming. Struggling.

And angrier than I'd ever felt before.

"My car wouldn't start again." I finally found my voice, quiet in the dark. "My teacher, he offered to give me a ride."

There was silence, as Oliver methodically worked his way through the rest of the fries. I wanted to scream, to shake him, to ask if he had heard a single word, but something stopped me. Ethan would be all over me now: demanding we go to the police, asking if I needed the hospital, protective and concerned. I would be back there again, describing it, reliving every terrible moment and trying my best to calm *him* down.

Oliver just slurped his milkshake, watching the distant lights on the highway snake past in a stream of red and gold.

I exhaled. As the silence stretched, I found myself reaching for the fries. I chewed slowly, tasting salt. Took another. Before I knew it, I'd eaten the whole package, and my throat was dry.

Oliver passed his milkshake without a word.

"Thanks," I murmured, tasting the cold sweetness, feeling it shiver down my throat. It felt too normal, all of this did, but now that normalcy gave rise to a small flicker of hope.

Maybe I could pretend none of it had ever happened. Maybe nobody would make me speak of it again.

Except Ashton was out there, and I knew now, he wasn't the kind of man to let things go.

Oliver finished his food and neatly folded our wrappers into the bag, holding it out for mine too with an expectant look. I passed my debris and he got out of the car, walking back to the trash-can by the main building.

I watched him in the faded neon: unhurried, casually sauntering, his face shadowed in the dark. I never knew what he was thinking, it was infuriating like nothing else, but tonight, I found his mystery was almost a relief. I wasn't responsible for his thoughts, trying to navigate them, keep him happy the way I did with Ethan. He was as inscrutable as ever, and I was left alone with myself.

He slid back in.

"Ready to go?"

I nodded slowly. I wasn't shaking any more, and my heartbeat had slowed. Now, I was just tired, bone-deep, my limbs aching from the struggle, my body crashing after the surge of adrenalin.

Now, I just wanted to sleep.

Oliver drove us back on familiar roads, winding through town until they reached my neighborhood. There were lights on in the houses as we passed; neatly-cut lawns and old front porches.

Safe.

He pulled up outside my house. I hugged my purse to my chest.

"Thank you," I said quietly, already reaching for the door.

Oliver's hand shot out, capturing my wrist. I flinched. He tugged again, and I had no choice but to turn. His eyes were watching me, dark in the night.

"Did anyone see you get in the car with him?"

I thought back. "I ... I don't know. The parking lot was empty, but, we were at the college, there could have been people around."

Oliver nodded, and I could see his brain working, turning things over. "What about at his place?"

I shook my head. "It was dark ... I didn't see anyone around."

"Then he took you straight home. If anyone asks, he dropped you off, safe and sound. Nothing happened."

I paused. I wanted to ask what he would do, but I knew it was safer if I didn't.

"Don't tell Ethan," I said instead.

Oliver's lips curled in a smile. He released me. "It'll be our little secret."

I climbed out, walking slowly towards my front door, but something stopped me and made me turn back. Oliver had his window down. I met his eyes, dark in the night. "What are you going to do?" I asked, my voice shaking.

He looked at me. "What do you think?"

THEN

Ashton was found dead in an alleyway two days later. The reporter said he'd been beaten and mugged in a drug deal gone wrong. The college board sent out an email, saying there would be a replacement lecturer for his classes. His pregnant girlfriend was shown, weeping on the news. Nobody knew he had a problem, but everyone in class agreed there had been something off about him all along.

I found the newspaper left on my front step, tied up with a red ribbon. I kept it in my top dresser drawer and re-read it every night, searching for clues.

Deep down, I knew, I didn't need them. Oliver had worked that intricate brain of his and found a solution, just the way I'd wanted.

Just the way I'd known he would.

NOW

"You think Oliver killed your professor?" Weber looks at me, his eyes wary and searching. We're still alone in the empty room across the hall from Ethan, the neon hum of the hospital filtering in bright strips through the blinds while we sit here on hard plastic chairs, dredging through every detail and lie.

I nod, shredding tissues in my hands. Tiny strips, over and over, I can't keep still. I thought telling Weber about what happened would help my story – paint Oliver as a monster, capable of anything.

"Why you didn't say something? You could have come to me," he points out. "You could have told a teacher, your mom . . . What about Alisha? She didn't mention anything to me."

I have to hold back a sorrowful laugh. As if my mother would have been any help at all. And as for my teacher ...

"I was scared," I whisper, shivering in my sweater. It's lost property, maybe, or belongs to one of the doctors: an oversized grey hoodie that dwarfs my frame, wrapping me in the bold team logo of some sports club or major league team. I don't know. I never followed sports all that much.

"Chloe?" Weber's voice rises, and I realize he's still waiting, still watching me with that expression that's equal parts sympathy and confusion. He's been wearing it all night, just like every other adult whose tiptoed around me, speaking in hushed tones. But now I realize, there's something more there too, a new emotion flickering to life in his eyes.

The steely glint of suspicion.

"I saw you together," he adds slowly. "Around town. At the station. It didn't look like you were scared of him. It looked ..." He pauses, then glances away.

Fear strikes me. "I didn't know what to do!" I lie, my lips already trembling, tears stinging the back of my throat. "He was so ... charming, everyone in town thought he was so great. I tried to tell, I really did." I babble, trying to get my words out. The right ones, the words that will make him see. "But I didn't know what to say. He killed someone, and I was scared he'd do the same to me! It all sounds so crazy, when you say it out loud."

"Then why did you go to the house?" Weber asks, changing tack, catching me in one of my earlier lies. "If you were so scared, why go meet him, all alone?"

"Because he threatened to tell," I say quickly. "He was going to tell Ethan, about the kiss – only he made it sound like something it wasn't. I wanted to talk him out of it, I thought I could keep the secret. I didn't want to hurt Ethan!" I fix my eyes on his, pleading. A girl broken and bruised, with blood still drying on her skin. A victim. "And I didn't know for sure he killed Ashton, not really. I had no proof, nothing real to prove any of it."

Sheriff Weber stares back at me, almost regretful, but unmoved.

"You still don't."

There's silence. Panic blossoms in my gut, sharp and bold. He's supposed to believe me now. He's supposed to be on my side. Instead, I can see the gears turning behind those small-town eyes, already weighing up my story against what he's seen, what other people might have already been whispering.

"You didn't tell anyone about Oliver's harrassment, nobody who can back you up?" he asks again, a last note of hope in his voice.

I'm shaking my head slowly, numb with resignation, when a voice comes from the doorway.

"She told me."

I snap my head around. It's Annette Reznick, her slight frame wrapped in a navy wool coat. Even in the dead of night, even for this, she has a full face of makeup on: her brows arched defiantly, her lipstick bright against her lifeless skin.

She strides over and stands behind me, placing a hand on my shoulder. To anyone else, I know, it would look like a supportive gesture, but I can feel her fingers desperately digging into my skin. Holding on for dear life.

"She told me." Annette speaks again. Her voice is shaking, but it rings out in the room. "She said she was worried about Oliver. He was acting strangely, obsessive. I should have listened, but I thought ... it all seemed like childish rivalry to me. Oliver always wanted what Ethan had, even when they were kids, he'd steal his toys just to spite him."

Weber looks from Annette to me and back again. "When was this?" he asks, checking his notes.

"A couple of weeks ago," I lie. I don't know why Annette is supporting my lies, but I leap on her excuse like a life raft in the storm.

"We were out of town," Annette adds quickly. "She called me, but, I was running late. It all sounded like high school drama. You know kids and their relationship tangles." She gives a weak laugh, but it fades on her lips. "I didn't realize ... How could anyone expect this?"

She turns to look across the hall at Ethan, pale and unmoving, strung up under the tangle of breathing tubes and IV wires. In the lull, we can hear the faint beep of his heartbeat monitor, steady and too slow.

I turn back to Weber. He's watching the two of us, trying to make sense of it. I can see he wants to push harder, but it's not just about me anymore. Annette is on my side now, and what can he say to that?

Is he really going to call a grieving mother a liar?

"Will you be making an official statement?" Weber presses gently. "We'll need to get it on record down at the station."

Annette nods once, briskly, wiping at her eyes. "Can it wait? I don't want to leave him."

"Of course." Weber is chastened. He clears his throat, uncomfortable. "Now, Chloe, you were saying—"

"Uh, excuse me, Weber?" One of the other police officers interrupts, lurking in the doorway. "The guys from the fire crew were looking for you."

He looks annoyed, but he rises to his feet. "We'll talk more later," he tells me, almost like a warning.

"I'm not going anywhere," I reply quietly.

The men leave, and Annette and I are left alone. A phone rings down the hallway, voices sound, muffled, and through it all, Ethan's monitor keeps on.

Beep. Beep. Beep.

Annette's head lifts, as if she's hearing it for the first time. She drifts across the hallway like she's sleepwalking, and I follow, two steps behind, watching as she fusses over Ethan: smoothing back his hair, adjusting a tube, tucking the blanket carefully around his body. Finally, she stands still, trembling, her hands folded together, clutched at her chest.

"When they called and said something had happened with the boys, I thought, 'Oh God, he's finally done it.'"

A laugh bubbles up, hysterical. She clamps a hand over her mouth, white-knuckled. Shaking.

"What do you mean?" I ask slowly, not taking my eyes off her.

Annette doesn't answer. She stands, watching over Ethan, and I wonder if she's even heard me at all. Then she turns to me and her eyes are bright, wet with tears, and a nervous flicker.

"I knew," she whispers. "Right from the start. The very beginning. Oliver was wrong." She says the word like a curse, and then again. "Wrong."

"Annette?" I reach out a hand to her and she flinches back, quickly walking over to the window. It's dark outside, the blinds lowered, but she stares into the faded yellow fabric for a moment, collecting herself. When she turns back to me, her face is composed. Resigned.

"He didn't stop crying." Her voice is steady now, like this is a story she's been rehearsing for years. "From the day he was born, he just howled and howled. Nothing I did was right. He wouldn't sleep, he wouldn't eat, and then when he did, he would bite down so hard, I swear, it was just to spite me." She swallows. "I know they're just babies, they don't even know themselves yet, but that boy . . . He never let me get a moment's rest and, Lord, I hated him for it."

I slowly close the door behind me, so there's just an inch of space left. I move closer to her and sit on the edge of a chair. Waiting.

"I didn't know what to do," she continues quietly. "Derek was away for work all the time, and it was just me, stuck in that house with that crying . . . thing. All day and all night. I used to dream about making it stop. Pressing down with a pillow, gently. Just ending it for good." Annette meets my eyes, sharp. "Maybe it would have been better for everyone if I had."

I inhale in a rush.

"But I didn't, of course." Her face twists. "And then the guilt, to even think about doing that, to my own child. What kind of mother was I?"

I don't answer, I just wait.

"After that, I thought, it was my fault," Annette continues, glancing down. She twists her rings around her fingers, the gemstones catching in the light. "He could tell I didn't want him, so he was doing it to punish me. I deserved it. But then, Ethan came ..." Her face relaxes. She looks across to his body, tender. "He was a dream. So sweet, he would lay there, cooing for hours. He was my boy, my good boy. And I thought, maybe Oliver wasn't my fault, after all."

Her lips press together determinedly and that's when I realize, she's absolved herself. If this sounds like a rehearsed speech, it's because it is. All these years, she's been waiting for the call: waiting for the day when she'll have to explain herself. Justify her choices. Lift herself neatly off the hook of responsibility for anything that Oliver became.

"I couldn't leave them alone together," Annette continues, her face clouding at the memory. "Oliver was still just two, three years old, but already ... I had to answer the door to the mailman once, I left them together in the crib. When I came back, Oliver was twisting his arm, just pulling it further and further while Ethan howled in pain. I asked him why he would do that, why he would hurt his brother. He just stared at me. 'My toy,' he said. 'Mine.'"

Annette shudders.

"All these little things. Signs. Finding the hamster dead in its cage, its head smashed in with a rock. Ethan would have strange bruises on him and, Oliver, he always knew what to say, how to be cruel, to twist the knife. I kept them apart, I didn't take my eyes off them, not for a second, and as soon as he was old enough, I got Oliver away." Annette's expression brightens. "We were moving so much for Derek's work, I told him it wasn't fair, to keep pulling Oliver out of schools when he had so much potential. I planned everything. Those boarding schools damn near bankrupted us, back then, but it was worth it to keep my boy safe. Of course, there were always reports from the schools," she adds dismissively. "Incidents with his friends, feuding . . . There was a suicide, his junior year. A boy jumped from the roof, and I always wondered . . ." Her face twists, a look of perverse pride. "But Oliver was smart, smarter than anyone. They never got anything on him. He stayed gone, living the high life with all his rich friends, and Ethan was just fine. Safe at home, with me." She pauses, looking up with an accusing stare. "Until you."

THEN

The New Year dawned, crisp and bright. Ethan and Oliver's family went out of town for the holidays, visiting family in Colorado. Mom and I ate Christmas dinner at the diner, then watched New's Year's celebrations on TV, sitting together under a blanket on the couch, like we had done every year since I could remember.

But this time, it was different. Everything had changed.

All week, Ashton's death had been the only thing on my mind, haunting me. I read that newspaper article over again, turning up the volume on the TV whenever the news reports came on. Part of me couldn't believe that Oliver had killed him; the other half saw it made perfect sense. But still, all I had were suspicions, waiting, half expecting someone to challenge the official verdict and demand answers.

But of course, nobody did, and soon the reports were replaced with holiday gift guides and celebrity breakdowns, and stories about polar bears mating at the national zoo.

At first, I'd felt guilty. I *should* be guilty: horrified that I could have done that to him, even worse, to have been complicit in his death. This was a man with family and a future, and now he was nothing but flesh and bone rotting in a grave somewhere.

Because of me.

I even visited the cemetery. I snuck in, one dark rainy evening, and stood over his grave, waiting for the guilt and misery to wash over me, even a small dose of the regret I'd felt for Crystal, but instead I felt something else, a clear, sharp burst of satisfaction.

Ashton had deserved to die. I was glad he was gone.

The knowledge settled around me, a thick cloak knitted from the terrible secret I could never tell. I knew I must be an awful person to be this way, but once the realization came, I didn't fight it anymore. I sank into it, reveling in the thought, wondering just what Oliver might have done to end him.

Did he beg, the way I'd begged him? Did he fight for his life?

No, I decided. Oliver wouldn't have gotten his hands dirty. It would have been swift, an unfair fight. Caught by surprise, just as he thought he'd escaped from me.

I hoped he regretted ever assuming I would just lay back and give him what he wanted.

I hoped he died thinking of me.

Ethan arrived home and called me right away. We made plans for that night, but Oliver found me first, like I knew he would. I was running my route around the lake, my breath fogging the early-morning air, when he fell into step beside me, matching pace for pace.

I didn't speak for another mile until I felt the burn in my lungs and slowed, bending double in a clearing.

"Did you have a very merry Christmas?" Oliver asked, arch as ever.

I straightened up. "No," I replied, studying him. That night had shifted something between us too. I wasn't intoxicated anymore, breathless and off-balance. I still felt the curious pull, that desire snaking through me just to look in his eyes, but there was clarity too; hard-edged, cautious.

I knew his secret, and he knew mine, too.

"Anyone ask any questions?" Oliver began walking, and I followed through the woods. The path was frozen, but we hadn't had snow for weeks. "About your dear professor."

"What kind of questions?" I replied quickly, looking around. "It was an accident."

Oliver turned, his lips tugged upwards. "Nobody's here, Chloe. You don't need to act the fool with me."

His eyes met mine, dark and victorious. The truth was there, clear as day.

He'd done it.

He'd killed Ashton.

A wicked thrill spiraled through me. "It was a tragic crime, miles away," I said carefully. "Nothing to do with us."

He gave me an amused smile. "Someone's learning fast."

I held his gaze, bold. "I had an expert teacher."

He laughed, walking for a moment before he spoke again. "You know, there was a chance you'd go running to your sheriff the minute my back was turned." Oliver said it conversationally, but I detected the faint thread of tension in his tone.

"What would you do?" I asked, on edge. "If someone did come asking about it."

He paused, looking thoughtful. "I could run, but running says you're guilty. Far better to stay and stick it out. See if they could get anything on me. I doubt it. The police in this town . . ." He rolled his eyes. "Please. I was careful, I didn't leave any loose ends."

"Except me," I realized with a shiver.

Oliver turned. "Except you," he agreed.

My heart beat faster. We were standing here, talking about a murder and cover-up as if it was no big deal, and the most chilling thing of all was that it wasn't, not to me.

Not anymore.

Now, I met his eyes and wondered about Ashton's final moments all over again.

"Ask me." Oliver leaned closer, knowing in an instant the question I was holding back. He knew, he always knew. "Don't you want to know?"

I bit my lip. Would anything be as good as the deaths I'd imagined for Ashton, the many dark scenes I'd played out in my mind since then?

"It didn't take much," Oliver added, dropping a kiss on the hollow curve of my neck. I shivered. "You did a fair amount of damage yourself," he whispered. "Poor guy was barely walking."

His lips lingered over mine. I caught my breath, barely moving, feeling the light shock of his touch.

"But you were careless," he whispered against my mouth. "You left a scarf in his car."

I jerked back, my blood rushing in panic. I saw police and sirens, lawyers and a cell. And questions, so many questions—

"Relax." Oliver laughed, looking amused. "I caught it. The scene was clean. I don't make mistakes."

I wondered for the first time if he'd done this before, but then he was kissing me, hard and slow, and I realized I didn't care. I felt the adrenalin crackle through me, exhilarating.

"We got away with it," I whispered, feeling a secret thrill. Oliver looked at me with an expression I couldn't decipher. "What?" I asked.

He shook his head slowly. "I just . . . I don't know. I didn't think you'd be like this."

"You thought I'd be guilty and weeping?" I challenged him boldly. "You told me not to pretend anymore."

"I did, didn't I?" Oliver watched me. "And here you are, the real Chloe. At long last. It's a pleasure to finally meet you."

He took my hand and bent his head, touching his lips to my knuckles in a grazing kiss. He lifted his eyes to me, bright and victorious. "What fun we're going to have."

We ran, steady, along the rest of the loop, emerging from the woods that bordered the back of my house. I opened the kitchen door, and he followed me in to find Mom trying to make tea, mopping spilled milk off the table.

"I'm sorry," she said quickly, shrinking back. "The carton slipped."

"There, there." Oliver spoke up. "No use crying. Spilled milk, get it?"

I quelled him with a look before turning back to Mom. "It's OK, I'll clean it up. Did you eat?"

She nodded. "Toast and honey."

"Good." I nodded. "Go to the craft room now, you can watch TV until lunch. I'll finish this."

"Thank you, sweetie." Mom managed a trembling smile before slipping obediently from the room. When we passed her on our way upstairs, she was sitting quietly, knitting yet another scarf.

Oliver arched his eyebrow. "Look who's behaving," he drawled.

"She just needed some incentive to keep it together," I told him, closing my bedroom door and stripping off my jacket. "It's either me or a psych ward."

"Why don't you pick the latter?" Oliver sauntered closer, slipping his arms around my waist. I breathed him in, the shiver of connection that laced us together. "You should commit her, it would get her out of your hair."

"I can't," I said. "She's depressed, not crazy."

"So, what's the difference?"

"I just can't. Not in a place like that."

"You're going to have to leave her eventually." Oliver pulled me back towards the bed. "A month from now, or a year from now, you'll go. The only difference is how much time you've wasted here, waiting around for her miraculously to be healed."

I shivered at the picture his words painted. "Another year? God, I'd rather kill myself."

Oliver's lips quirked in a smile. He lay back and I climbed beside him. "That's rather unproductive. And unnecessary. You can escape this life without it being permanent."

I looked over.

"Disappear," Oliver continued. "Change your name, start fresh somewhere."

"But I like my name." I leaned closer and bit down lightly on his shoulder.

Oliver made an impatient sound. "Chloe doesn't suit you."

"What's wrong with it? I think it's a pretty name."

"Pretty, sweet, *nice*." Oliver announced them like cardinal sins. "But we both know, you're none of those things."

His eyes caught mine. I caught my breath. "Are you saying I'm not pretty?" I teased him.

"You're fucking beautiful and you know it."

I felt my cheeks color. Even after everything, he could still affect me, right to my bones. "So what should I be called, O wise one?" I said lightly.

"Hmm, let me see." Oliver studied me, propping one

hand under his chin in an exaggerated pose. "Something bold and dramatic, I think."

"Scarlett," I suggested, smiling. "Juliet. Boudicca."

Oliver shook his head impatiently. "You're ... Vivian."

I blinked. "Vivian is my middle name." I sat up, thrown. "How did you know that?"

"I know all sorts of things about you." Oliver smiled up at me. "Anyway, you're missing the point, *Vivian*. It's already listed on your birth certificate. You wouldn't even have to get it legally changed."

I laughed again. "Now wait a minute, who said anything about legal stuff?"

Oliver looked at me, as if I was talking crazy. "If you're going to be Vivian, you need to do it properly. No use half-assing when you're creating a whole new identity. You want your mom showing up out of nowhere?"

I felt a flicker of unease.

"Let's not talk about it anymore," I said quietly, tracing circles on his chest. "I'm not going anywhere, not right now."

"But you can't stay here." His voice was quiet. "It's killing you, slowly, every day. I see it when you're with him."

He didn't say Ethan's name. I hadn't asked him not to, but somehow, it had become the unspoken rule.

The loose end. The one thing still keeping me from Oliver.

"He loves me." I said it matter of fact. I didn't have to pretend to be guilty or shameful, not with Oliver. "He tells me all the time."

"Of course he does." Oliver pulled back, angling his head to look at me. "You're the best thing that ever happened to him," he said, almost amused. "But he's just another mediocre thing that's keeping you down."

"Don't," I said, but he sat up.

"You really don't see it, do you?" His eyes were hard on mine. "Your potential, what you could be if you just let them all go. Your mom, Ethan, everyone holding you back, making you pretend to be less than you are." Oliver gazed at me and I could see the promise there, the glimpse of something brighter.

I ached for it, that other life. At first, it had been wistful, a soft and melancholy kind of longing that drifted over me, late at night; but every day that passed now, it grew sharper, taking on a life of its own. It was demanding. It refused to be silenced.

Why should you be stuck here, playing nursemaid for the rest of your life? it asked me, every time I fixed her dinner. *Why do you have to worry about pleasing everyone else? Why can't you get what you want, just once?*

"We should get going," I said. "I have to go to work."

"Not yet." Oliver's hands stopped me, closing around my

body. He wrapped his arms around me from behind, his lips resting against the curve of my neck.

"You could come with me," his voice whispered.

I froze.

His hands roamed lower, possessive.

"Where?" I said softly.

"Anywhere. It doesn't matter. New York, LA. London. Europe. I know people all over."

I closed my eyes, letting myself sink against him, into the sensation of his hands, and the vision he was promising. Gone from here, from Haverford, and with him . . .

No guilt. No hiding. Free.

"One day," I promised myself.

His hands left me, and suddenly I was alone in the cold.

I turned. He was already at the door. "Don't wait too long, darling." Oliver gave me a look. "I'm not like baby brother. I won't hang around here for long."

THEN

After that, I knew, I couldn't stay. I was drowning there. This town had made a liar of me; an adulterer, a caged animal chasing my own tail.

A murderer.

More and more these days, I felt like a bundle of broken edges bound together with razor wire, swallowing down the sharpness, painting on a smile. I would find a way out, a way to be with Oliver, before he left me here for good. Before the cage burst open and the person I was hiding broke free.

So, I sat down at the table where I'd made that first, desperate plan, all those months ago. I dragged out Mom's old address book and flipped through the pages, looking for answers. She was an only child, fallen out of touch with her college friends, drifted apart from the couples she and Dad had known as newlyweds.

It was useless. She had nobody who really cared but me.

But maybe I was looking at it all wrong, I realized hopefully, looking at the dog-eared pages. I didn't need someone to agree to take her on; after all, I never had. I just needed the door to open, for someone to invite her in.

I called Mom's cousin Carol in Atlanta, anxiously drumming my fingertips on the table as we exchanged pleasantries and fake laughter. She was in her forties, still unmarried. They'd had some kind of rift, years ago, and now, the only contact was the Christmas card that arrived every year, showing Carol with her arms raised on the finish line of her latest charity fundraising marathon; sinewy and determined.

"We're planning a trip," I told her brightly, tracing the beaming face on the front of her latest card. "Just a little getaway, Mom's been down since the divorce, so I thought this would cheer her up. We'd love to come visit."

"Oh. Sure." Carol's instinct for hospitality took over. You didn't turn away family, it wasn't polite. "I'd love to see you both. I mean, you wouldn't be staying long?"

"No, just a night or two," I reassured her. "We've got tons to see!"

I hung up with a promise to send our flight details so she could meet us at the airport. But I knew, only my mom would step off the flight.

Everything was falling in place, but still, I felt that treacherous pang of guilt. The pages of my plan were spread around me. I had last month's paycheck coming and money set aside for household expenses. I would get by just fine, but what about her? Could I really send her off to be somebody else's problem, wash my hands for good?

I walked silently to her bedroom and cracked the door. She was sleeping, tucked under the covers, motionless in the dark.

My mother. My anchor.

I felt a sob rise up in my chest. Despite everything, I didn't want to leave her, but I knew, I couldn't do this anymore. I could feel my love for her being choked away with every passing day, stifled under the sheer weight of her helpless need. I was snapping at her more often now; every tiny little irritation a spark to my endless reserves of anger.

I didn't like the person I was becoming around her, so impatient and brusque. I didn't want my last well of affection to be smothered clean away. It would be better this way, I told myself, silently closing the door. It wouldn't have to be for ever. Maybe Carol could succeed where I had failed: sell the house, get Mom into a treatment center. She was a grown-up, after all. She would know what to do.

All I knew was sending Mom away was my only chance of escape, to get away from this town. My heart ached for everything we'd become, but I knew, I'd spent too long trying to fix her, to hold what was left of this family together.

I called Oliver from down the hall, lowering my voice to a hush. "Next week," I said, hearing the finality in my voice. "The eighteenth. I'm leaving. Are you in?"

"I already have plans for New York." Oliver sounded amused. "I'm going to stay with friends."

New York. I felt a shiver of pure desire at the words. Busy streets and endless sidewalks. Bookstores and bars, and a whole world on one tiny island.

"Can I ... come?" I asked, hating that I needed to ask permission, feeling the weight of my future hanging on those few words.

Silence stretched, long enough to chill my blood, but then Oliver's voice came again, amused.

"I suppose there's always room for one more."

I hung up and stood there in the dark, my breath coming fast, feeling the wide expanse of possibility open up in front of me for the first time in what felt like forever. My world had been shrinking every day, penning me in, but this time, it felt wide open.

Some pieces couldn't be glued back together. Some people weren't for fixing.

Sometimes, the only thing to do was burn the whole fucking world down and start again.

NOW

Weber finally agrees to let me leave the hospital to pick up fresh clothes and supplies. Still, he's not so lax as to let me step foot outside alone. He sends Blake along for company. "Protection," he says, but we both know the truth, it's for him, not me.

I'm restless, still picking polish off my fingernails as Blake drives me silently through the dark neighborhood and pulls up outside my house.

"You need any help?" he asks, already reaching for his cellphone.

I catch a glimpse of Candy Crush on-screen, and shake my head. "No, I won't be long."

"Uh-huh," Blake murmurs, already absorbed. I feel the

same spike of resentment that I do every time he's around. He's moved on from Crystal's death with barely a backwards glance. Nobody called him wrong or bad, they just sighed over the tragedy, and said how brave he was to keep going.

Would they be so kind to us about Oliver?

I open the door and step inside, my mind already racing. Annette may be backing up my version of events, but until Ethan wakes up, I'm the only one left unscathed to face the questions.

So many questions.

I've been in slow-motion for hours now, but suddenly, there's a panicked itch in my veins; the haze of shock and waiting giving way to something sharp and insistent, crying out for action. I race upstairs and go straight to my closet, pulling down the duffel from the top shelf. It's already half packed, so I throw it on the bed and go to my dresser, yanking open drawers and hurling things on to the bed in a blind flurry. Underwear, shirts, jeans. I have the money I put aside to leave with Oliver, some of Mom's credit cards if I need. They won't get me far, to the West Coast, maybe. A big city, somewhere to lose myself in the crowds. A place nobody knows my name, the way I always wanted.

And then what? And then what?

I sink on to the bed, still clutching a sweater. I look around the room, at my books and trinkets, the framed photos on the dresser and the old stuffed toys on the shelf: a life that feels already like it belongs to someone else.

If I run, there'll be no coming back. I'll have nothing, nobody, and although the thought doesn't chill me like it should, I can't stop my brain from ticking forwards, playing two moves ahead the way Oliver always taught me.

How do I get out of town?

Blake is oblivious out front. I could be out of the window and away through the back yard before he even makes the next level, but I'd have only a twenty-minute headstart before he thinks to look for me; another thirty at most before it gets back to Weber and they start checking the roads and bus stations.

Weber.

I stop, imagining his face as he hears the news.

If I run now, he'll know I'm guilty.

If I run now, I won't make it far.

I take another breath, forcing myself to calm, then I finish packing the duffel with essentials. I stash it back up on the closet shelf, out of sight. It's there if I need it, I tell myself, still feeling the itch to run.

If everything goes right for me, I won't need it at all.

I take a shower, standing under the scalding shower jets until the hot water runs out and the dirt and blood are rinsed clean away from my body. Then I wrap a towel around my body and smear the steam from the mirror, assessing my reflection; trying to see myself through somebody else's eyes. The bruises are still ringed around my neck, and there's an ugly welt above my right eye. I don't try to hide them. Instead, I pick a green sweater that brings out the purple in the bruise, and leave the smudged shadows under my eyes. I braid my hair neatly, pull on jeans and winter boots, and pack a different bag for the hospital: a small backpack I fill with text books, a spare sweater and toiletries. I'll be keeping vigil at the hospital as long as it takes, so I grab a pillow and quilt from my closet too, then head out front to where Blake is still waiting in the car.

"Good news," he tells me, when I pile in the front seat. "Boyfriend woke up."

I freeze.

"He did? When? Is he OK?" I demand, panic running like ice through my veins. They said he wouldn't be awake for hours, maybe even days. It's the only reason I figured it was safe to leave him, to take one tiny moment away from the hospital.

I was wrong.

"Who knows?" Blake shrugs. "They just said he's out of the woods. That's good news, right?" He frowns at me, and I manage to smooth my panicked expression into a smile.

"Uh-huh," I murmur, but all the drive back to the hospital,

my heart races with fear. He could be talking to them by now, telling him everything. I was supposed to be there, to make my case. To get our stories straight.

The moment we arrive I leap out of the car, sprinting back through the lobby and leaving Blake behind. I'm breathless by the time I reach Ethan's room, but my footsteps fade to a falter when I see him through the glass, sitting up in bed.

His face is pale, his body still hooked with wires and tubes. Weber is sitting in the chair by the window, taking notes, and there's another man in there too, someone I've never seen in a heavy overcoat, his expression stern.

Ethan meets my eyes through the glass. He stares at me a moment, his expression unreadable. Then he turns away and I know it's over.

He's telling them everything. He's telling them the truth.

I stabbed him. It was me.

THEN

We had a plan and I was foolish enough to think it would work. I'd come a long way from that tentative, waiting girl at the end of summer, but I was still naïve, expecting everything to fall into place just because I so badly needed it to.

But desperation gives rise to its own kind of hope, and as I set the pieces in motion, it was almost laughable how simple it was: just a long list of tasks to be checked off in turn, small cogs that would wind the machine of my freedom, one by one. My days were full of planning, fevered and drifting; my nights became dreamscapes of skyscrapers and busy, rushing streets. Of kisses I didn't have to hide in the dark, and a life that would finally – finally – be mine.

I was close. I could taste it. Soon, I would be gone.

All that was left was Ethan.

I deliberated all week as I made the rest of my plans, blowing off our date nights under the pretext of work, and stress, and Mom. I didn't want to lie to his face, but a part of me couldn't bear the thought of letting him down.

He believed in me. Like nobody had before, he wanted to protect me, and love me, and keep me safe. The problem was, I didn't want protecting. That girl he loved didn't exist, not anymore.

Maybe she never had.

Finally, after too many texts and missed calls, he dropped by unannounced and found me packing Mom's things into her case.

"We're taking a trip," I told him brightly, ducking out of his embrace to go fetch my toiletries.

"What? When?" he blinked at me in surprise.

"Tonight," I announced. Mom's flight was early in the evening, I would drop her off, and then meet Oliver. It was all planned.

"It's last minute, but her cousin invited us, and I figured the change of scene would be good for her. I was going to come by later," I added, "and say a proper goodbye."

The final one.

"But I'll miss you." Ethan stuck out his lower lip, all puppy-dog eyes.

"I won't be gone long," I lied, not wanting to get into it now. I needed to think of the perfect words to let him down with, but more than that, I wanted to be somewhere I could walk away when it was all done; not here, without an escape. "Just a week or so. You'll survive."

"I could come with you." Ethan looped his thumbs into my pockets, keeping me in place. "Help you out with your mom."

"No, it's fine," I replied quickly. "You have work, remember?"

Ethan sighed. "You're leaving me all alone. Olly's going away too."

"Oh yeah?" I tried to sound disinterested. "I forgot."

"He's going to stay with friends in New York, try and get a job." Ethan rolled his eyes.

"Sounds fun," I murmured, but Ethan just scowled.

"Probably just sponge off some other poor schmuck for a while."

"Hey," I scolded him, feeling a flare of defensiveness. "Don't say that. Oliver pays his way."

"Sure, in flattery," Ethan muttered. "I'm getting sick of his games. I swear, Mom would sell the house out from under us and give him the check just to keep him happy."

"Don't be jealous," I told him, fighting to keep my tone even. Ethan would never know what his brother had done for me. "It's not cute."

"Aww, I'm sorry." Ethan smiled again, his hands on me, grabbing. "And I'm not jealous. How can I be, when I've got the one thing he hasn't?"

His words sliced through me. I pulled back. "I don't belong to you," I said, frowning at him. "Is that what you think?"

Ethan blinked. "I didn't mean it like that. Just, you know. I'm yours. You're mine." He kissed me, pulling me back against him until we were horizontal on my bed. I kissed him back, knowing it was a goodbye, wanting to give him something before I left him forever.

But it felt all wrong. A betrayal – but of Oliver this time.

"I've missed you," Ethan grinned, slipping his hands up under my shirt. "It's been too long."

His hands slid against me, soft enough to send a shiver through me. I kissed him back, slow and sweet like he wanted, wrapping my legs around his waist, trailing my fingers over the ridge of his shoulders, dropping butterfly kisses on the sensitive parts of his neck. I tended to him, doing everything right, fighting that unease curled around my organs. He deserved this, I told myself, arching against him, but I couldn't shake the sense of wrongness vibrating in every cell. Each touch felt like a promise I wouldn't be keeping. Every kiss was a lie.

Ethan panted against me, sliding his hands across my stomach and lower still.

I recoiled from him, before I could stop myself.

Ethan looked at me with confusion.

"I'm not feeling it," I apologized quickly, avoiding his gaze. "It's, umm, that time of the month."

"It's OK." Ethan stroked over my bare shoulder. "There's still stuff we can do," he smiled, trailing his hand down over my breast.

I flinched back again. "I said, I'm not in the mood."

"But it's been forever." Ethan's voice was edged with complaint. "You're always busy, or running late for class."

I fought to keep my temper in check. I'd wanted this to be a good night, one last sweet memory for him. "I'm sorry, babe." I forced a smile. "I'll make it up to you."

"I know one way you could do that . . ." Ethan gave me a suggestive smile. He took my hand and moved it to his crotch, pressing against the hard denim.

Something inside me snapped. "I said, I'm not in the mood!" I scrambled away from him, getting to my feet. "Or don't you care how I feel just as long as you get off?"

Ethan looked wounded. "I didn't mean that!"

"No, you did!" My voice rose, frustrated. "I told you I didn't want to, and you still wouldn't listen. I'm not some fuck toy you can pick up any time you like!"

Ethan's face changed. "You're just feeling emotional," he said, looking cautious. "PMS. It's OK, I'm sorry, babe. We can just cuddle."

I wanted to scream.

"I can't do this anymore." The words were out of my mouth before I could take them back, but once I heard them, loud in the silence, I felt a swell of relief so sharp it could have knocked me off my feet.

Yes. This was it. I couldn't pretend any longer. I would tell him now, before I left. Wipe the slate clean before I even left Haverford, so that tomorrow, I could depart with nothing holding me back.

Ethan sat up slowly. "I don't know what you're saying." His eyes watched me, still cautious.

"Us. This." I caught my breath. "I'm sorry, I'm so, so, sorry, but . . . it's too much. I can't."

Ethan's mouth fell open. I could see the realization settle across his face. "You're breaking up with me?"

His voice was a whisper and, despite everything, I felt an ache slice through me.

"I'm sorry." A sob rose up in my throat. He was the one good person left in my world, and I was hurting him anyway.

Hurting him to be free.

"What did I do?" Ethan swallowed, springing to his feet. He crossed the room to me, grabbing my hands. "Was this because I pressured you? I'm sorry, I was being a pig. I won't do it again, I swear."

"No." I pulled away. "It's not that. It's not you! It's ... everything."

"I don't understand." He looked bewildered, his blue eyes wide with emotion. "Tell me what to do, Chloe. I'll do anything!"

"You can't," I cried. "It's over, OK? We're done."

There was silence.

Ethan caught his breath, his chest rising and falling as he clenched his jaw and looked around the room. "You're just stressed, I get it," he said, sounding determined. "With your mom, and school, it's all been too much for you."

"Ethan ..." I protested weakly.

"It's OK." He gave me a tight smile. "You're right, you need a break. Some space to think. This trip will be good for you, and then we'll talk when you get back."

I watched him helplessly. He wasn't listening. He didn't understand. That was Ethan, right from the start. He'd decided on me, that day in the diner, all charm and boyish enthusiasm, talking me into our very first date by sheer force of will. He'd picked me, and that was it. In his mind, we belonged together.

But I didn't belong to anyone at all.

I exhaled. "Fine," I lied, not wanting to hurt him anymore. "We'll talk when I get back."

"Do you need a ride to the airport?" he offered, pulling his sweater back on.

I shook my head. "No. We're good."

Ethan smiled at me again, tender as ever. "We'll be OK," he reassured me. "I know things are tough, and you feel like you can't handle it. But you can. I'm not giving up on you yet."

He leaned down to kiss my cheek as he passed me towards the door. I felt the brush of his lips against me and turned my head away.

"Goodbye," I whispered, knowing it was the last time.

"See you soon."

I listened to him thump downstairs and let himself out, closing the door softly behind him. The last threads of guilt strung up around my heart finally snapped.

I thought that was the last I'd ever see of him.

I was wrong.

NOW

I pace, panicked, down faded hospital hallways and back through endless swinging doors. I'm trying to keep myself together, keep the terror hemmed inside, but how can I keep pretending now that Ethan is awake?

I can feel him now, taking a crowbar to my delicate cages, cracking them wide open and letting the darkness loose. All my secrets and fear and tangled, twisted lies, taking flight around me, and there's nothing I can do to stop him.

I should have run, back at the house, when I still had the chance. I should have got the hell out of town before it locked me up here for ever.

I circle back to the ICU, expecting to meet a pack of deputies at any moment. The curtains to Ethan's room are pulled closed, and I can just imagine Weber's woeful expression, noting down the long list of my crimes. I shiver, already feeling the sting of metal on my wrists, the harsh glare of the interview room.

I know what's coming to me, the only question is, when?

"Chloe."

I hear Weber's call from by the elevators and turn, confused. He's not in there?

"I thought you were talking to Ethan," I say, my voice shaking slightly.

Weber doesn't seem to notice. "I was, but the doctors needed to check him out first."

"Is everything OK?" I ask, my mind still racing. "They said he was fine."

"Nothing to worry about." Weber scrutinizes me now. "Just some more tests. He's been through a lot."

I nod, forcing myself to seem calm. "Did he, say anything?" I ask, casually.

"Not much yet. He was pretty confused, and out of it from the drugs." Weber pauses. "When the doctors are finished, I'll sit down for a real chat."

"Right." My heart pounds. "I don't know how much he'll remember," I add, "he was already unconscious when I dragged him out. I think he hit his head pretty hard."

Weber narrows his eyes. "We'll see about that."

The door opens and the doctor emerges. Weber moves to enter, but he blocks the path. "Ethan needs to rest now," the doctor informs him.

Weber scowls. "I have to speak to him. This is a murder investigation, remember?"

The doctor holds fast. "It'll have to wait. He's been through a severe trauma. I want to minimize any additional stress, at least for a few more hours until we see how he stabilizes."

Weber shoots me a look. "Then nobody goes in, you understand."

I take a step back. "It's OK, I was just going to find Annette. I think she's in the cafeteria. I could get you something," I add, with a helpful smile.

Weber shakes his head, and turns back to the doctor. "I want to see his medical records, I need to know everything that happened to him."

"Of course."

The doctor gestures for Weber to follow him, but Weber doesn't take a step until I do.

"I'll be downstairs if you need me," I tell him, still sounding upbeat. I walk carefully down the hall towards the elevator, feeling his eyes on me. As the doors close, I see him finally turn and follow the doctor away.

I wait until the elevator reaches the basement, then I hit

the button again and head straight back up to the ICU. I walk fast back down the hallway and check around, but nobody is in sight. I crack the door to Ethan's room, and step inside.

It's dark, and it takes my eyes a moment to adjust to the dim. I edge towards the bed, tip-toeing silently, but suddenly, the lamp turns on and the room is flooded with golden light.

My heart stops.

Ethan is sitting up in bed.

"I was wondering when you'd show up."

THEN

I took Mom to the airport and hugged her goodbye with tears stinging in the back of my throat.

"You've got magazines for the flight," I told her, fussing with her scarf in the tiny local departures terminal. "And I packed you a snack too. I wrote down all your details for the connection. Carol will be there to pick you up at the other end."

I tried to think if I was missing anything, what more I could have done. "I packed a file of important papers in your luggage," I added, remembering the folder of insurance documents and bank details. "Give them to Carol, she'll know what to do."

Mom's eyes filled with tears. I hadn't told her what was

really happening, that when Carol called to find out where I was, I would already be gone. But she knew, this was an ending, I could see it in her expression.

"I'm sorry, sweetheart," she whispered, hugging me tight. "I tried, I really did."

"I know." My voice cracked, breathing in the scent of her shampoo, and the lavender lotion she always liked to use. "Me too."

I watched her join the line for security, her steps hesitant and slow. A guard patiently showed her how to put her things in the bin for the scanner and step through the metal detector.

She would be OK, I told myself. People would be kind to her, kinder than I could manage, and perhaps she would get better because she had to now. She had no other choice and, as I'd discovered these past months, necessity could drive you to things that seemed impossible, once upon a time.

She turned back, her eyes catching mine for a moment. I felt a deep ache cut through my chest at the plaintive look in her eyes. It wasn't too late, I could run to her, take her home again, and keep her safe, just the two of us. I could get another ticket and go with her, just as we'd planned; find a way to start fresh somewhere else, together.

It was a wild longing, a child's futile wish, but even as the thoughts whirled through my mind, I felt something rise up in me, resistant and cold.

I was close, so close to being free. Being with Oliver. This was my escape.

I deserved this.

So I walked away from her, out of the airport buildings and back to my car. I sat there, waiting, until her flight took off, then made the drive to Haverford one final time. As the harsh winter landscape sped past my windows, that resistance became a chorus, humming inside me like an anthem.

You're better than this. You always have been.

I was so close.

I was twenty miles outside Haverford when my phone rang. I glanced over, expecting another message from Ethan, but it was a different number this time. Oliver.

My pulse kicked as I answered, keeping one eye out for Blake or one of the deputies, bored on the side of the road and eager to ticket. "Hey, I just dropped her off."

"Good." Oliver's voice was even. "Swing by the lake house on your way back. There's something I want to show you."

"How mysterious," I teased. "What's going on?"

"Let's just say I have a surprise. A way to send this town out with a bang."

I smiled. "I'm on my way."

I hung up and took the turning that would lead me out

past the lake to the site. As I rounded the curve, I saw lights flickering in the far house, so I pulled up in the dark drive beside Oliver's car and turned off the engine.

"Hello?" I called, pushing the open door. The electricity was off, but inside, I found candles flickering on the edge of the stairs. Night-lights were set in a path, leading upstairs. I followed them, my curiosity building. In the hallway, I found another trail of candles, and a scattering of rose petals on the floor, leading to the master suite.

I pushed open the door. "Oliver? What's going on?"

The room was lit up with dozens more candles, flickering from every window ledge and mantel. There was a blanket on the floor; sultry music playing from his phone on low.

"What, you don't like it?" Oliver strolled out of the shadows. He had a bottle of something in his hand, and a wry expression on his face as he gestured around the room. "I thought we could celebrate your newfound freedom."

I blinked. Oliver wasn't the type for big gestures, but the room was set up like a scene from a movie: the perfect romantic hideaway.

"What's really going on?" I regarded him carefully. "This, flowers and candles? This is so not you."

He grinned. "You know me well. No, I thought I'd see how the other half lives. Try a little Hallmark sentimentality. What do you think, darling? Doesn't it make you want to move to a nice house in the suburbs, get ourselves a couple of rugrats and a dog?"

Oliver pulled out a knife – Ethan's hunting knife, I recognized – and used it to lever the cork from the bottle. It came free with a hollow "pop", and foam flooded over Oliver's wrist. "Damn," he cursed, but I laughed, and lifted his arm to my mouth to lick it off.

"Champagne?" I raised an eyebrow.

"Only the best for you, my dear." Oliver took a long swig. "After all, it's the first day of the rest of our lives."

"Start as you mean to go on," I quipped in response, taking the bottle from him.

"Carpe diem."

I drank long, feeling the effervescence of the bubbles shimmer through my bloodstream.

I felt reckless, and golden, and bright. Oliver was joking with his trite sayings, but they were true. This was my beginning, and I felt reborn, fresh from the shadows of the past year.

"Thank you." My voice was quiet. Oliver looked up. "For ... everything. Not just ..." I paused, trying to explain what he'd done for me, but failing all the same. I shrugged. "I don't know what I would have done without you."

Oliver tilted his head, and the smile he gave me was one I'd never seen before: quieter, and sincere. Almost sad.

"It's my pleasure," he said softly, reaching to stroke my cheek. "All this time ... I never thought I'd find someone like you."

His eyes were dark, but I recognized the expression there. To be seen, and truly understood; we both had found that in each other. No need to hide the sharp edges and smooth ourselves down, play-acting at being just the same as everyone else.

We were different, in all the same ways.

I reached for him, kissing him hard until I was breathless. We tumbled to the blanket, lips and hands and gasping breaths. This was what it felt like to truly lose myself in someone for the first time, to be more than myself, gone. I poured myself into him, in every kiss and touch, giddy with the possibility of tomorrow.

I didn't hear the car pull into the drive outside, or the door pushed open. I didn't hear the footsteps on the stairs until it was too late. I didn't have time to do anything but pull away from Oliver and see him there in the doorway, staring at us in furious disbelief.

Ethan.

THE END

Oh God. I push away from Oliver and scramble to my feet, fumbling to fasten my jeans.

"What are you . . .?" I glance back to Oliver, but he's just sitting there, expressionless. "Ethan—"

"No." Ethan shakes his head slowly. "No, you don't say anything. Don't say a fucking word!" His voice breaks. He's breathing heavily, agitated, hands reaching and then closing into fists, like he doesn't know what to do with his own body. "This is why you broke up with me? It's him, it's always him."

I catch my breath. "I'm sorry," I whisper, but he isn't listening.

"I should have known you'd get to her." Ethan paces, jittery. "You have to have everything, don't you? You always find a way to wreck everything. Well, you're not doing this. You don't get to take her!"

Oliver watches him. "Don't do anything stupid, baby brother."

"Don't call me that!" Ethan roars.

I flinch back at the fury in his voice. I've never seen him like this, so angry and unhinged.

"Ethan ..." I start, but Oliver speaks over me.

"I mean it. You don't want to go crazy and do something you regret." His gaze shifts away from Ethan and I follow it. The knife, resting on an upturned box.

I suck in a breath. Ethan notices. He looks across and sees the knife. Oliver makes to move towards it, but he's strangely sluggish, and Ethan beats him to it. He grabs the knife and ducks back, pointing the blade towards the both of us.

"Get up," he orders.

Oliver obeys, unfolding himself slowly from the floor. I stand there, stranded, fear racing through every nerve in my body.

What are we going to do now?

Our lives are made up of choices, you see. Big ones, small ones, strung together by the thin air of good intentions; a line of dominoes, ready to fall. Which shirt to wear on a cold winter's morning, what crappy junk food to eat for lunch. It starts out so innocently, you don't even notice: go to this party or that movie, listen to this song, or read that book, and then, somehow, you've chosen your college, and career; your boyfriend or wife.

So many choices, we stop counting after a while. They blur into an endless stream, leading seamlessly to the next question, the next decision, yes, no, no, yes. The line of dominoes falling one by one. Click, click, click, they tumble faster until you can only see the two that really mattered:

The beginning, and this, the end.

Oliver, and Ethan, and I.

After the fighting, and the blood. After I almost talk Ethan down; after Oliver makes his murderous plan clear, we're left, the three of us.

Two boys. One knife, heavy in my hand. And a way out of this, so simple, I can't avoid it, however horrifying it seems.

"Do it," Oliver orders. "Chloe, I'm warning you. If you don't, I will."

"You can't be serious," I protest weakly, even as I know he is. My fingers wrap around the hilt of the knife, gripping tight. "He's your brother," I whisper, fascinated and horrified all at once.

"And I'm choosing you." Oliver meets my eyes, and the expression there is chillingly matter of fact. He's weighed the calculation between us and, somehow, the scales have tipped. To me.

It's crazy, but that knowledge sends a surge of power through me. He's chosen me, over Ethan. I'm the one he wants.

"We're the same, you and me," Oliver continues, hypnotic. "You know it, you can stop pretending."

"So we go, just leave here, right now," I say. "Nobody has to get hurt."

Oliver shakes his head. "He's a loose end. You know I don't leave any evidence behind. Besides," he adds with a dark smile, "I need to see what you're made of. Are you the girl I think you are, or just another one of these pathetic sheep?"

I catch my breath, blood racing, boiling in my veins as I realize it was set from the start. Bringing me here, the roses and champagne; calling Ethan to discover us. Even the way he pushed Ethan towards the knife was a manipulation – Oliver knew all along, this was where he wanted us.

It's another of his games. The final test.

Who am I?

"You want me to kill him?" I ask quietly, calm rushing ice-cold through my body.

Oliver's lips quirk in a smile. "I want you to do whatever you want."

Slowly, I turn to Ethan. His eyes widen, as if he sees the darkness in me for the first time.

"Chloe, no!" Ethan pleads. "Whatever he says, it's not

true. You're a good person, you always have been. You won't, please. You can't!"

He's begging, no pride left in those broad shoulders; no easy swagger now. Ethan begs for his life and I watch him, horrified I could reduce him to this.

Horrified and thrilled, all at once.

"Don't you see?" Oliver takes another step towards me, hand outstretched for the knife. "It was always going to end this way. Him or me. You can't have us both, Chloe. You can't leave with him still hanging on. You have to choose."

"Please, Chloe, don't!"

"Do it." Oliver is relentless. Another step, he's closing in now, and I feel myself sway towards him, the way I always did. "You're curious, aren't you? To see what it feels like to have that power. You wanted to know, before. Now's your chance."

He's right. I feel it, deep inside, the rage that won't be quieted; the hunger only he could ever satisfy. Ethan smiled and petted at me, kept me up on his gleaming pedestal so pretty and sweet. He never knew me at all. He never wanted to know this part of me. But Oliver ... he knew, right from the start. Everything I could be if I could just let go.

He showed me what it meant to feel power, and anger, and desire. To be the one calling the shots, never to cower and beg like I used to.

That's what I want my life to be.

I close my fist around the knife, the hilt tucked snug in my palm.

"That's right." Oliver smiles. "I knew you'd realize."

"No," I tell him, steely. "You said, this was my choice, and I haven't decided yet. Who knows?" I add, arch. "I could choose to kill you instead."

Oliver laughs, his eyes glittering at me in the dim light. "You decided the minute you picked up that knife, sweetheart." He grins. "You could have given it to him, you could have thrown it clear. But you like it, you like being the one with all the power."

I held his gaze. I wasn't going to deny it, every word was the truth. I had the power now, but what was I going to do with it?

Suddenly, Ethan lurches towards me, hands outstretched and desperate. Grabbing at me, clinging like he always did.

"Stop it!" I recoil back. "Let me go!"

"He's crazy," Ethan gasps, face twisted with fear. "You can't listen to him, you're my Chloe. My good, sweet Chloe. Remember? Remember we said we'd always belong to each other. Please!"

He sobs, clinging to me, but now my shock is hardening into disdain. He could take the knife from me in an instant if he wanted, but he's too weak to even try. He thinks he can blackmail me instead, wrap that old affection around me like a deadweight, pulling me down.

"Get off," I tell him, shoving at his limp body.

"You love me," Ethan whimpers, pathetic. "You wouldn't hurt me. I believe in you!"

He claws at me again. Revulsion rises in me. I can't take it: the guilt and the obligation he's using to trap me, all the broken hope in his eyes. I don't owe him anything, I never did. He was the one who grabbed me tight and didn't let go. Didn't let me breathe.

I meet Oliver's gaze over his head. "Do it," he whispers, and I see the thrill in his eyes. He's waiting for this, holding his breath, watching his brother fall apart. The darkest soul I've ever known. The mirror of me.

I remember watching the deer through the cross-hairs, my finger on the trigger. Ashton's head smashing into the wall, the lightning fury in my veins. What would it feel like this time? To be the one who decides.

I feel that surge again, lifting me, pulsating, something white-hot and undeniable.

"Are you going to stay?" Oliver demands. "You'll die in this godforsaken town."

I think of snow on the dark roads, the screech of tires. I feel hope rise in me, stronger than anything. Fight or flight.

"Do it," Oliver orders.

And I do.

THE END

A heartbeat, a split-second's whim, that's all it takes to change your life for ever.

But what happens when you get it wrong?

When you feel the sigh of the knife sliding in, and hear the low, pained gasp; disbelief in his eyes that he could misjudge you so completely; the sticky wet smear of red on your hands.

What happens when you realize in that sick, bloodied moment – *no, no, no!* – that you can't take it back?

You chose wrong.

NOW

I approach the bed cautiously. Ethan doesn't take his eyes off me, but his expression is unreadable. I feel a faint glimmer of hope. The doctor said he was confused, maybe he doesn't remember.

"Thank God you're OK." I sink into the seat beside the bed and reach to clutch his hand. "You lost so much blood – and the fire . . . I didn't know if I'd get you out alive. Your parents are here, did they see you already? I can get them if you want, I just had to see you for myself." I babble, the words tripping over themselves. "I'm so glad you're OK!"

"Are you?"

"Of course!" I exclaim. "We were so worried, you were in

surgery for hours, and even then, they said you might never wake up." I catch my breath, squeezing his hand tightly. "But here you are, look at you. You're going to be OK."

There's a pause.

"I'll never be OK," Ethan says quietly, steel in his voice. "Not after what you did."

Oh God.

I meet his eyes and the accusation there robs the breath from my lungs.

He remembers. He remembers everything.

"Ethan . . ." I gasp, my mind racing for something to tell him. Anything to pull him back from the edge. "You don't understand, let me explain—"

"Don't." Ethan looks at his hand in mine, then slowly pulls it away. "Weber will be here in a minute and then I tell him everything. The truth, this time." His jaw is set in determination and I realize, with a sinking heart, he means every word.

He's done with me, the way I was done with him.

It's over.

A coldness slips through me, settling deep in my bones. Resignation. All night, ever since I made that choice, part of me has been waiting for this. I thought I could claw my way out of the wreckage, with lies and tears and twisted truths, and I came close, so close, to slipping loose of their chains.

But the panic is over, now, there's nothing but inevitability. An ending, instead of my beginning.

"There's only one thing I need to know from you," Ethan adds slowly. "They said you saved my life. They said Olly's ... Olly's dead."

I nod silently, looking down.

"Why would you save me?" Ethan asks, his voice lifting. "After everything you did to be with him. Why did you save me from the fire?"

I force myself to glance up again and find him looking at me with an anguished expression on his face. "I don't understand," he says. "You picked him. You looked me in the eye and you picked him."

"I know," I whisper, my voice breaking. "And I know, I can never take that back, but I was wrong. It was all wrong." I gulp a breath, my voice desperate, trying to make him see. "The second it happened, I knew I'd made a terrible mistake. It was, I can't explain it, it was like I'd been under Oliver's spell and, suddenly, I woke up." I meet his eyes, tears already wet on my cheeks. "You know what he's like, he made everything seem so ... simple. Like it wasn't real, it was all just a game. But when I hurt you ... " I take his hand again, gripping tight. "It was real. Suddenly, everything was real, and I couldn't let it happen. I had to keep you safe from him."

I hold on, waiting for some reaction. Ethan takes a long breath, still so pale. He's got wires trailing from his body, an IV hooked to his arm.

"What happened?" he finally says. "I remember the knife, and then ... I was on the ground. He said something about starting a fire, to make it look like an accident." Ethan shakes his head, frustrated. "But everything else is gone."

"You passed out," I tell him quietly. "You were bleeding and you passed out. Oliver was lighting the fires. He'd brought kerosene with him; he'd planned it all, even calling you over to find us." I shiver. The candles and the rose petals were all props in his final game: to make it look worse, when Ethan walked in. To help him hide the evidence when we were done.

"You were laying there; there was so much blood. I already knew, I'd picked wrong." I lifted my eyes to his, plaintive. "You were the one who believed in me. It was you, it was always you – but he would never let you go alive. I never realized how much he hated you until then. So, I went after him when he was about to start the fire. I took the pipe, the one he'd used on you, and then ..."

Ethan searches my face. "What did you do, Chloe?"

"I made sure he'd never hurt you again."

There's a long silence. I'm clinging to Ethan's hand, waiting for him to say something. Anything.

There's a noise; the door opens. "I'm just going now . . ." Weber is on his cellphone, but when he sees us here together, he hangs up without another word.

"I told you to stay out." He glares at me. "You're interfering with a witness, get the hell away from him."

My heart drops. I send a desperate look to Ethan, but he turns away.

This is it. The end.

I force myself to rise out of the chair. My legs are trembling, my whole body is thick with fear. I slowly walk towards the door, knowing that these are my last few moments of freedom. I should have run when I had the chance. I should have done so much differently. But it's too late.

It's always too late.

"Wait." Ethan's voice comes, breaking through my terror. "She can stay."

I turn, confused. Ethan reaches out his hand to me, giving me a private look. "I want her to stay," he says again.

Weber looks back and forth between us. "But I need to get your statement."

"I don't remember much." Ethan meets my eyes. "I just know she's the one who saved me. That's all that matters."

He's covering for me.

I gasp an inhale of pure relief, crossing the room in an instant to be by his side. "I told you what happened," I tell

Weber, holding Ethan's hand tight. "Oliver was obsessed with me. He stabbed Ethan, and Ethan hit him in self-defense. It was all an accident."

"Is that right, son?" Weber looks furious, but there's nothing he can do. He's on the other side of the room from us; Ethan and I, a united front. "You don't have to say anything right now," Weber adds. "Take your time, see what you remember."

"There's nothing to remember." Ethan looks defiant. "It was Oliver. I was just defending us. That's what happened."

Weber lets out a long breath. "We still need to go through it."

"Fine," Ethan says.

"Alone." Weber glares at me.

"It's OK." Ethan squeezes my hand. He gives me a brief smile. "I've got this. You go find my parents."

"You're sure?" I linger, still feeling the dance of panic in my veins. What if this is some kind of game, to lull me into security before he brings the truth crashing down?

"I promise." Ethan's eyes are clear and true. He lifts my hand to his lips in a kiss. "You saved me," he murmurs. "I knew you wouldn't let me down."

I cup my hand to his cheek. "You believed in me," I whisper, dizzy with relief.

Weber clears his throat.

I pull away. "I'll be back," I tell Ethan. "I'll get you some jello. It's gross, but it's the least of all evils in this place."

He cracks a smile. "Don't be gone too long."

I walk past Weber and out of the room, my heart pounding. That future that seemed a distant dream suddenly bursts into view again, bright and close enough to hold. The hospital walls fade away around me, instead, I see busy streets and strange new cities; college classrooms and crowds of people.

"I'm not finished with you yet."

THE END

I chose wrong.

I felt it, the minute the knife slid in and I felt that rush, the glorious rush of power. Better than any drug or glittering orgasm, better than anything I'd ever tasted before.

This was mine.

Ethan gasped, his expression desperate. I didn't care. I felt the power take me over, and I knew in that moment, it would never be enough. To feel this way, to know I could hold a life in my hands and rip it away for good . . .

I wanted more, already. I wanted it for ever.

Oliver gave a slow clap. "Beautiful work, my dear."

I turned. He was watching Ethan's gasps with a dark look of victory. This was his prize. Not just that Ethan was dying, but that I was the one who'd done it. His student. His instrument. The ultimate betrayal.

And that's when I realized, through the haze of blood and power, I would never be safe with him.

If he could watch his brother die with a smile on his face, then what would become of me? I'd built my dream of a future on his promises, his seductive words, but one day, he'd turn on me too, and I'd never see it coming.

He'd killed before. He knew this thrill.

One day, it would be me.

I pulled the blade out and Ethan crumpled to the floor, broken and bleeding.

"I'll set the fires downstairs," Oliver told me, all business again. He swept over the candles nearby, sending them spinning to the floor. "You clean up here. There's kerosene in the bathroom, to make it spread. This place will be ashes before anyone thinks to look."

He exited the room, footsteps receding on the stairs.

I gasped for air, thinking wildly. Fire. Yes. I'd need it to hide what happened, to give me time to spin my story. I quickly wiped the knife handle down with my sweater sleeve and dragged Ethan closer to the doorway. The candles' flame was spreading, tiny pockets of flame, but there was still time.

I picked up the length of pipe from the floor and crept downstairs.

Oliver was sloshing kerosene from plastic gallon jugs, all through the kitchen and dining rooms. He was humming, cheerful, even after everything, and he didn't hear me as I moved up behind him, stealthy and silent.

I caught my breath. I raised the pipe, gripping with both hands. Then my boot hit a stray nail on the concrete and it skittered aside with a metallic ring.

Oliver turned.

I'll always remember the expression on his face: the confusion, turning to bewildered outrage as he realized what was to come.

He underestimated me. They always did.

I brought the pipe up with all the force I had. It cracked against the side of his skull with a glorious dull ring; he lurched backwards, falling heavily to the ground, face-down.

Silence.

Quickly, I pulled the knife from the back of my waistband and dropped it at his feet. I grabbed the kerosene and poured, shaking it over his motionless body until his clothes were damp through, the floor wet around him, the whole house reeking and ready.

I found the matches in his bag by the door. Ethan was still upstairs, the fire already burning. I could have dragged him clear first, but it didn't matter whether he made it out alive. All I needed was a body to back up my story. I would be a hero if he made it; a wretched victim if he didn't. The only part that counted was here: Oliver, unconscious on the floor.

The man who'd made me, unleashed everything I was.

The only one who ever knew me at all.

"Thank you," I whispered.

I struck a match, feeling the drag of friction. The flame flickered and then flared up, bright with promise. I stared into the fire for a moment, until spots danced in my eyes and I could see nothing but the black center of the flame, then I let it fall to the ground.

The kerosene ignited with a hiss and a flare, flames racing outwards, hungry and consuming.

I stood and I watched it all burn.

NOW

"Chloe. Wait."

I turn. Weber is following after me, striding down the hallway. It's morning – with the endless strip lamps, I didn't notice until now: pale light streaming through the far windows and the new shift nurses changing with a bright chatter.

A new day for me.

Ethan is selling my story, Annette backing us up too. All the pieces fit together, there isn't anything left to explain. At least, I don't think there is.

"Can I help you with anything else?" I ask him, careful.

"I talked to the medical examiner." Weber stops, standing too close, looming over me. "He said Ethan was likely stabbed by someone left-handed. And the blow on Oliver's skull, it was someone swinging upwards, someone shorter than him. His report will say, your story doesn't add up."

My heart shivers in my chest, but I don't let the panic rise. He wants to scare me, but I'm done with that now. Ethan is on my side, his parents too. All that matters is the story, and I spun it just right.

Just the way I planned.

I coolly meet his gaze. "Sometimes it's better to let things go. That's what you told me, isn't it? Maybe a pipe will burst," I add, giving him a look. "You know how evidence can get destroyed."

Weber's jaw goes slack. His eyes widen with realization: of his lies, and my silent threat.

"Oh, and consider this my notice for work," I add brightly. "I'm not staying."

I watch it click into place in Weber's mind: suspicions becoming fact, with all the horror that truth contains. But even as his eyes fill with shock and betrayal, I'm not afraid. He knows he can't touch me, he knows I've won.

I learned from the best, after all.

I walk away from him, and the last claim this town will ever have on me. Oliver was right, I was always better than this place, and now I never have to hide again.

My world. My rules.

"Where will you go?" Weber calls after me.

"San Diego, I think." I turn back and beam, victory thick in my veins. "It's about time I paid my dad a little visit."

Turn the page for a tantalising
preview of Abigail Haas's

two girls plus one boy
equals murder

DANGEROUS
GIRLS

ABIGAIL HAAS

Elise is dead.
And someone must pay.
**But the truth is more shocking
than you could ever imagine . . .**

NOW

Would it have made a difference if I had cried? I've had long enough to think about it, but even now, I can't know for sure. If I'd fallen apart, and wept, and screamed. If I'd curled up, shaking, into a ball in the corner of the police station and refused to speak. Would they have believed me then? Or would they have just found another way to spin it: that my grief was remorse, for the terrible thing I'd done. That my outbursts were too fevered, too public, too much for show. An act, to cover my tracks.

The truth is, once Dekker got it in his head that the break-in was staged and one of us killed her, there was nothing I could do. He was coming for me, and every little detail of my life was evidence, if you held it up to the light and looked at it just right.

He was coming for me.